W9-BRM-690

TELLING LIES

A
MAGGIE MACGOWEN
MYSTERY

Wendy Hornsby

AN ONYX BOOK

ONYX
Published by the Penguin Group
Penguin Books USA Inc., 375 Hudson Street,
New York, New York 10014, U.S.A.
Penguin Books Ltd, 27 Wrights Lane,
London W8 5TZ, England
Penguin Books Australia Ltd, Ringwood,
Victoria, Australia
Penguin Books Canada Ltd, 10 Alcorn Avenue,
Toronto, Ontario, Canada M4V 3B2
Penguin Books (N.Z.) Ltd, 182–190 Wairau Road,
Auckland 10, New Zealand

Penguin Books Ltd, Registered Offices:
Harmondsworth, Middlesex, England

Published by Onyx, an imprint of Dutton Signet,
a division of Penguin Books USA Inc. Previously published
in a Dutton edition.

First Onyx Printing, May, 1993
10 9 8 7 6 5 4 3 2

Copyright © Wendy Hornsby, 1992
All rights reserved

 REGISTERED TRADEMARK—MARCA REGISTRADA

With thanks to Detective Dennis Payne,
Robbery-Homicide Division, LAPD, for introducing
me to Mike Flint and for watching out for
his interests. And to all the knotheads
in RHD-OIS: Just get to steppin'.

Chapter 1

After the third firebomb smashed through the front windows of my parents' Berkeley house, I was parked in a walled convent school sixty miles down the Peninsula. Other than swimming and nuns in black habits, there wasn't much worth remembering about St. Catherine's Academy for Young Ladies. At least, nothing in relation to what was happening at home. I was still doing time there on December 20, 1969.

It was cold on December 20. That I recall clearly, though most of the details of the day have been either lost to me or distorted by the lies memory plays. Oddly, an anomaly of memory, a few of the ordinary events of the morning have attached themselves to my keener recollection of that evening, little shards of trivia that spill out whenever the horror comes to mind.

If I'd had my cameras then, I might have been able to keep the pieces together more coherently. But I didn't. The few photographs and bits of film footage I have managed to scrounge all came from sources alien to my point of view. I don't trust them. Especially where Emily is concerned. And if there is connective tissue in this flawed history, it is Emily.

This I remember about December 20. I was barely sixteen. It was the last day of the fall term and I had a swim meet. The bleachers were unusually full because a lot of families had come to St. Catherine's to fetch their young home for the holidays. My own parents were still tied up with final exams and holiday preparations. Marc was still in Vietnam. I hadn't seen my sister, Emily, in the flesh for months, so I hardly expected her to come to anything as unspectacular as a swim meet.

I was swimming a medley, breaststroke and freestyle. The water seemed strangely dense that day and I lagged the field badly. Cold was only part of the problem. I had a lot on my mind: How do you survive at school when the *Time* editorial for that week is about your big sister and is assigned reading for the entire junior class? I felt isolated, abandoned among the academic virgins.

I had given up halfway through the first lap of my first heat when I heard Emily yelling from the bleachers, "Do it, Maggot. Do it, Maggot. Do it."

Inciting to riot had certainly developed Emily's pipes. Every time I raised my head for a breath, I could hear her over everyone else. I counted off my strokes, one, two, three, four, before I earned a breath. All I wanted was to hear her voice, so I stroked faster, harder, slicing through the water, counting to four to earn another earful: "Do it, Maggot."

I won the heat. Actually, I set a meet record. I don't know how, exactly, because I wasn't racing. I was only trying to hear Emily.

When I came out of the water, I found Emily sitting in a clearing among the parents in the bleachers, with her two FBI shadows behind her. I've always been a natural showboat, so I should have been having more fun. But I was sixteen, remember. My sister, Emily, could cause me humiliation like no one on earth. And I loved her.

I still loved her. So, there I was, on another December 20, exactly twenty-two years after that day, this time in Los Angeles, cold and wet again, and once more searching for Emily. Only now the crowd was an entire city, and no matter how hard I tried, I could not find her voice anywhere.

It was rush hour and pouring rain. I was somewhere south of Santa Monica, driving Emily's ancient Volvo station wagon. The gas gauge didn't seem to function and the oil indicator light kept flashing at me. The last thing I needed was for the car to die on me. Avis at the airport had turned down my Visa and I didn't have enough cash for a second taxi ride to Emily's apartment in Chinatown.

It's not that I was destitute. The week before Christmas my charge cards are usually maxed out. And so are airport cash machines: I had hit three in a row that were down. So, temporarily, my economic situation was tight. If I'd had a little more warning, I would have been better prepared. Emily's summons to L.A. hadn't even left me time to go home to pack a toothbrush and a raincoat.

My destination at the moment was Grace House, a moveable soup kitchen run by a fellowship of nuns. It took getting lost three times before I finally found it in an abandoned bait shop a block south of Ozone Street. Short of cardboard shelters in the alleys, Grace House was unquestionably the most destitute of the places where I might find Emily.

Grace House was also the last place I was going to look for her. I promised this to myself. We'd had a date for four o'clock, and she had missed it. This wasn't unusual in my experiences with Emily. I had given her an hour, hanging out on the stoop of her building. But waiting is where I generally fail. She had called and said she needed to see me *now*. And *now*, one way or another, was what I was holding her to.

Silver needles of rain streaked the dark sky and bedeviled a ragged column of homeless men and women struggling along the street headed toward the light coming from Grace House. Swathed in makeshift raingear, burdened with carts or bundles of possessions, they looked like peasant refugees fleeing from some catastrophe. As I drove past them, I couldn't help but visualize the scene as it might be on film—an occupational hazard: silver lines against black, the rounded contours of the gray mass of people moving inside the frame. Seen from the perspective of a camera lens, they were no longer individuals. I could deal with them better that way.

I found a place to park at the curb directly in front of

Grace House. I got out and made a dash for the sidewalk, seeking shelter under the rotting remains of shop awnings.

"Ma'am? Excuse me, ma'am?" A clean-shaven man wearing a white apron over his jeans and T-shirt intercepted me. "You the caterer, ma'am?"

I thought about the Glad Bag–garbed crowd surging around me and wondered how to respond to this question. Grace House was a seat-of-the-pants, nonprofit operation. True, this was L.A. But how many soup kitchens are catered?

"Sorry," I said. "I'm not the caterer."

"Elks had a salad bar at their lunch today," he said. "They said they'd send over the leftovers. They'd better hurry 'cuz Sister says the soup's ready."

"I'm sure you can depend on the Elks," I said. "I'm looking for Emily Duchamps. Is she here?"

"The doc? Ain't seen her."

"Earlier today, maybe?"

He shrugged. "I only got out this morning."

Out from where I didn't want to know. I thanked him and pushed through the cluster of smokers finishing their butts beside the no-smoking sign on the door.

The small storefront was packed. Half-a-dozen women were setting out eating utensils and tending huge, shiny vats of soup. Among them, only one wore a traditional wimpole and navy jumper. Civilian dress or not, there is something about nuns, and I couldn't say what exactly, that tags them as brides of the church. I searched among them for the S.I.C.—Agnes Peter, the Sister in Charge.

Most of the narrow room was taken up with rows of Abbey Rents tables and folding chairs. I spotted Sister Agnes Peter setting up chairs around a back table. She had a helper who was so filthy he could have been white or black—it was impossible to tell. The two of them were sharing a joke about something that I suspect was rather gamey because when I walked up, their laughter devolved into breathy chuckles.

Agnes Peter smiled up at me. In her thrift-shop jeans

and sweatshirt, generic short haircut, she was nothing
like the knuckle-rapping nuns of St. Catherine's.

"Maggie MacGowen," she said, surprised. "Are you
here working on a film?"

"No. I'm looking for my sister, Emily," I said. "Have
you seen her?"

"First thing this morning."

"Where?"

"The rectory at La Placita church, downtown. She was
giving T.B. tests to a new group of Salvadorans who are
taking sanctuary with Father Hermilio."

"You haven't seen her since?"

"Has something happened, Maggie? Your father?"

"No. Everything's okay," I said. People always seem
to be waiting for my father's obituary; when it comes, it
will be a lulu. "Emily called. We talked about our
brother, Marc. She said she had a surprise, said I had to
meet her at four. But she didn't show."

"You know Emily," she said, smiling as she shook her
head. "She resides in that space between this world and
her own. Sooner or later, she'll remember your date."

"Where is Dr. Emily?" Agnes Peter's hairy companion
demanded. "That woman's not doing nothing about my
new teeth. I told her the County won't give me any new
ones. What's she gonna do about it?"

"Nothing," I said. "Emily can only help you if your
problem is contagious."

"Yeah? Well, first one tooth fell out, then another.
You tell me that ain't contagious?"

"Will you settle for new socks, Mr. Barnard?" Agnes
Peter took a pair of clean, but used, cotton socks from
her jeans pocket. "Better hurry. Time to queue up for
dinner."

Mollified by the socks, Mr. Barnard tucked this boon
inside his coat and hustled toward the line forming for
soup.

"Where might you find Emily?" Agnes Peter mused
as she unfolded the last of her chairs. "She's been work-

ing on the measles epidemic for the last month or so. Have you tried County Health?"

"Yes," I said. "And the Free Clinic, Harbor General, and the Clinico de la Raza. I have called or visited every place I could think of. I would have called you, if you'd had a telephone."

"Maggie, we don't even have a permanent zip code." She touched my arm. "Are you worried about Emily?"

I shook my head. "No. It's the date. Makes us all a little crazy. Emily sounded so happy when she called me. I need to know why."

"Stay put," Agnes Peter said. "The Elks are here."

The Elks, five of them, in ties and raincoats, came in struggling under enormous plastic salad bowls. Agnes Peter was effusive with them, but they seemed ill-at-ease, eager to deposit their salad and leave. Perhaps they had been snared by Agnes Peter before.

With a skill that was half Fred Astaire and half Rambo, she somehow maneuvered the Elks toward the poor box at the end of the serving table. She gave them plenty of time to grope for their wallets before she shook each hand and allowed their exit.

Outside, it had started to rain again, harder now. The latecomers, androgynous in their plastic drapings, surged in and filled what space was left in the small shop.

I was keenly aware of the smell, of wet clothes and infrequent showers, the remnants of bait shop stench that even the onions in the sisters' soup couldn't cover.

It was time for prayers and the room fell still. Agnes Peter fingered her beads. She'll always be a puzzle to me; a notorious rabble-rouser, she still closed her eyes for prayers. I read the familiar litany of grace on her lips but didn't recite along with her. I had put all of that away a long time ago, at about the same time I packed away my bobby socks and blue plaid jumpers.

The diners looked more hungry than prayerful, but they waited patiently—the price to pay. Some of them kept their eyes open, like me. I always loved the secret feeling of spying on people during prayers, hoping to catch someone unawares, find out something useful. For my benefit, my older brother, Marc, used to pick his nose and pretend to eat it. He did this with his eyes closed to protect his place in heaven. For his sake, I hope it worked.

I gazed up, not toward heaven, but at the posters tacked to the walls. The messages were an odd mix. Obviously, some had moved in with Grace House, while others had been left by the previous tenant. A butcher-paper banner on one side wall promised JESUS LOVES YOU, its opposite offered FRESH NIGHTCRAWLERS. Both seemed appropriate.

When I looked down again, I found I was being stared at. A tiny little girl with enormous brown eyes peeked out at me through a curtain of ponchos. When I smiled, she only stared. She looked pitiful, shrouded in an adult's cheap plastic raincoat. But her hair was carefully combed back into a tight ponytail and her face was clean. She never took her eyes off my face, as if I was some sort of oddity, an interloper in the world she knew.

Agnes Peter crossed herself and came back to this mortal sphere. She followed my line of sight to the little girl.

"How's your daughter, Maggie?" she asked.

"Casey's fine. She's spending the holidays in Denver with her dad. You know Scotty remarried?" I asked.

"Did he?" she asked, watching me closely. "How old is Casey now?"

"Twelve," I said. "She's already as tall as me."

"Good nutrition," she said knowingly.

I looked again at the little girl in the line. "Does she have a home?"

"Now and then. We got her and her aunt into a family shelter last week, but the aunt got into some problem there. Tonight they'll probably go on the Salvation Army bus to the downtown mission."

"On Skid Row?"

"Unless you have a better idea." There was no challenge in the way she said this.

"You're busy," I said. "I'll call tomorrow at the church. If you hear from Emily, I'll be at her apartment."

"Do you have a car?"

"Emily's. She always leaves the key under the front seat. It's hardly worth stealing, is it?"

"The VA hospital is pretty lenient about admissions when it's raining. Don't suppose you'd be able to drop a few of our vets off there on your way."

"The VA isn't on the way to Chinatown."

"Worth a try, though, wasn't it?"

I noticed Agnes Peter had walked me toward the poor box as she talked. I peeled off my last five and said a little prayer that the Volvo made it back to Chinatown.

Agnes Peter gave me a hug that smelled equally of onions and Zest.

"Don't worry about Emily," she said. "She's somewhere, trying to keep busy. This morning, she asked me to light a candle at mass for your brother."

"Did you?"

"Yes," Agnes Peter said. "Twenty-two of them."

Chapter 2

I had no idea what Chinatown did about Christmas, but votive candles in little jars pasted with decals of a blond Virgin Mary seemed an unlikely part of local tradition. I counted a dozen candles flickering on the covered stoop of Emily's apartment building.

There hadn't been any candles or pots of flowers on Emily's stoop when I had arrived there straight from the airport at four o'clock. At four, it wasn't dark enough for candles. Agnes Peter told me that Emily had spoken to her about lighting candles for Marc. That's what I was thinking about when I saw them. Maybe Emily had set out the candles, I thought, as either a gesture toward custom or, more likely, some sort of nose-thumbing at Establishment rituals.

Whatever the reason for the candles, I was encouraged: if Emily had set them out, she couldn't be too far away.

It was almost seven. I tried Emily's apartment, and when there was no answer, buzzed her landlady, Mrs. Lim. Still no response. I pulled the collar of my sodden wool coat higher on my neck and went to the edge of the stoop to watch the rain and try to decide what to do next. If Em didn't show soon, I had friends in L.A. I could impose upon for at least a ride back to the airport.

Across the street there was an eight-foot plaster Buddha with a line of Christmas lights strung between his hands. He grinned malevolently on traffic flowing north out of Downtown toward the Pasadena Freeway, traffic that was still heavy long after rush hour. I watched the cars, and the people trudging along the sidewalk, looking for Emily in everyone who passed.

I was beyond cranky. Except for a few doughnuts during filming breaks, I hadn't eaten since dinner the night before. I thought there might be funds enough available on one of my MasterCards to cover moo shu pork and a few drinks at Hop Louie's, a restaurant a block over on Gin Ling Way. The company of people who had homes to return to would be a nice change. What I really wanted was a hot bath and a warm bed. I had put in a long day even before I got on the plane from San Francisco.

Basically, I'm self-employed. I make documentary films. There isn't a lot of money in it. Most of my films are co-produced by the PBS affiliate in San Francisco, now and then by WGBH Boston or the BBC. It's good work, it's what I want to do. The tough part is selling the product. Like most arts-related industry, selling the product really means selling myself. My image, that is. Now and then my soul; I have a daughter to feed.

I had spent the day filming promotional spots for PBS affiliates. You know the sort of thing, "If you enjoyed this presentation of 'Aged and Alone,' and want to see more quality programming like it, then the most important gift you may give your family this holiday season is a membership in Wichita's only viewer-sponsored television station, WKRN." Or Duluth's, or Honolulu's.

Someone with more zeroes in his contract than I have thought I should look network-slick for fund-raising, so a wardrobe/makeup person had been brought in to give me a commercial veneer. I didn't mind at first. It was like the old days when I used to anchor the evening news. But every time the camera stopped, this makeup person, Stella, pulled out her sponges and brushes and patched my face.

We had started before five that morning. By one, when my producer, Errol, came back from a liquid lunch, my coating of matte-finish goo was pretty thick, and I bore little resemblance to the portrait that sits on my mother's baby grand.

Errol's own cheeks glowed like Max Factor crimson number six. He gave me a boozy leer when he said: "Aleda Weston surfaced today."

"So?" If I could have moved my lips I would have said more. But my face was clenched in Stella's hand while she painted over break-through freckles and under-eye shadows that I thought gave my face character.

"After twenty-two years, Aleda picks today to come out of hiding." His eyes had a morbid sparkle. "Something's up, Maggie. Something very interesting."

"Can I quote you?" I asked, released from Stella's clutch at last.

"I want to quote *you*. I want to hear what your sister, Emily, has to say. And your father."

"My father has quit talking," I said.

"Don't let me down, Maggie. We can do a beautiful, exclusive piece on this."

The gleam in Errol's eye reminded me of a funeral director I once interviewed. Ever since Abbie Hoffman's suicide, Errol has been hot for stories about the heroes of the old New Left, their demise, their parole, their transformation into middle age, their occasional reappearance after years in hiding. He finds them poignant.

"The time is right," he said, trying to hold my eyes with his. "It's the twentieth day of December, Maggie. Think about it."

For an hour before this conversation, I had been trying to figure out a way to persuade Errol that he should let me leave the studio before we had taped the spots for Cincinnati, Seattle, and Tupelo, Mississippi. I hadn't told him yet that Emily had called me while he was out drinking his lunch.

"It's mandatory, Maggot," she had said. "Meet me at my apartment at four."

She must have forgotten to tell me about the rain.

Errol was watching Stella daub white makeup in my chin cleft.

She said, "Little collagen injection would fill that right in."

"I've thought, Errol," I announced, hoping that I oozed conviction when in my heart I was lying. "Get me on the first available flight to L.A. I'll see what I can talk Emily into."

He had bought it, both the promise and the ticket. So there I was, standing on Emily's stoop the second time, waiting for a break in the downpour.

The rain sluiced down in straight, vertical sheets that flooded the streets and poured down the eaves and made the votive candles sputter.

I was nudging the candles toward a drier area when a woman swathed in a heavy black shawl dashed in beside me. She wore crude, peasant sandals, and her sodden skirt clung to bare legs. She shivered. I assumed that she had only stopped for temporary shelter, until she reached into the folds of her clothes and brought out a candle of her own. When she struck a match over the wick, I saw her face clearly: she was no more Chinese than the blond decal Virgins flickering in the candlelight.

She could have walked up from one of the Latino neighborhoods around Downtown. But why? To leave a candle in this doorway?

"The candles are pretty," I said, but she gave me a *no comprendo* shrug. She dropped the lighted candle into a small baby food jar and set it down among the others. I tried to speak with her, but she was finished with her business before I got past *hace frio*. She said a quick Hail Mary and headed back out into the night.

I watched her go, thinking that maybe she was on some sort of pilgrimage and this stoop represented one of the stations of the cross or something. Whatever she was doing, she shouldn't have been out: It was late, the weather was extreme, the neighborhood was none too good and the woman was very pregnant. I thought she should be home in bed, and hoped she had a bed to go home to. Emily would have known exactly what to say and do.

I tugged up the collar of my coat and followed the woman into the rain. Before I gave up on Emily and went in search of a bed of my own, I thought of one more place to look, though I dreaded it. Emily was on staff at French Hospital, three blocks down Hill Street from her apartment.

She didn't do rounds, she wasn't that sort of doctor. Instead, she checked on things she had growing in the laboratory, staph and strep and various other agents of modern plague. The hospital itself was okay, a small, neighborhood place. But Emily's little corner of its labs was the stuff of nightmares.

I walked in an ankle-deep stream of frigid runoff, shivering in my wet clothes. Every doorway I passed had a night tenant huddled under plastic drapings. Seeing them only made me feel colder. When I saw the lights of an open bakery on the opposite side of Hill Street, I dodged the splash of a pair of cars and crossed to it. A sign in the window promised fresh coffee.

A tiny man in starched white baker's coveralls and cap stood in the open door, watching impassively as I leapt over the runoff in the gutter.

"Is your coffee still hot?" I shook out a shoeful of water beside his threshold.

The baker nodded and backed into his shop. I hesitated before following him. I didn't want to soil his immaculate floor, but the lights inside and the smell of fresh-baked something overcame any fastidiousness on my part.

By the time I had my shoes back on, the baker had filled a Styrofoam coffee cup and was fitting it with a lid.

"You go," he said, pushing the cup toward me.

I didn't want to go. It was warm inside and I couldn't drink the coffee out in the rain. There were some round tables by the front window. My intention was to sit down for a few minutes and get warm. If Emily came past on her way home, I would see her. But when I started to shrug out of my coat, the baker snapped open a white paper bag and put the coffee inside it.

"You go," he repeated.

"I go," I sighed, rummaging in my pocket for money. I thought he must be ready to close.

"You go." He pointed toward the door and waited for me.

"Whatever you say," I conceded. My coat was cold when I shoved my arms back into the sleeves. I picked up the bag and dropped a couple of sodden, crumpled dollars onto the counter.

He brushed the money back toward me. "You no pay."

"I insist."

"You no pay." He folded his arms as if offended. "You go."

I was stung. I thought I might have committed some cultural gaffe and didn't argue further. I stuffed the bills back into my pocket, grabbed the white bag and went to the door.

I turned for one last whiff of the place and saw the baker dialing a wall phone. He spoke into the receiver in rapid Chinese. I clearly heard him say "Lim" twice. To tell the truth, everything he said sounded like "Lim" to me. His manner was so much like Em's landlady, Mrs. Lim, brusque and grouchy, that I might have been listening for her name, assuming a kinship. Wondering what I was doing that made me so offensive, I admired Emily anew for her ability to get along peacefully with so many people.

I went back out into the rain, wondering whether hotels ran credit card checks before they handed out room keys.

Down at the corner, French Hospital was a lighted block against the dark of a school playground beyond it. I hugged the coffee close to me, hoping for some warmth to seep through the cup.

"I am Caesar." A man shrouded in a tattered tarp held a gloved hand toward me, offering a limp square of paper. "I'm deliverin' to you the message and the truth."

The scrawny brown dog he led on a shoestring leash

cowered behind him and growled at me. I took the man's paper, assuming it was some sort of religious tract, and pressed on him the wet money the baker had refused. I felt it wasn't rightfully mine, anyway.

"Bless you." He looked closely at me through the downpour. "I don' want no money. I already received my reward."

He reached toward me and frightened me. I started to run back toward the shelter of the bakery lights.

"Wait," he cried with such anguish that I stopped. "Pretty lady, don' be scared. Jus' take your money."

"What's wrong with my money?"

"I can't take nothin' from you."

"Go buy the dog a meal, he looks hungry."

"We're okay." He had to hold the money against his upturned palm to keep it from being washed away. "Please, I can't take it from you."

"Keep it," I said, and rushed past him. "It is the message and the truth."

Outside the hospital entrance there were more candles. And flowers, too, several little pots of them, and one good-sized spray of white carnations. The ribbon sash across the carnations had DOLOR spelled out in gold letters. Pain, it meant. Stuck to the flower easel was a round pro-choice sticker. I wasn't sure what the message was, except it had nothing to do with Christmas.

The small waiting room inside was crammed with people, a mini U.N., a fair representation of the city's immigrant makeup. The information pamphlets on the wall came in five different languages, but they all looked poor. Women held sleeping children in their laps, men stood along the sides, clustered in pairs or trios, with their heads together. A brace of nuns averted their eyes as I passed.

Behind a window at the far end of the lobby, I found a receptionist. She was a round little woman, about my age, with TRINH FREEDMAN pinned to her stiff white bodice. When I cleared my throat, she looked up from the stack of file folders she was sorting.

"Is Emily Duchamps here?" I asked.

"The hospital has no comment to make about Dr. Duchamps."

I stifled a laugh. The hospital must have learned over the years how to deal with Emily's crusades. I had heard the State Department use nearly the same phrase when Em took off on an unauthorized medical mission to Cuba during a typhus epidemic. I hoped that this was only a flash of déjà vu and not a clue that Em was in trouble again.

"I'm Dr. Duchamps's sister," I said. "I've come to fetch her home with me."

"Oh! Miss MacGowen." Trinh Freedman's head snapped back and she blushed. "I didn't see it was you. We don't say nothing to the press about Dr. Duchamps."

"Glad to hear it. Will you please page my sister or point me in her direction?"

"Page her?" She looked around the lobby, meeting the dozens of eyes turned on us. Then she got up and smoothed the seat of her white uniform. "Come with me, please."

"If she's in the lab, I'll wait here," I said.

"Doctor is not in the lab. Please, this way."

She led me into the maze of slick, polished corridors.

I'm not sure when denial kicked in. I was considering offering Trinh my unpaid-for Ferragamo pumps in trade for her worn, white oxfords instead of thinking about where she was leading me, or why everyone we passed stopped in their tracks and stared. Even when I'm dry, I don't have the sort of looks that make people stop and stare. I should have tumbled.

Because of my line of work, I found the scene we walked through thoroughly familiar: big city hospital, knots of uniformed police and paramedics sloping against the walls, plainclothes detectives with guns on their belts, medical people in white lab coats and soft-soled shoes bustling among them, the smells of coffee and disinfectant.

Trinh checked back to make sure I was still with her,

waited for me to catch up. The door I followed her through was marked INTENSIVE CARE, AUTHORIZED PERSONNEL ONLY.

When I went inside, I saw panels of monitors, the back of a uniformed nurse hovering over a patient on a raised hospital bed. The patient lay absolutely motionless.

"Barbara," Trinh said to the nurse. "Miss MacGowen has come to see Dr. Duchamps."

The nurse stepped away from her patient.

I stood frozen, dazzled by all the white—white sheets, white gown, masses of white gauze bandages, dead-white skin.

Incredibly, in the middle of the whiteness, all six feet of her stretched the length of the high bed, was my sister, Emily.

Chapter 3

My brother, Marc, came home from Vietnam in a bronze box with a bronze star on his chest. I was barely sixteen. I remember edging up to his coffin, expecting him to throw open the lid, shout boo and laugh and pass out some of the righteous grass he had promised to smuggle home. An elaborate prank would have surprised me less than watching his box disappear, seals intact, under a load of gray cemetery dirt.

On December 20, 1969, Marc died. Now he had been dead for exactly as long as he had lived. Twenty-two years. The two halves of his life, measurably the same, seemed so unequal; one too short, the other endlessly long.

Now here was Emily, his twin in life, perhaps in death as well. It was a strange and horrible irony.

I edged over to the bed and found Emily's hand under the sheets. Her icy fingers didn't respond, but I held on to them anyway. "Emily?"

"She can't hear you," Nurse Barbara whispered.

"How do you know?" The situation was so weird I couldn't take it in. What I wanted to say to this nurse was, "Emily always hears everything." Instead I put my face so close to Em's that her soft gauze turban brushed my cheek. "Em, it's me, Maggot."

"Honestly, Miss MacGowen, she can't hear you."

"What's happened to Emily?"

Trinh Freedman hovered at the end of the bed. "I'll get Doctor Song."

I looked at her, stopped her flight toward the door. "What happened to Emily?" I demanded.

"We're not authorized to say."

"Authorized, hell," I snapped.

"I'll get Doctor."

I appealed again to Barbara, but from the anxiety in her face I knew there was no point in pursuing it.

Under the fluorescent lights, Emily was impossibly pale. There was a network of fine lines around her eyes I had never noticed before. In my mind's eye, she is still the young woman on the cover of *Time*, fresh and earnest and powerful. Here in front of me was Emily the middle-aged woman. How was it possible I hadn't noticed the passage?

Emily's mouth was drawn into a hard O, like a maiden aunt puckered for a duty kiss. I felt I should kiss her.

"Maggie MacGowen?"

I wheeled at the deep voice behind me. He was dark and slender, a tall Asian wearing a crisp white lab coat.

"Doctor?" I said.

"Albert Song." He extended his hand. "I'm glad you made it so quickly."

"I can't believe this."

"None of us can."

"What happened to Emily?"

Dr. Song narrowed his black eyes. "You weren't told?"

"No."

"Who contacted you?"

"No one. I just came. Please, tell me."

"Emily was brought in a few hours ago." He whispered, "She was shot."

"Shot? Gunshot?"

"I'm sorry."

"How?"

He shook his head. "She was found in an alley off Gin Ling Way."

I thought again of Marc's coffin disappearing into the ground while I waited for him to jump out. Emily teased, but she never played practical jokes. This whole scene made no sense and I would not buy into it. I crossed my arms. "Not Emily."

"So pointless," he said. "Whoever did this had to be some newcomer to the streets. Every bum in town knows that Emily Duchamps will give him anything he needs."

Except for one thing. I turned away from Emily to ask: "Was she raped?"

"No," he said.

I leaned over Em again, searching for some reaction. "Is she in pain?"

"We don't think so."

"Tell me everything."

"We don't know much, police don't either. She was shot from the side, probably taken unawares. A single bullet pierced the skull, passed through her right temporal lobe and exited over her left eye."

Through her brain? I looked at her profile, our father's profile, until it was blurred by tears.

"I'm truly sorry," Albert Song said. "Emily is a singular treasure."

"How bad is it?"

He turned his attention to her, delaying his answer. He laid his palm along her cheek and flashed a light into her right eye. When he spoke again, his words came slowly, full of sad knowledge I thought he was reluctant to share.

"Right out of medical school, I would have told you it was hopeless. But I've learned never to predict with brain injuries— I've seen too many miracles.

"She's strong," he continued. "She's world-class stubborn. If she wakes up, who knows? We're amazed she's made it this far without mechanical intervention."

"*If* she wakes up?" I couldn't hear her breathe. "Are you saying that if she wakes up she'll be okay?"

"Okay?"

"Will she be able to practice medicine?"

"No." His dark eyes had gone very liquid. "Miracles

don't come that big. There is significant damage, loss of brain tissue."

I couldn't take my eyes off her.

Every day of my life, I still missed Marc. There was so much I wanted to tell him, so many things we needed to discuss. I still listened for his voice every time I opened the door to our parents' house, waited for him to jump out and do something new and annoying to me. He had left me too soon and I had trouble forgiving him.

I'd had Emily for twenty-two years longer than I'd had Marc. The time made no difference; it was still too soon to lose her.

I stood beside her, trying to make her cold hand warm, trying to make her respond to me. I couldn't hear myself breathe.

I wiped my eyes and turned to Dr. Song. "What now?"

"She seems to have stabilized," he said. "We installed a shunt to relieve some of the pressure on the brain, and maybe it helped. I'm glad you're here to represent the family. We don't have facilities to properly treat Emily further. If she remains stable until morning, you might consider moving her to Cedars-Sinai or UCLA."

"I hate talking over her as if she isn't here," I said.

"If she could hear, she wouldn't mind." Dr. Song had been looking around for something. Barbara, the attentive nurse, picked up a clipboard and handed it to him.

"Do you want the forms now?" she asked.

"The forms?" He took the clipboard and flipped through the attached pages. "I heard that Miss MacGowen stopped by Lee's bakery. I thought maybe the coffee would do her good."

I had forgotten the white bag clutched against my coat. I held it out to him. "Heard how?"

"Community grapevine. Mr. Lee called and said you were on your way."

"How does he know me?"

"Emily brags about you. The whole neighborhood watches your films, even without Chinese subtitles."

"Oh, Em." The room became a spin of white until my

feet seemed to lose contact with the floor. Dr. Song caught me by the arms before I fell and sat me on the edge of Emily's bed.

"I'm eternally sorry." His voice was husky.

"Doctor," Barbara prodded. "The forms?"

"Right." He took a breath and passed me the clipboard. He spoke quickly, getting something unpleasant over with. My ears were ringing so it was difficult to concentrate on what he was saying.

"Take your time," he said. "But not too much. Emily listed you as next of kin on her personnel records. The hospital needs your signed consent for the surgery we have already performed, just to cover our ass. The other, well, I know this is a tough time to be making decisions. You'll want to talk with family, maybe a lawyer. But I'm warning you, time is of the essence. So far, Emily is holding her own. But if there is a crisis, she stops breathing unassisted, or she goes into cardiac arrest, and we don't have a signature on your desires about medical intervention, then the hospital board will make the decisions for you."

"Can I trust them?" I asked.

"You can trust them to do what's safe for the hospital. They'll plug her in."

I moved further onto the bed and squeezed Emily's foot through the covers. She didn't react. Even when I pinched the corn on her little toe, there was nothing. I looked at the forms, a blur of black-and-white legal mumbo-jumbo. I read the word *respirator* a few times, and the words *food* and *water*. The question was not what I wanted, but what Emily would have wanted me to do in her interest. I thought I knew, but who can be sure?

Albert Song looked at me expectantly.

"What's in the frontal lobe?" I asked.

"As to function? Thinking, judgment, reasoning."

"How about speech?"

He nodded. "And speech."

In profile, Emily truly was incredibly like our father.

I imagined them sitting side by side on the back deck of our parents' house in the Berkeley Hills, staring up at Grizzly Peak or out across San Francisco Bay, locked together in endless silence. I knew what my father would advise.

I signed the consent for the surgery that had already been performed. Then I checked no in the box next to mechanical respirator and yes in the box next to food and water. I signed the bottom with my legal name, Margot Eugenie Duchamps MacGowen, and handed the clipboard back to Dr. Song.

"Here," I said. "But ask me again in the morning."

Chapter 4

The hospital staff had left me alone with Emily for a few minutes. I clung to her hand in the antiseptic room, feeling useless, growing angry. I needed more than anything to talk to my twelve-year-old daughter, Casey, to make sure that she was all right. To make sure that I was all right. I wanted desperately to hold her. A telephone connection was the best I could do.

It was late in Denver, where Casey was spending the holidays. Maybe she was in bed. I went to the bedside telephone anyway, and dialed her father's number. I didn't relish running the gauntlet long-distance of ex-husband and new wife, of explaining why they should rouse Casey to speak with me. But I needed to hear Casey's voice more than I didn't want to hear theirs.

Worse luck—Linda, the second Mrs. Ian Scott MacGowen, answered the telephone. She sounded sleepy. I had a sudden, uncomfortable flash as I imagined Scotty snuggled beside her under the covers.

"It's awfully late to be calling, Maggie," she said. "Casey's asleep. She skied all day and went to bed exhausted."

"May I speak with Scotty?"

"He's asleep, too."

"Please wake him. This is an emergency."

"Is it your parents?"

"No. It's Emily."

"Emily?" There was a reverential pause. "I'll go down and get Scotty."

Go down and get him? I thought about that while I

waited. Either she had lied to me and he wasn't asleep, or they weren't sleeping together. Both prospects were interesting. I hold nothing against Linda, though she detests me the way The Other Woman generally hates the first wife. It's guilt. There had been times when I could have made her more comfortable, reassured her that she had moved in on a moribund marriage and was only a small factor in our breakup. But I kept quiet. Caveat emptor, let the buyer beware.

Scotty sounded wide awake when he picked up the phone. "Maggie, what's happened?"

"It's Emily," I said. "She's been shot."

"Dear God. Is she . . ."

"She's in a coma. She's stable, but, Scotty, her prospects are grim."

"How are Mom and Dad taking it?"

"They don't know yet. I want to talk to Casey. Will you waken her?"

"She's not asleep. She's right here. We've been playing chess." I heard an extension phone somewhere in the house hang up with a bang.

"Maggie," Scotty was saying, "if there's anything I can do. Anything."

"Thanks. Where's Casey?"

"Here she is."

"Mom?" Casey's voice seemed tiny, too far away from me. "You okay?"

"I'm fine, baby. How are you?"

"Bored. Why'd you call?"

"Aunt Emily's in the hospital. She's been seriously hurt. I wanted you to hear about it from me before you saw it on the news."

"It's really bad then, isn't it?"

"It is."

"Will she die?"

"I don't know."

"God, Mom, you must be real sad, I mean because she's your sister. And you already lost your brother. I never had a sister or a brother, so I don't know what that's like exactly, growing up with someone and then they die. Aunt Emily's pretty weird, but I know you laugh around with her a lot." Casey never bothers with polite bullshit. I love her. "Was it, like, some disease she picked up?"

"No. Emily was shot."

"Oh! Gross!" She took a couple of deep breaths. "Does she look bad?"

"There are a lot of bandages, but she looks beautiful."

"Am I going to come home?"

"I wish you could, but I think it would be best if you stay with Daddy while I take care of Aunt Emily."

"I could help you with things."

I heard the undercurrents. Casey is a patient, loyal soul. She hadn't said much about the divorce, except that she didn't want to lose her father. This holiday trip to his new house had been essential to her, reassurance that the cement between them still held firm. She would never complain to me about Scotty, or about Linda. So, I knew that if she was looking for an excuse to come home, something had happened to make her feel more than just uncomfortable. I also knew, knowing Casey as I do, that I couldn't force an issue.

"Linda said you had been skiing," I said. "Having fun?"

"Colorado's okay," she said. There was a pause. "Mom?"

"Yes?"

"Remember, after the earthquake when our house was all a mess and we had to stay with Grandma? Remember how fun it was?"

I remembered. The experience had been a nightmare for all of us. "Give Dad a little more time, honey. You've only been there a few days."

"You still going to Ireland to film?"

"In January."

"You'll be gone so long, Dad wants me to register for school here next term."

"Is that what you want to do?"

"Linda's pregnant."

"So?"

"Take me to Ireland with you."

I thought about it for maybe three seconds. "Okay," I said.

"No bull?"

"No bull. You're old enough. Maybe you'll learn something useful."

She gave a teenagery squeal. "Dad, I'm going to Ireland."

Scotty's voice in the background did not sound happy.

"Dad wants to talk to you," Casey said. "I'm sorry about Aunt Emily. I love you, Mom."

"I love you, too, baby."

"Here's Dad."

Scotty's voice was on the cusp between control and fury. "Are you nuts? Belfast, Northern Ireland, is a fucking war zone."

I squeezed Emily's hand. "The whole world is a fucking war zone, Scotty."

Dr. Song burst into the room and brushed me aside. "Emily, Emily, what are you doing?" he moaned.

His face was the ashen gray of a funeral guest. I stood there, panicked, while he took Emily's hand from me and probed her wrist for a pulse. His eyes were on the heart monitor screen. The regular blip I had been watching before I called Casey had changed to wild fluctuations, sharp peaks and profound valleys. Then, suddenly, the peaks straightened into a flat green line.

"Please, Em," I begged. I moved over her, as if I could shield her from some outside danger. But her battles were all being fought inside. There was nothing for me to do except watch her impassive face for clues to the outcome.

After a long pause, Dr. Song sighed and tucked away his stethoscope. I thought it was all over. I was trying to cry out, plead for him to do something. He wiped sweat off his face and smiled.

"Sorry for the scare," he said. "She's okay. Monitor

sensor slipped, that's all. I freaked like a first-year med student when I saw the monitor going crazy. I'm sorry."

"Em's okay?" I had to say it myself.

"Yes. Her pulse could be stronger, but it's steady."

I held Emily's hand again, still scared, afraid to be encouraged by Dr. Song's smile or the warmth he had left on her palm. He was now happily whistling "Jingle Bells" while I was still juiced from the panic he had carried into the room. I felt like decking him.

Dr. Song had peeled back Emily's gown to get at the sensors strapped around her chest. While he worked on the sensors, Em's torso was bare. I'm no prude, but I felt very uncomfortable being in the room with him while Emily was naked. When I last shared a room with Emily, she had still been a modest teenager. At that time, this situation would have mortified her.

I looked at her.

At forty-four, Em still had a nice, athletic body. Her belly was flat and well-muscled, the taper of her narrow hips was graceful. Her bare breasts were larger and fuller than I remembered them, certainly larger than my own. Hers were truly beautiful, well-shaped and firm even though she was lying on her back. This fascinated me. I remembered Em slipping foam inserts into a strapless high school prom dress. Too odd, I thought, that sometime between that night and this one, she had become so voluptuous.

It took me a few moments to realize that the thin red lines under her breasts weren't impressions made by her bra. They were surgical scars. Emily had breast implants.

The pure hedonistic extravagance of this act threw me. Not financial extravagance, because she probably exchanged freebies with another doctor to acquire these accessories. It was the unprecedented attention to herself, and her appearance that was a shocker. Why had she done it?

In transit between my news-writing job at WHCK radio in Des Moines and an anchoring spot at KMIR-TV in Palm Springs, I had traded in my father's hook nose for a pert Marlo Thomas special. It took a lot of soul-searching before I could do it. I liked the original better, but the change was a professional, video necessity.

Emily had given me a lot of heat for undergoing this "mutilation." So what had compelled her to enlarge her bust? A lover? The disappointment of a lover?

I realized I had begun to think about Em in a nostalgic way, as if the sum of her existence had drifted into the past. Discovering Emily's secret voluptuousness shook me, made me wonder what else I didn't know about her, gave her new life.

"Maggie!" I heard Scotty's voice, anguished but very faint. At some point I had dropped the telephone receiver. I reeled it in by the cord.

"I'm here," I said.

"What the hell happened?"

"Nothing. Mechanical glitch. I'll call you later. Take care of Casey." I hung up.

Trinh and Nurse Barbara had slipped into the room. Barbara bustled over to help Dr. Song, while Trinh guarded the door.

"She's okay," I said to them.

Trinh nodded, though she didn't seem persuaded. She looked at me and said, apologetically, "Some of those policemen in the hall want to talk to you."

"Good," I said, helping Dr. Song to redress Emily. "I want to talk with the police. Ask them to come in."

Trinh brought in two of them. Both wore banker-gray suits, both had police photo I.D.'s clipped to their handkerchief pockets. There were four rain-spattered black wingtips on the floor. In spite of this plainclothes uniform, the two couldn't have been more different. One was tall, slender, gray-haired, his face set in an expression of quiet, almost reverential watchfulness. His partner was a solid block of man, from his Brillo pad mat of red hair to his box-shaped feet. If he hadn't had tears in his eyes, he would have been thoroughly intimidating.

The big redhead moved toward me first, offering his massive hand.

"Detective T. O. Bronkowski," he said. "You're McGee, Doc's sister?"

"MacGowen," I said. "Maggie MacGowen."

"Right. Saw on the tube that thing you did about the 'Frisco quake. Thought you'd be taller."

"I'm tall enough," I said. At five-seven, I'm no midget.

"I guess because the Doc's such a stretch model, I thought you would be, too."

He carried a white plastic trash bag that he carefully set on the floor. "I'm so damn sorry about the Doc. How's she doing?"

"Holding on," I said. "Who did this to her?"

"Don't have much to tell you," Bronkowski said. "But, count on it, we will. In the middle of Chinatown, in the middle of the day, someone heard the gunshot, someone saw something. People around here can be pretty tight around the police. But for the Doc's sake, they'll come around."

Bronkowski leaned over and took a long look at Emily. His face flushed with blood. "Bastard must be some kind of animal to leave her out in the rain."

"Emily was left out in the rain?" I hated the picture that flashed behind my eyes. "How long?"

"Hour, maybe two," Bronkowski said.

"Where?" I asked.

"Alley off Gin Ling Way. Around six, a busboy from Hop Louie's ducked out for a smoke and found her lying behind some lettuce crates."

I turned to Dr. Song. "If someone had found her sooner . . ."

He shook his head. "Wouldn't have made any difference."

When I looked away, I met the stare of the second detective. I had nearly forgotten about him. He stayed behind Bronkowski, quietly, constantly watching me. I couldn't tell his age; his face was young but his short hair and his carefully trimmed mustache were silver-white. If

I were a criminal, I think he would be the one to worry about.

We engaged in a bit of a staredown. I think I won, because he was the first to smile. He offered his hand.

"Detective Michael Flint," he said. "Emily and I go a long way back."

"Detective," I said, taking his hand. His fingers were still cold and damp from outside.

"You live in the Bay Area?" he asked.

"San Francisco."

"Down visiting for the holidays?"

"No. I flew down just for the day, to see Emily."

"Someone called you about the shooting?"

"No."

"You just happened to come down. Today?"

"Is this the third degree?" I asked.

"This is conversation." He smiled again. "I leave the third degrees to Bronk."

"Okay, then," I said. "I didn't just happen to come down. Emily called me. We were supposed to meet at her apartment at four."

"Did you meet?"

"No. She never showed."

"Any idea what she was involved in?"

"Other than a measles epidemic and TB testing, no. I could probably sketch in her day until about noon. Then I lost her trail. She missed some appointments."

"Noon? That gives us a big gap. We think she was most likely shot between four and five."

"Jesus." I felt nauseous. "At four I was sitting on her doorstep, waiting for her."

"Alone?"

"Alone with everyone in Chinatown."

We were interrupted by the priest I had seen in the lobby. He pushed open the door and looked around the room. "May I?" he said.

"Father Hermilio," Dr. Song said. "Please, come in."

The small room already held a capacity crowd, so one more soul made tight quarters intimate.

"Albert, Michael, Bronk," Father Hermilio greeted each in his soft, accented voice. Then he reached out for me. "You're Maggie. Emily always speaks of you with affection. She is very proud of you."

I almost lost it then.

"I ask you for permission to administer the sacraments to Emily," Father Hermilio said.

"The sacraments?" I had to think about it. Emily had fallen away from our parents' Catholicism long before I had. As far as I could remember, her last religious excursion had been a summer trip through Buddhism. If there seemed to be a lot of church-related people in her life, it was only because church volunteers staffed so many of the city's social-service programs.

"Is it all right, Maggie?" Father asked.

"Yes, please," I said, not for Emily's sake, but because I knew my mother would ask about it when I called our parents.

When I called our parents.

Father Hermilio slipped a purple stole around his neck and took out a little bottle of annointing oil. Bronk laid his big arm around me, Albert Song took my hand, and we all watched the priest. Maybe someone in the room was waiting for a miracle to come from the prayers. I was not. I was only glad for the moment of silence to gather myself, because I did not want these people to see me cry.

The situation was doubly hard for me because it was all déjà vu, a rerun of the night of December 20, 1969.

Someone, the Pentagon maybe, had leaked an unconfirmed report that my brother, Marc, had been fragged, killed by his own men, in Vietnam. Coming at the same time as Emily's indictment, with her face on the cover of *Time*, this was big news. The press descended on my parents' house in Berkeley, corralling them inside, as it were.

When a picture of me in my school uniform appeared in the early television newscasts, my father had sent Emily to fetch me from school. We made our escape from St. Catherine's Academy, to the principal's great relief, directly after the swim meet. I remember little about the ride up the Peninsula in the car beside Em, except that my hair was still wet and I couldn't stop shivering.

At home, we found the usual undecorated Christmas tree in the living room, and the accumulation of lights and ornaments stacked in boxes beside it. Mother always waited to decorate until we were all home for the holidays. That year she had defied tradition and hung a snapshot Marc had sent from Vietnam. We never got around to hanging anything else on that tree.

For the rest of the afternoon, we had sat silent vigil. There was nothing safe to say. Sometime during the evening a detachment of officers arrived from the Presidio across the Bay, bearing the official message. They had filed in and stood in our living room, ramrod straight, all starched and pressed and spit-polished, as my parents crumbled. It had been brutal.

And now it was my turn to deliver the message. There was no way, in the end, to soften the truth except to tell them in person. But I could not leave Emily.

I thought that the best thing would be to call on my father's brother, Max, impose on him as I had so often before, persuade him to prepare the ground.

Everyone in the room was watching me, half a dozen pairs of tear-filled eyes. Their sadness made me feel better for Emily, knowing there were so many people who cared about her. Em, always on a crusade, didn't always spend enough time nurturing friendships. Or little sisters.

Father Hermilio finished his prayers, annointed Emily, blessed her, blessed the rest of us, then knelt quietly at the bedside.

Michael Flint touched my elbow and I moved with him toward the door.

"You okay?" he asked.

"I'm upright."

"Can I ask some questions?"

I shrugged. "Can I stop you?"

He smiled. "Not likely."

"Go ahead."

"The name Aleda Weston mean anything to you?"

"Of course."

"She made some deal with the FBI in New Hampshire. She's coming to L.A. to surrender."

I looked up at Detective Flint, but his face gave away nothing. "You know about Emily and Aleda Weston?"

"I told you, Emily and I go back a long way. When I was a rookie, she was one of the first famous people I arrested."

"A feather in your cap," I said.

"Where are you staying in town?"

"I don't know yet."

"Emily's apartment key is in that bag Bronk brought in. You'd be close by if she needed you. She wouldn't mind."

"You know this for a fact?" I said.

He smiled, a full, tooth-showing smile. "I know this for a fact."

Flint picked up the white plastic bag. "This is the personal property Emily had with her when she was brought to the hospital. We've finished with it, so you can have it, if you want it. I'm warning you, it isn't real pretty."

"Thank you," I said, taking the bag. It felt heavy, and I could see moisture beading inside. I could also see a khaki field jacket and a pair of white Reeboks. The rest looked like more clothes.

Dr. Song tucked his stethoscope into his pocket. "It's settled? You'll be at Emily's?"

"I think I should stay here."

He shook his head. "Emily's okay for now. You get some rest while you can. You're in for a long haul."

I didn't want to leave Emily. But there was no way to avoid it. I'll never forget how hurtful it was to learn about Marc, and to grieve for him, under the public gaze. I wanted to buy my parents as much time and privacy as I could. From Emily's apartment I could speak with them alone. I planned to be away from Emily for no more than an hour.

I went over to Emily and kissed her cool cheek. I turned to Dr. Song. "Do you have the number at Emily's apartment?"

A chorus of four responded, in unison, "Yes."

"You have a car outside?" Bronk asked.

"She walked," Flint said. He took the bag from me and reached for the door. "I'll take you home."

He was pushy, and I don't like to be pushed. But it was still raining outside and my feet were still cold. So I went with him. Why not? If Flint felt better carrying Em's bag and holding doors for me, let him.

Father Hermilio walked out with us into the crush of people hovering outside Em's room. The two men fended off queries from the crowd and I walked quietly, as if in a cocoon, between them, noting faces, attitudes, separating the morbidly curious from those genuinely grieving. I figured the two categories were about evenly represented.

Father Hermilio talked to me as we walked, but I hadn't been listening.

"So you will come?" he said.

"Where?" I asked.

"Midnight mass at La Placita. The community will offer prayers for your brother. Emily arranged it. Now, of course, we will pray for her, too. It would be nice for you to speak for the family."

"I'll come," I said. "But I can't speak. I could never get through that."

"I understand," he said. "But you will come?"

"Yes." I was trapped again by my upbringing. And puzzled. "She set up this service for my brother, Marc?"

"*Sí,*" he said. "*Por toda la familia.*"

For the whole family, he said. More likely, for Emily. The years my brother was in Vietnam were tough on all of us, but especially tough for Emily. It was embarrassing for her, one of the nation's leading antiwar rabble-rousers, to have her twin in the Marines. She gave him

incredible grief for dropping out of Stanford and en-
listing. When he signed up for his second tour of duty,
one would think, listening to Emily, that he had done
something criminal.

Marc and Emily were close, as twins are. But they
always fought. They couldn't help it; they both had ex-
ceedingly strong personalities—that is, egos. Their battles were more wars of domination, one over the other,
than expressions of independence. They could never suc-
cessfully separate from each other. Even when Marc
died.

As we entered the lobby, the crowd rose for us. That's
when it hit me, the purpose of the flowers and candles,
the neighborhood people crowded in the hospital. It was
all for Emily. I had been so preoccupied with looking for
Emily that I hadn't put it all together before. Word about
Emily had gotten out through the community grapevine
very quickly. Again, I thought it was nice so many cared
for her. At the same time, I began to feel very uneasy.

Sometime after Em had been found in that alley, she
seemed to have undergone a transition from Emily, doer
of good things, into Saint Emily. Mythic, heroic, mar-
tyred Saint Emily. I didn't like it very much. Emily would
hate it. For her, I would not enable the myth makers. I
would not become the keeper of Emily's flame, as she
had been the keeper of Marc's.

The crowd pulled at me with their sad faces, as if by
their concern they could will from me better news than
I had to give them.

Father Hermilio leaned his head close to mine. "Will
you stay for a moment and share their prayers?"

"Please, I can't do it now," I said. I walked the narrow
path that opened for me through the crowd, acknowledg-
ing their murmured blessings, touching the hot hands
that reached out for mine. There was a general sighing,
low like wind in your ears when you're running very fast.

"I will see you at mass tonight, my child," Father Hermilio said. He made the sign of the cross over me, and
I bolted.

It was a short run for freedom. When I saw what was waiting for me outside, I stopped so abruptly that Flint nearly collided with me.

Poised among the flowers and candles in the covered entry, a three-person TV news crew lay in waiting: a reporter, a cameraman and a soundman-gofer.

I didn't know the reporter's name, but I recognized the hairdo. When she caught sight of me, I saw her check her reflection in the end of the camera lens and plump the lacquered hair.

I didn't want to go through this new ordeal. I might have backed out, except that I was on foreign turf, and I might need a few favors on account. I plumped my own hair, or tried, and took a handful of Flint's gabardine-upholstered elbow.

"Call your mother," I said to him. "Tell her you'll be on the eleven o'clock news."

He chuckled and pushed open the door.

The camera was already rolling on us.

I held my hand in front of my face. "Hold it a sec," I said. "I'll do this for you, but a couple of requests first."

"Sure," the reporter said. "Pause it, Tony."

She came over to me with her hand extended. "Inez Sanchez, KABC news. What can I do for you?"

"I need some time. As far as I know, my parents haven't heard about Emily yet. Can you hold the story until eleven? Promise me, no news breaks?"

"I think so."

"And keep it low key?"

"Sure."

"Now, what can I do for you?" I said.

"If you don't mind, just stand here with me while I do the set up." She looked closely at me. "My makeup kit's in the van. We'll wait for you."

I checked myself in the nearest window. My hair was flat, I had no lipstick, Stella's makeup job was long gone. I turned to Inez. "Let's just do it."

"Whatever you say."

The soundman dropped a cord down my back, clipped the attached power pack to my belt and found a place under my lapel for the mike. He positioned me so that the carnation spray and its message, DOLOR, made a backdrop. He moved Flint tight beside me and arranged his jacket so that his detective shield caught the light.

"Okay, Inez?"

"When Tony's ready."

"Go ahead," the cameraman said, and I saw the red filming light come on.

Inez went into her spiel:

"We're standing outside French Hospital in the heart of Chinatown. It is sadly ironic that this institution, built a century and a half ago by French missionaries to provide succor for their countrymen, pioneers in the untamed environs of early Los Angeles, and who then stayed to give assistance to the Chinese immigrants who followed, should now offer its services to one who seems to have followed in the footsteps of the original missionary doctors.

"Dr. Emily Duchamps, one of our nation's leading figures in health care for the poor, was found earlier this evening, gravely wounded by an unknown assailant.

"With me now is Dr. Duchamps's sister, award-winning filmmaker Maggie MacGowen." She closed toward me as the camera pulled back. "Miss MacGowen, what is your sister's condition?"

"She's stable and comfortable. Out of pain."

"And the doctor's prognosis for her recovery?"

"Hopeful."

"The name Aleda Weston is also in the news tonight, a name once closely associated with your sister's. Have you spoken recently with Miss Weston?"

"No."

"She is due to arrive in Los Angeles within the hour. Will you be in contact with her?"

Ms. Sanchez was no dummy, damn her. I decided I had been cooperative enough. "Detective Flint can answer more of your questions than I."

I backed out of the camera frame, leaving Flint in the red beam of the lens. I unhooked the mike and the power pack and handed them to the soundman on my way past.

I had gone less than fifty yards through the drizzly prelude to another downpour when Flint caught up to me.

"I said I'd drive you," he said, panting a little from his sprint.

"I want to see Aleda Weston," I said. "Can you arrange it?"

"Depends. I'll try."

Flint's city-issue, green four-door was at a curb marked OFFICIAL VEHICLES ONLY. He opened the passenger door and I slid in across the scratchy imitation tweed upholstery. Flint didn't bother with his seat belt. And he didn't bother with conversation, either.

All the way up the hill to Emily's apartment, I listened to the rain hammering against the car roof and the calls coming across Flint's police radio: "Any unit in the vicinity of the southeast corner of Third and San Pedro, four-five-nine suspect in the building. Handle code two." "Any unit in the vicinity, one-ten South Hope, see the woman, two-eleven purse snatch." It was a dangerous world out there.

"It's painful, but we need to talk about Emily," Flint said, finally.

"Sure," I said. "Just give me a little time to get pulled together."

"Whatever you say."

That's when I saw the flowers in the street, a bright spill along the dark pavement in front of Emily's building. The candles had been tossed out among them, helter-skelter, a few of them still glowing. All the little pots and jars filled with flowers and candles for Emily, all the offerings that had so neatly lined Mrs. Lim's stoop, were smashed. Not randomly broken—every one smashed.

Broken glass crunched under Flint's tires as he pulled to the curb.

"Kids," he said.

"Uh huh." When I opened the car door, I could smell crushed flowers and burning wax. Behind me I heard Flint's radio: "Any unit in the vicinity, Echo Park and Logan, assault in progress. Handle code three."

There were sirens in the distance, and I wondered if they were already rolling in Echo Park. It was only a couple of miles away. Truthfully, what I wondered was, how fast could they get to me?

I can take care of myself. And Flint was only five feet behind me with his automatic holstered on his belt. Didn't matter—what I saw scared me.

Spray-painted on the wall beside Mrs. Lim's front door, two feet high in a very careful script, were the words DIE FAST, BITCH.

Chapter 5

Em's landlady, Mrs. Lim, must have been lying in wait for me while I said goodbye to Flint. She was out of her apartment and rushing down the hall in my direction before I had rebolted the front door behind me. Mrs. Lim grasped my free hand and pressed it against her bony chest.

"Emily, Emily," she wailed. With her gray bun disheveled, the gaps among her teeth, the shocked pallor of her face, she was scary to behold.

I didn't know whether she had seen the mess that had been made of the candles and flowers, or the graffiti painted on the front of her building. Maybe she had heard it all happen. She was certainly frightened.

Not knowing what else to do, I put my arm around her thin shoulders. She was so tiny, it felt like holding a child. I tried to sound reassuring, "The doctors are taking good care of Emily. They're doing everything they can."

She started talking at me in a rapid-fire, high-pitched monotone. I couldn't understand much of what she said. It may have been Chinese, it may have been despair. Whatever it was, she kept it flowing all the way up the stairs to Emily's third-floor apartment. I nodded or tsk'ed when it seemed appropriate.

As I read it, the gist of her anguish was deep guilt that she had not somehow better protected Emily. In other circumstances, the notion was ludicrous of Mrs. Lim, maybe five feet tall if she stretched, physically shielding the gigantic Emily. Unless physical protection wasn't what she was talking about.

I had Em's keys in my hand, but Mrs. Lim was faster with her passkey. She opened Emily's door and kept up her stream of talk. I needed to be alone for a while and didn't want her to follow me inside. To my relief, though she kept talking while I slipped past her, she came no further than the threshold.

"You tell me," she demanded. "Doctor call, you tell me."

"Absolutely," I nodded. "I'll let you know as soon as I hear anything."

She brushed the sleeve of my wet coat. "You change. I get eggroll."

After the intimate tone of our conversation all the way up the stairs, by the time she padded away down the carpeted hall, I was almost sorry to see her go.

I went into Emily's empty apartment and closed the door. I stood there for a moment, hesitant, thinking about Emily, listening for her voice. All that I heard was rain falling on the tile roof above me. A desolate sound, a solo drum tattoo.

I had never spent much time in Emily's apartment. From what I saw, she hadn't either. She certainly hadn't gone to any pains to make the place comfortable. Her rooms had a Zen simplicity. They were small, sparsely furnished, efficiently proportioned. The entry, where I stood, served as a sort of hub, with a bath to my left, the bedroom Em had converted into an office to the right, and through the double doors ahead a combination kitchen and sitting room where she slept, when she slept, on a sofa bed.

The bulb in the entry ceiling fixture was out, so there was very little light, only the general city glow coming through the sitting-room windows and a small night light plugged into a socket beside the bathroom door. Feeling like an intruder, I picked up the only familiar object I saw, a framed photograph of our brother, Marc, and carried it into the sitting room with me.

Still hugging Marc's picture against me, I closed the curtains, switched on a lamp and looked around.

The house I had left in San Francisco was a mess. I live in the Marina District, a block behind the block that was leveled by the big earthquake a couple of years ago. I lost some very good neighbors, as well as the back wall of my restored woodframe Victorian.

Under normal circumstances, reconstruction on the house should have been completed, the frame bolted to a reinforced foundation, and all of it painted a bright new color. But the year of the earthquake had also been the year of my divorce.

Scotty and I had invested our time, more money than we had, and a few layers of skin in that house. I suspect that we lavished so much energy and affection on the place because we had nothing left to give each other. By the time the big quake came, the house was a showplace, the marriage was a shambles.

At the present, I have two-thirds of a house, two-thirds of a family. And debts stretching into the millennium.

The contrast between my house and Emily's could not have been greater. I had left carpenter's dust, tools, construction debris everywhere. Emily's apartment, in contrast, was absolute order. Her place wasn't merely clean, it bordered on being sterile.

Except for Marc's picture, there was no evidence of emotional baggage hanging on her walls, no eccentricities draped over chairs. I hated the lack of her presence. The only sign that anyone lived here was a copy of Camus's *The Stranger*, in the original French, on the table beside the sofa, and a few breakfast dishes draining in a bamboo rack beside the sink: one plate, one cup, one spoon, one knife.

I wanted to know what she had eaten, probably her last meal in her own apartment. I went to the refrigerator to look. With the exception of a very good bottle of chardonnay, I found what I had expected: a block of tofu, a quart of nonfat, unflavored yogurt, a small loaf of dark-brown bread, and a lot of fruit that wasn't very pretty—probably organically grown. It was boring fare. It was a boring room.

Twenty-two years ago, Emily had personified revolutionary youth: brilliant, beautiful, dangerous. What I missed in her apartment was some evidence of that passion. I held up Marc's picture, seeking an answer from his well-remembered face. I found only more questions. Emily had altered the photograph, performed plastic surgery of another sort.

I shivered, and it had nothing to do with wet clothes. On my dresser at home, I had a framed print of the same photograph. Everyone who knew Marc had one. It was the Christmas greeting he had sent from Vietnam, the same shot my mother had hung on the Christmas tree. The prints had arrived in the mail the day we learned he'd been killed, the same day Emily's face appeared on the cover of *Time*.

What made the original snapshot so poignant, besides the timing, was that it was so typical of Marc, so silly. He stands in front of burning latrine barrels with a big grin on his face. He's barechested, wearing fatigues and combat boots. Though he is dirty and sweaty, the smile on his face is truly sweet. In one hand he holds up a red Christmas bulb, in the other a hand-rolled joint that is, in his words, as thick as his dick.

Emily had had her print enlarged. That would have been touching, except that she had had it airbrushed. Censored, if you will. Erasing the shit barrels was one thing, but to wipe out Marc's joint was tantamount to emasculation.

I was shocked. Why would she do such a thing? I ran over the obvious possibilities: trying to boss him one last time, purging his icon to bring him into line with the new political correctness, a posthumous "just say no"? Emily, as I remember her, would have called this sucking up to the Establishment, caving in to the status quo. I usually thought she was a bit wacko when she spouted off this line, but for her it was completely natural. As natural as seeing Marc with marijuana.

Some of my fondest memories of youth are of walking with my big sister and brother in the hills behind our parents' Berkeley house. Walking and sharing a joint. For this sin I am now, of course, deeply regretful, but the sky was so blue then, the jokes so funny, the discussion so profound.

Passing me a joint was the first act of recognition by Em and Marc that I was growing up, was becoming somewhat interesting, was more significant than the maggot they labeled me when I was a baby. Tainted as we were by the evil weed, without question those were the best times I can remember.

Recently, I was talked into attending an anti-drug fundraiser cocktail party by an old friend who had gone on a few of those walks with me and Marc and Em. In spite of this folly during his formative years, our friend has gone on to become a very successful, and very straight, investment banker. He was to give a prepared speech at this "do" about drugs and the ruination of America's youth. But he was pretty bombed on martinis by the time he was to take the podium. He wanted me to go up with him and give a testimonial, admit our youthful sins.

"Glad to," I said. "I'll tell them that now and then I used to share a joint with friends and lovers, and I'm sorry as hell about it. It nearly cost me my job. I could handle heightened orgasm, not be misled that conversation was made more brilliant. My downfall was what it did for banana-nut ice cream. Banana-nut ice cream is why I gave up smoking grass. I couldn't have a joint and not crave banana-nut, I couldn't eat ice cream and keep an on-camera figure. The choice was clear—career future or marijuana. I gave up the weed."

"Never mind," he said.

"It's the truth," I said.

"Fuck it," he said. That evening was the last I ever heard from him.

I was following my wet footprints back toward Em's sofa when the doorbell rang.

I opened the door and said, surprised, "Ah, Detective Flint."

"This neighborhood's a bitch to find a parking place," he said, taking off his raincoat.

"In a police car? Can't you just park it anywhere?"

"Not unless I want a ticket." He was looking around for someplace to hang his coat. "In this town, they even ticket the mayor."

"Very honorable," I said, following him into the bathroom, where he draped his coat over the shower door. "Why are you here?"

"You should change out of those wet clothes," he said. "And turn up the radiator. This place is colder than the morgue."

"Detective," I said, "I have things to do, some phone calls to make. Then I plan to take a hot bath and get right back to the hospital."

"No tub here," he said. "Have to settle for a shower."

"When I said I wanted a little time, I meant more than five minutes."

He was already in the sitting room, looking around.

"Go ahead," he said. "Go change. I'll look after myself."

"Go away," I said.

"Not a chance." He sat down on the sofa and crossed one knee over the other. He had long, runner's legs, and I liked the way the gray pinstripes stretched across his thighs. I found this observation to be vaguely disturbing.

Flint put on a thin smile and looked around, taking inventory. "Not much of a decorator, was she?"

"She didn't spend much time here," I said. I stood in the middle of the room, wet and shivery and shocked numb.

"You should get out of your wet clothes."

"Right," I said, too miserable to object anymore. "Don't touch anything until I get back."

He smiled. "Wouldn't think of it."

There was a walk-in closet off Emily's office. I rummaged around and found a set of navy sweats and a pair of thick ski socks. I shed my clothes and hung them up to dry, the holiday-red suit I had worn for filming, the

sodden camel coat, my underwear. The ruined pumps I
tossed into a corner, then, remembering that Em's feet
were several sizes larger than mine, set them upright and
stuffed the toes with tissue. After I spoke with my parents, I planned to call Lyle, my tenant, and have him
send me down a bag of essentials.

Though I hadn't even thought about lighting a joint
for fifteen years, before I left the closet I looked inside
Em's little redwood jewelry box, just in case, for old
time's sake, she still kept a stash there. I found some
pretty good jewelry. But that was all.

There was a knock at the front door and I beat Flint
to it. I found Mrs. Lim, holding a covered tray.

"I make eggroll and tea," she said, with a little bow.
"Very hot."

"Thank you," I said. She came in, hesitated when
she saw Flint, then went through and set the tray next
to the sofa. As she uncovered the eggrolls and poured
tea, she kept looking over at him, something building in
her mind.

"Smells wonderful," I said.

She handed me a cup of tea, then pointedly recovered
the pot with a starched linen napkin without offering anything to Flint. Instead, she pointed a finger at him and
scolded, "You no good police, Michael, this happen for
Emily."

"I'm sorry, Mrs. Lim," he said, looking abashed. "Believe me, I'm sorry."

"No good police, Michael." She jabbed her finger in
his direction once more, looked to make sure I was
drinking my tea, stopped to adjust the radiator, then
turned and padded out the door.

"She blames me for Emily," Flint said, chagrined,
when she was gone.

"She's upset, she needs to blame someone," I said. I
went to the kitchen to get him a cup. "I'm just glad she's
mad at you and not me."

"I've known her for years. She'll calm down."

"You seem to know everybody in town."

"Basically." He poured himself tea and sipped it as he made a slow circuit around the room. "You haven't checked the messages on Doc's answering machine."

"They may be personal."

"Maybe." He punched the replay button and I went over and stood beside him to listen. He seemed a lot taller all of a sudden, now that I was in stocking feet. I stood as straight as I could while we waited for the machine to rewind. There were a lot of messages, so it took a while.

My mother was first. "Good morning, sweetheart. Dad and I were thinking about you. Give us a call. I love you."

There were a couple of calls from someone named Jose at County General delivering incomprehensible lab information, something about hemocytes.

An almost familiar man's voice: "Four o'clock, Em. Chill the wine."

"She did," I said, pausing the tape.

"What?" Flint asked.

"Chill the wine. It's in the refrigerator."

"So, did they meet at four?"

"If they did, they didn't open the wine. I wish I knew who that was."

"Yeah." He restarted the tape.

Most of the messages were business, delivered in the sort of shorthand evolved by people who speak together frequently. Some left names and times, some didn't.

The first call I found ominous came from someone named Leroy Bates, from Health and Human Services in San Pedro. "Dr. Duchamps, it's one-ten now. Did I get our appointment time wrong? I have a two o'clock flight to Sacramento. I'll be back tomorrow. Call me and we can reschedule." Where had Emily been?

He was followed by a very familiar voice. "Emily, you're nuts. Don't do a damn thing until you talk to me. I have a room at the Bonaventure now, and I'm waiting for your call. I love you like crazy."

Flint played that one again.

"It's my uncle, Max," I said. "He's Emily's attorney."

"You know what he's talking about?"

"I intend to ask him."

I heard my own voice next, the first message I had left that afternoon.

"What time was that?" he asked.

"Around three-thirty, a little before. I called from the airport."

"Cutting it close, weren't you?"

"It was the only flight I could get."

He nodded and listened through two hang-up calls before Emily's four o'clock date made a second call:

"It's almost five, Emily. Where are you? I'm still waiting . . ."

Then I called again. "Come home, Em. I'm in the booth across the street. I'm cold, I'm wet, I'm hungry. And get out the penicillin—I had to use the bathroom at the Chevron station on the corner and I know I picked up something lethal."

Max again. He sounded angry, said it was after six and he was tired of being room mother. The tape ran out before I could make sense of the comment.

Flint lifted the tape out of the machine. "Damn it, Emily. Where were you?"

"May I have the tape?" I said, holding out my hand.

"Later. It has to go downtown first. You'll get it back, I promise."

I was going to argue, but the telephone rang.

"Hello," I said.

"Emily, thank God you're there." The four o'clock date. "What's happened?"

To Flint I mouthed, "It's him." Into the telephone, I said, "What could happen?"

"Why didn't you come?"

"Where?"

There was a long pause. "Emily?"

I was afraid he would hang up if I played this any further. "This is Emily's sister. Please, who are you?"

"Maggot?" It was almost a sob. I wished I could place

his voice. I was sure I had heard it somewhere, some-time. He sounded desperate. Emily had been giving sanctuary to desperate people for a long, long time. He could easily be one of them. He called me Maggot. A lot of her friends from the old days called me Maggot.

"Are you still there?" I asked.

"Yes. How are you, Maggot?"

"So so."

"Where is Emily? I have to talk to her."

"Emily can't come to the phone now. I'll relay a message for you."

"Just tell me that she's all right."

"She isn't all right." I started to cry. It made me mad, but there was nothing I could do about it. The pain inside simply took over. Then he was crying into the telephone, too, in short choking gasps, the way my father, and probably a lot of other men, cry. When I could, I said, "Who are you?"

"Not yet, Maggot. Not yet." Then the line went dead.

I stood there, sobbing. It felt good to let go, but I was still embarrassed that Flint had seen me come apart. He handed me the linen napkin from Mrs. Lim's tea tray.

"You're a real brick," he smiled.

"Fuck you," I gasped, wiping my face and blowing my nose into the napkin.

"A real brick and foul-mouthed." He put a tentative arm around my shoulders and held me stiffly. He patted my back. I thought he was being so nice because I was Emily's sister. Maybe he hurt, too. He crooned, "Go ahead and cry."

"I'm finished." But I let my head drop against his lapels. It wasn't very comfortable; all the paraphernalia on his belt—holster, beeper, shield—came between us. But I could hear his heart beat, hear the air going in and out of his chest, and that made me feel better. I started to breathe regularly after a few minutes.

"You okay?" he asked.

"Yes."

"If you're sure you're okay," he said, "maybe we could talk about that phone call."

"I'm okay." I moved away from him, blew my nose again, and managed a steady breath. I sat down on the sofa and thought about what the man had said.

"So?" Flint asked.

My voice sounded shaky and thick, but it served. "I don't know who the caller is, but he knows me. Or knew me a long time ago."

"What makes you think so?"

"The way he reacted when I told him who I was. He called me Maggot."

"That's significant?"

"Very," I said. "There's something about his voice that's familiar, and at the same time, it isn't. I wish I could place him. Maybe it was just the tone of the conversation that was familiar. He seemed very nervous. He wouldn't say anything that would identify him, as if maybe he thought the conversation was being overheard. I used to take a lot of nonmessage messages for Emily, from people who wouldn't leave their names."

"Married men who take lovers don't leave their names, either."

"A lover?" I thought about the bottle of wine, Em's beautiful new breasts. "That's a possibility."

"Anything else about him?"

"Just impressions. He's not especially young, not especially old. No strong regional accent. He sounds educated, but not academic, not like the stiffs on the faculty with my father. The rest you know: He had a date with Emily at four, and she missed it. About that, he seemed worried, maybe frightened, rather than angry. One other thing," I said. "He asked awfully quickly whether she was all right. When I said she wasn't, he cried."

"*He* cried?"

"What, you never cried?"

"Never." He picked up an eggroll and bit into it. "Almost never, anyway."

"You're some tough guy, Flint."

"Comes with the territory." He smiled. "You know, you're perceptive. You'd make a pretty good detective."

"I was a reporter for a long time."

"If you ever decide to convert to the good guys, give me a call."

"I'm tired, Flint," I said. "Will you go away?"

"Let's call Uncle Max."

"After you leave. It's a personal call. I might cry again."

"Go ahead." He tossed me the napkin. "There's still a dry corner."

I laughed. "You a married man, detective?"

"Twenty years," he said.

"Amazing," I said.

"Not really. Twelve with Leslie, eight with Charlene. I don't count the year between them, or the two after."

"So you're not married."

He shook his head. "Go on, call Uncle Max."

"What time is it?"

"Ten-fifteen."

I went to the telephone, but dialed my parents' number instead of the Bonaventure.

Nine o'clock is the beginning of the evening for my parents. Over the last few years, they seem to have given up on sleep except as a way to fill the hours before dawn. I believe my father is afraid to sleep. It reminds him that one day fairly soon he won't wake up at all. And when he does sleep, he dreams of Marc in his coffin.

My mother answered on the first ring. "Emily?" she said, without bothering with hello.

"Mother, it's Maggie," I said.

"Are you with Emily?"

"I just left her."

"Tell her the guest room is all ready for her mystery guest." She sounded artificially cheerful, fueled by an extra martini after dinner, I thought. Maybe two.

"Mom, is Dad with you?"

"He's at the faculty club playing trio sonatas with the Helms. Margot, they ran your new promos after *Mac-*

Neil/Lehrer tonight. You looked lovely. Your hair seemed lighter. Have you done something to it?"

"No. It was probably the lighting." I took a breath. "Who is Em's mystery guest?"

"If I knew it would hardly be a mystery, would it? All she said was, that it's someone we have all been waiting for. Think it's a romance?"

"Mom," I said, getting a toehold before she took off on another tangent. "Emily is in the hospital."

A pause. "Working late?"

"I don't know how to say this. She was injured this afternoon. She's in intensive care."

"Intensive care?"

"Yes. Mom, Em was shot."

I waited until she clued me she was ready to hear more, expecting either sobs or a flood of questions to bridge denial. When she finally spoke, I was nonplussed by the calm in her voice. And by what she asked first.

"Did Emily shoot herself?"

"No," I said quickly.

As she asked about the details of Em's condition, the hospital, the people taking care of her, I began to understand that Mother had been expecting something dire. I don't mean to suggest that she was not upset about Emily. Certainly she was. There was also a quality of relief about her, as if the monster that had been lurking in her closet had finally shown his face. He was fearsome, but apparently not as horrible as she had imagined. At least, his name wasn't suicide.

"Dad and I will get the first plane down," she said. "We'll look after Emily. The rest, Margot, my darling, we'll leave to you."

"The rest?" I asked.

"Find the truth."

She said good-bye and hung up and left me dumbfounded.

"Everything okay?" Flint asked.

"I don't know," I said. "Let's go see my Uncle Max."

Chapter 6

One nice thing about Los Angeles, you can never look too strange. It was very late. I walked through the lobby of the Bonaventure Hotel wearing Em's too-big sweats, her black Burberry raincoat slapping around my ankles, a Dodgers cap over my wet hair, and red spike-heeled pumps.

Flint, who walked beside me, looked like a straight john in his suit and trenchcoat. I think the contrast should have elicited at least a leer, and would have in a hotel of this caliber almost anywhere else in the world. The desk clerk who took care of us was nothing but obsequious. He rang Uncle Max's room, announced Miss MacGowen and a gentleman, and sent us up to the eighth floor.

"Tell me about Max," Flint said on the way.

"You'll meet him for yourself. Don't be surprised by how young he is. Max is my father's baby brother. I think he's only four years older than Emily and Marc."

When the elevator doors opened, Max was there waiting, pacing the hall in his stocking feet. He did a double take when I stepped out.

"Where's Emily?" he asked, looking past me and into the empty elevator. Disappointed I think, and puzzled, his eyes came to rest on Flint. "Who's he?"

I said, "Can we go inside?"

He looked again at Flint. "I'm not sure."

Ordinarily, Uncle Max is a gorgeous man with dark, polished good looks. But even on camping trips, I had never seen him as bedraggled as he appeared in that hallway. He wore the remains of business attire, a rumpled dress shirt and suit pants with red suspenders hanging loose. But it wasn't his clothes that made him seem such a mess. Something about his posture, his expression, his aura, if you will, was disordered. His face was pale and blotchy—stress, I thought, or too much booze. When he got around to hugging me, I could smell him, the acrid sweat of a man with something eating at him.

"Is Emily following you here?" Max asked.

"No," I said. "Max, we have to talk. But inside, okay?"

"Without Em?" He was still bothered by Flint. He gave him another long visual going over, from the top of his short haircut to the tips of his well-waxed shoes. He asked, "FBI?"

"LAPD." Flint showed his ID. "Detective Michael Flint."

"Damn, Maggie." Max pulled me aside. "Does Em know you're bringing him?"

"No," I said.

"It's her party. No one gets in without an invitation."

"I invited him," I said. We were the only people in the hall, but there were a lot of doors to listen behind. "You have a room here, Max? Or are you working the halls?"

Max threw up his hands. "Whatever you say. Let Emily's wrath fall upon your head, not mine."

As we walked toward Max's room, he and Flint did a sort of parry-thrust routine, spraying off their particular legal territories.

"Emily is my client," Max said. "I will say nothing until I have consulted with her. You know the bonds of lawyer-client privilege."

"I know they're not absolute," Flint said. "When you're briefed on the situation, you'll want to talk with us."

"We'll see." Max unlocked his door, but held up his hand for us to wait. He leaned inside and said something.

The response I heard was some quick shuffling of feet, an inner door closing. Then Max waved us in.

He stopped me as I passed him and fussed with my cap. "Maggie, did I forget to say I'm glad to see you?"

"You did."

"Well, all things considered, I am." He took my hand and led me inside. "All rise. Our Maggot is here."

The Bonaventure Hotel is comprised of five tall glass cylinders standing in a bundle. The roundness of the hotel is striking on the outside, but it gives the rooms inside awkward shapes, triangular like slices of a pie. In Max's share of the pie, his rumpled bed occupied the crust end and two sofas and various tables filled the point.

Max needed to call housekeeping. At least to make the bed. Tangled among the sheets were the tumbled contents of two large briefcases and the remains of several room-service dinners. On the low table between the sofas there was a bucket of ice, half a bottle of scotch, a pyramid of beer cans, a collection of used coffee cups, all surrounded by sloppy, wet rings.

I smelled the sweet, heavy fragrance of pot hanging in the air. A familiar, nostalgic aroma in keeping with the presence of the two men occupying the sofas.

California State Assemblyman Rod Peebles and the Reverend Lucas Slaughter rose to greet me. I doubt whether I had seen either of them in the flesh for fifteen years or more. They looked essentially the same, just incongruously older: young people disguised behind the masks of middle-aged folks. Beyond the good wool clothes and the expensive, Establishment haircuts, a micromillimeter under the surface, I knew I would find the same old radicals.

Flint was literally sniffing the air. But he said nothing. He went straight to the television, turned it on, and with the sound off, watched the screen out of the corner of his eye.

Rod and Lucas were both reaching for me.

"Good to see you, kid," Lucas said. He mashed me

against the packets of room service sugar and a hotel pen he had squirreled away in his shirt pocket. "Déjà vu, huh? All of us waiting for Emily."

"Where the hell is Emily?" Rod Peebles gripped my hand quickly. "We're worried sick. We've been here since five o'clock."

"She isn't coming," I said. I dropped the bomb: "Emily has been shot."

Suddenly Max had no color. "How bad?"

"She's in a coma."

"But she's alive?"

"Technically," I said. "There's a lot of brain damage. Even if by some miracle Emily survives, we've lost her."

Max looked as if he would collapse. I took him by the hand and guided him to sit beside me on the sofa. Lucas clearly was devastated, speechless. Rod Peebles's face I saw only through the bottom of his scotch glass.

Flint perched on the edge of a table facing us. He was the first to break the shocked silence. "Need anything?" he asked.

Max slowly shook his head.

I squeezed Max's hand. "What was this meeting all about?"

"I don't know."

"I don't believe you. Please, for Emily, help me."

"I wish I could." He stood and made an attempt to pull himself together. At least, he tucked in his shirt and pulled up his suspenders. "Where's the goddamn coffee I ordered?"

He settled for the bottle of scotch. I gave him time to down a hefty shot before I pressed him.

"Please, Uncle Max," I said. "I need you."

"Uncle Max," he repeated, slurring his words a little. He swallowed another shot. "Therein lies the problem. *Uncle.* Uncle sounds so dependable. They always made me babysit you three, you and Marc and Emily. I was just a kid, too, for chrissake. Whatever mess you got into, I couldn't say no to because it was always more interesting than anything I could think up. And more dangerous. You just sucked me along in your wake. All of you. When you got into trouble, everyone thought it was my fault. I was the fucking uncle. I always had to tidy up after you. And the bigger you three got, the tougher the cleanup got."

He glared at me, his body swaying boozily. "Don't you sit there, little Maggot, with your eyes wide and innocent. You were as bad as Marc and Emily. No, you were worse. You never knew when enough was enough." He pointed at me. "But I do. I've had enough. Your messes are too big now for anyone to fix."

Flint, Rod, Lucas, took this in with grim-faced chagrin. I think they were all too embarrassed to look at me.

"Sit down, Max, before you fall," I said, getting up and walking over to him. "You delivered that speech very well, sounded just like Marc. Have a tantrum when someone calls you to account, and they back off. But it's me you're sounding off to, and I'm inured. I also know you're one of the most capacitous drunks in town. Half a bottle of scotch shared with friends and spread over an evening is nothing for you.

"You've got good technique," I said. "But save it for the uninitiated. Tell me what Emily was up to."

Max had the grace to smile.

Lucas applauded. "God, how I've missed this."

"Max," I said. "Now that you've circled the camp, don't you think it's time to enter the breach?"

Flint gaped. "I can tell you're related," he said. "What's it like when the whole family is together?"

"Noisy," Lucas said.

"It used to be," I said. "But it's gotten awfully quiet. Go ahead, Max."

He nodded toward Flint. "What about him?"

"He stays," I said. "And no more bullshit. Emily was planning to do something dramatic today. It has to do with Marc, and the date, and Aleda, and a man I think I used to know. And that's why she was shot. So, what was up?"

"I don't know." Max was back at the scotch bottle. "What did she tell you?"

"Nothing. She said to meet her at her apartment at four. She told Mom and Dad she would be bringing someone home for the holidays."

He thought about that for a moment. "She told me to come down to L.A., get a hotel room in the general vicinity of Chinatown. She said people would be coming to see her—she didn't say who—and that I was to keep them all fed and entertained until she arrived. She said she had a surprise. She said she wouldn't be alone and there might be legal complications. But she was really happy."

"And?" I said.

"That's all. Except for mass. She arranged a midnight memorial mass for Marc and she wanted us all to go."

I turned to Rod and Lucas. "Is that why you're here? Emily called?"

"That's it," Lucas said.

"That's enough," Rod nodded. "But I can't stay for mass. Previous engagement."

"Oh, yes?" Lucas winked at me. "Don't get the idea that our Assemblyman Rod is a heathen, Maggie. It's just that he has persuaded himself that his constituents have forgotten about his radical origins. He doesn't want to be seen in public with his old comrades, lest his flock are reminded that he was once the personification of the 'L' word—Liberal. Our Rod has changed his political raiment. I always counsel him to summon the doubters as the Lord summoned Moses, and tell them, 'I am who I say that I am.' And if they give him any guff, he should follow the Lord's example and set the place on fire. Rod certainly remembers how it's done."

"Fuck off, Lucas," Rod said. He poured himself a stiff drink and drained it. "You always think you're so damned funny. Let's show a little respect here. Or didn't it sink in what Maggie just said? Emily was shot."

Lucas was puffing up for a retort, but Flint raised a hand and cut him short.

"Hang on," Flint said. He reached over and turned up the volume on the television.

On the screen, we saw the videotaped image of Inez Sanchez standing in front of French Hospital. There was some residual grousing between Lucas and Rod, so we missed part of her set-up speech. But Flint and I had heard it before:

"Dr. Emily Duchamps, one of our nation's leading figures in health care for the poor, was found earlier this evening, gravely wounded by an unknown assailant."

The camera pulled back, brought Flint and me into the frame. I did my short bit, Flint did his, then the screen faded to a piece of file footage from the late sixties: the front of the Federal Courthouse in San Francisco, zoom on a cheering group on the steps, all of them with raised fist salutes—Emily, Rod, Lucas, Emily's ex husband, Jaime Orozco, the late Arthur Fulham Dodds, Celeste Baldwin. And Aleda Weston.

The magic of television took us back to Inez, live now, at the Los Angeles airport. She wore the same coat, new makeup. She was standing on the sidewalk outside a terminal building, waiting for Aleda and her federal marshal escort to come out.

Inez was out of the rain, but the traffic around her was relentless. The effect was something like broadcasting from a freeway shoulder. Passing buses and vans regularly overpowered the sound transmission and blew her hair across her face, lifted her coattails.

Standing with Inez was Mrs. Tom Potts, Senior. I remembered her from the trial and all the press coverage. She was the mother of the graduate student who had been immolated in a lab fire during a Berkeley demonstration in 1969. He was the manslaughter on the indictment against Emily and her colleagues, the heart of the fire that had provided the backdrop for Emily's *Time* cover.

To my best recollection, Mrs. Potts was a schoolteacher, and Mr. Potts was some sort of civil servant. They were a family with more hope than money to invest. And young Tom Potts was the sum of their investment.

Mrs. Potts ignored Inez's questions to deliver her own message.

"I have waited the equivalent in years of my son's lifetime for his killers to be brought to justice," Mrs. Potts said. "I hear that Aleda Weston has been very ill. Maybe that's why she's come out of hiding. I'm here to make sure that some high-priced lawyer doesn't convince the people of this country that the twenty-two years she spent as a fugitive from justice can in some way equate to time spent in prison. Even if she was shut off from the company of her family, at least she was alive. Because of her actions, my son was not so fortunate."

She took a breath. "I offer my condolences to the parents of Dr. Duchamps. They also lost a son. But for the doctor herself, I am only sorry that she cannot feel pain the way my Tom did. The eternal fires of hell are nothing compared to what he suffered in that burning laboratory. My consolation is that Dr. Duchamps is about to find out for herself what the fires of hell are."

Her bitterness stunned me. Such hatred must have needed constant tending to keep it fresh for so many years. I looked over at Flint to check his reaction. I was thinking we had watched suspect number one spill her guts. Flint wouldn't look at me. He sat on the edge of the table with his arms folded across his chest, his face perfectly passive. Even when we caught our first glimpse of Aleda, he didn't change his expression.

Lucas gasped. "Dear God." He began to weep softly.

The lighting was spotty, but I saw Aleda's face clearly. She seemed much older than her forty-four or forty-five years. She was excruciatingly thin, stooped as with gross fatigue. The flashing cameras and the jostling press seemed to confuse her. My heart ached for her. Mercifully, her escort hustled her into a waiting car and swiftly drove her away.

Max turned off the set. "Lucas, what did you say earlier? Déjà vu? I look around this room, I see those faces on the tube, and hell, it's December 1969 again."

"There are a few faces missing," I said. "Is this all Emily had in mind? A reunion, with a surprise guest? Who would it be, Max?"

Max shrugged. "I don't know."

"But you must have some ideas," I said.

"I know this will sound crazy," he shrugged. "But Emily has been behaving so strangely."

"Strange how?" I asked.

"Happy. Think about it. Emily happy in December."

"So?"

"So." Max reached out and touched my cheek and looked deep into my eyes. His own eyes welled with tears. "I can't explain it, but I've had this weird feeling all day, Maggot, that Emily was going to bring Marc."

Chapter 7

Flint and I were alone in the hall outside Max's room, waiting for a down elevator. My head buzzed from too much coffee, too much talk, not enough good answers. It was late, and though I felt frayed, my mind was still racing.

Flint was awfully quiet.

"What do you think?" I asked him.

"About that mob?" He had a wry smile. "Bunch of commies."

"Actually, one reconstructed Trotskyite, an Episcopalian, and a Harvard man."

"You know what I mean."

I laughed. "Good bet none of them voted for Bush."

He was thinking about it as we got into the elevator. "Your uncle went to Harvard?"

"For law school only."

"Maybe that explains it."

"What?"

"He's either nuts, or drunk. Or both."

"Uncle Max?" I said. "I don't think so."

"What he said about expecting your brother to show up. Twenty-two years after his funeral. You don't find that strange?"

"Sure," I said. "But on a one to ten scale of strange things I've encountered only today, with rain in L.A. measuring one and the shooting of Emily hitting ten, I think the notion that Marc could be alive only rates a six, maybe a seven."

"You don't mean that," he said.

We stepped out of the elevator and into the lobby.

"It's the date, Flint. Max has been thinking about Marc. He feels him close by. I feel him, too, almost like being haunted. Though there's more to it than heavy remembrance." I looked over at him. "Something is up. Some bit of old, unfinished business wants to be taken care of."

He frowned. "This unfinished business has Max scared?"

"Not scared as much as frustrated. Unfinished business can be like *coitus interruptus*," I said. "You know how that sets you on edge, don't you, Flint?"

"The things that come out of your mouth . . ."

I have long legs, a family trait, and I was stretching them to get through the cavelike lobby and out the door. Flint had no trouble keeping up. When we were outside, in the rain again, I turned to him.

"Get me in to see Aleda Weston," I said.

"I'll try. I'll make some calls in the morning."

"Tonight, Flint. I want to talk to Aleda tonight."

"Jesus, lady. Aren't you worn out? I'll buy you a drink, take you back to Emily's apartment. You get some sleep. In the morning, when normal channels are open, I'll see what I can do."

"Never mind," I said. We stood on the sidewalk in front of the hotel, rain pelting the awning over our heads. The only way I can describe how I felt is itchy, itchy inside somewhere I couldn't quite reach. But I had to keep trying.

I looked sideways at Flint. "Tell me where they're taking Aleda tonight and I'll handle things myself."

"Be my guest," he challenged. "She's being booked into the Metro Detention Center, the new federal lockup on Alameda. Think you can talk your way in?"

"I think it would be a lot easier if I was with a badge."

He slapped his hand over his heart and grinned at me, "She admits she needs me."

"Jesus Christ, Flint, it wasn't a proposal."

"Ssh," he said. "Don't spoil the moment."

I turned and started walking again so he wouldn't see me laugh.

Flint was beginning to grow on me. In my line of work, I've met a fair share of policemen, a lot of them suits like Flint. Generally, I don't like them very much. They wear a tough veneer, armor I suppose, to protect the soft spots they manage to hang on to in spite of the shit they see during the ordinary course of their work. Emotional armor may be necessary to survive the job until retirement, but it makes them hard to get close to, too slick to get a solid grip on.

Outwardly, Flint was like his comrades: nosy, cautious, bossy, reactionary, opinionated. He made the proper tough-guy faces, held the right postures, but I suspected that all the time he was asking his questions, doing his cop thing, he was loving every minute. His hair had gone white awfully early in life, but he seemed otherwise unmarked by his dealings with the city's underside.

Flint hadn't let the valet park his city car when we arrived. So we had to retrace the long hike into the depths of the hotel garage to fetch it. When the car was in sight, he bumped my arm.

"Say it," he said. "Say you need me."

"If that's all it takes, okay. I need you, Flint. I need you to get me in to Aleda."

"Okay, we'll give it a try," he said. "But first you tell me why the hurry."

"I don't know. There just is."

"There just is?" he said. "How do I write that in the report?"

"You write this, 'Detective Michael Flint, serial number . . .' What's your serial number?"

"One-five-nine-nine-one."

"You can fill that in later," I said. "You write, 'Detective Michael Flint, after an exhaustive investigation, determined that Aleda Weston, located in the custody of United States Federal Marshals at the Los Angeles Metropolitan Detention Center, was a material witness in the shooting of Emily Duchamps."

"Did we just make another detour into Oz? Aleda was in an airplane somewhere over the breadbasket when Emily was shot."

"I bet you breakfast that if you check long-distance telephone records, you'll find some nice long chats between Emily's number and the general neighborhood of Aleda's most recent digs."

"Think so?"

"I just bet on it, didn't I?"

"If you're so damned smart, tell me what they were talking about."

"The timing of this little reunion. Aleda and Emily were very close until Aleda went underground. I know they worked this all out together."

He thought about it, frowning. "You can't be thinking that Emily expected Aleda to come and pour the coffee. They had to know she would be in custody for a while."

I took his arm. "Let's just ask her, shall we?"

Still he hesitated. "Do you eat big breakfasts?"

"Huge," I said. "This one will really cost you."

"We'll see." He unlocked the car. "*Vamanos*."

The car was cold when we got in. The windshield steamed up as soon as Flint turned on the heater. Flint smeared it around a little with his coat sleeve. I couldn't see anything out of my side. He strained forward as he drove us up out of the garage, trying not to hit any concrete pillars. He was awfully quiet again. He had turned down his dispatch radio so that we heard only a female-voiced hum over the sound of the engine and of tires squealing on the slick driveway. I kicked off my shoes and put my damp feet against the heater vents and tried to sort things out.

I had planned to stop by the hospital to see Emily. When I called Dr. Song before leaving Max's room, he told me my parents had arrived. My father, he said, was sedated and sleeping in the doctors' lounge. The nurses had set up a cot in Em's room for my mother. If, by some chance, Mother had managed to fall asleep, my arrival would waken her. She had to be exhausted. I wanted to see her, but, as Dr. Song had warned me, we were in for a long haul. Mom and Dad needed their rest. I could wait until morning. I prayed Emily held on that long.

The Metropolitan Detention Center sits next to the Hollywood Freeway, a cruel, transient view for the prisoners locked inside.

Flint parked in what he called city parking—a red zone in front of the building. He hung the microphone of his police radio over his rearview mirror to fend off parking cops.

The streets were deserted—downtown L.A. dies when the commuters go home for the night. Other than a few dark shapes sleeping in protected recesses around the entrance, there was no one around. Not even a news van in sight.

The detention center building is new. It looks more like a postmodern hotel than a prison. At least on the outside. The reception area beyond the front door is hard and polished and austere beyond any need.

There were two federal corrections officers manning the front desk. Flint handed his police photo ID to the older officer, a thin, balding man in his mid-thirties.

"Detective Flint," he said. "LAPD. Major Crimes Section."

"Officer Clark. Guest registration," the officer said, handing back Flint's ID. "I can recommend the accommodations, sir, but we don't offer room service."

Flint laughed politely. "Quiet night, huh?"

"Up here it is," Clark said. By now they were both leaning companionably on the desk. I might as well have been invisible. "New guest has things hopping in the booking area."

"Would that be Aleda Weston?"

Clark nodded. "Our star boarder."

"Is she processed in?"

"They're still at it. You want to talk to her, you'll have to wait."

"Who's the assigned federal attorney?"

"Ricardo Valenti."

"Richie Valenti?" Flint raised his brows. "Is he in the building?"

"Believe he is. You know Richie?"

"Hell yes." Flint grinned. "We been tangling for a long time."

Clark grinned his own grin and leaned closer to Flint, expectant. "Yeah?"

"He ever tell you about Señora Magdalena?"

"He never did." Clark turned to a second officer, an Opie-esque, freckle-faced redhead. "Hey, Ernie, Detective Flint here was on the Magdalena thing with Richie Valenti."

"Yeah?" Ernie joined them. "How'd that go down?"

"Classic lawyer fuckup," Flint said. "Can't blame Richie, though. You ever see Señora Magdalena?"

"Nice, huh?"

"Beautiful. Little bitty thing. Couldn't have weighed more than a hundred pounds. And tight all over. You know the type?"

Flint's listeners, lifted from their nightwatch boredom, pressed closer, waiting for more. I stood back a little, an interloper, and watched Flint work. He was good, with subtle hand gestures and facial expressions that said more than his words. This was male bonding at its richest.

"Beautiful little thing," Flint repeated. "And young. In this country we would have called her marriage statutory rape. How she hooked up with Señor Magdalena I can't figure. Except he was rich. What was he, Colombian trade consul or something? Anyway, he was older than shit and just about as ugly. I think Richie got a look at him and started to feel sorry for the *linda señora*. Stupid ass, huh?"

"Typical lawyer," Clark chuckled. "Dumb shit."

Flint cast me a sidelong leer. "Guess we shouldn't talk about a pending federal case in front of a potential witness, right?"

The two listeners swiveled to look at me.

"Hell," I said. "Don't let me interrupt a good story."

Turning from me, Flint gestured Clark and Ernie closer. "Help me out on a technicality here. Is it considered a conflict of interest if, when a federal case comes to trial, the prosecuting attorney and the chief defense witness are both still taking penicillin for something they picked up together in an interrogation room?"

They all laughed, a little too hard, I thought.

"So," Flint said. "Is Richie still in the building?"

"I can call down. What's your business?"

Flint nodded toward me. "Señora Magdalena's sister wants to see him."

"No shit?"

"Nah. Miz MacGowen is Aleda Weston's half-sister. I was told to bring her over here to see the attorney in charge. Guess that's Richie, huh?"

"Come on through," Clark said. "Ernie'll escort you back. Say hi to Richie for me."

"I'll do that," Flint said.

Ernie was still chuckling as he opened a side door for us. Flint waited for me to go ahead of him.

"You're a good liar," I whispered as I walked past.

"Standard operating bullshit."

"With you, it's a gift."

He laughed.

"I can't wait to meet Richie Valenti," I said.

Flint winked. "Neither can I."

I stopped in my tracks and laughed. Guffawed may be a better description. Ernie seemed to think I was fairly strange. The way I looked, baggy sweats and spike heels, and Flint's allusion to me during his Richie story, may have given him a certain impression. I didn't give a damn: he was handing us visitor's passes. Ernie clipped a plastic pass to Flint's lapel, but stood at arm's length to hand me mine.

"Through here, folks," Ernie said, and led us into a back passageway. "Down at the end of the hall."

I noticed the noise first, a stark contrast to the mausoleumlike quiet of the front lobby. A dozen or more peo-

ple hustled about or sloped against the walls in various
stages of boredom. The mob looked something like the
crowd that was keeping vigil outside Emily's hospital
room: clusters of people in wilted business suits, a peri-
meter marked by half a dozen uniformed officers. Most
of the activity centered around a gridded window, a cage,
set in the wall at the end.

On the far side of the cage, I could see the bowed,
graying head of Aleda Weston.

I felt a sudden rush of emotion when I recognized her,
equal parts nostalgic tingle and elation for having pulled
this off. I gently punched Flint's padded shoulder.
"We're in."

"Getting into a lockup is never the problem," he said.
"It's getting out again."

"I'll worry about that later. That's Aleda. How close
can we get to her?"

"You can just walk up and talk to her."

"Really?"

"Try it."

We were being watched, the newcomers. It was too
late and too damp outside for anyone to look freshly
starched, but I was certainly a contrast to the suits and
ties that characterized the group. I didn't want to stand
out, have all ears on me when I got my chance at Aleda.
I stayed close to Flint, using his respectable mien as cover
as we walked toward the end of the passageway.

"Maggot?" A primly suited woman with wide hips and
a frizzy perm detached from the knot closest to the cage
and bustled toward us. "Maggot, is that you, honey?"

It took me a moment, but I recognized her: Fay
Cohen, one of Emily's lawyers from the old days. Fay
had been the last word in fire-eating radical attorneys
during the sixties. A Red Diaper, Emily labelled her, the
offspring of Depression-era Leftist labor organizers. She
had sucked in the tenets of violent protest at her mother's
breast.

I had seen the scope of her fury in court, in defense
of Emily and Emily's ex-husband. I had once, as a kid,

literally trembled with fear in her presence. Now she appeared merely grandmotherly, a soft, postmenopausal woman whose feet seemed to hurt.

I walked ahead to meet her. Fay reeked of cigarettes and coffee and failed deodorant.

"I knew I'd be seeing you soon," she said. "But I didn't expect it to be here."

"I came to talk to Aleda," I said.

"Impossible."

"You've tried?"

She smirked. "I represent Aleda. No one talks to her."

"Until when?"

"Until I say so."

"You know about Emily?" I asked.

"Of course. I'm sorry, honey. It's a tough break."

"I need Aleda's help."

"Help for you maybe, but not for Aleda. Aleda has been as good as off the planet for twenty-two years. What do you have to talk about?"

"The good old days."

"Fat chance, baby girl. Aleda is here on a twenty-two-year-old fugitive warrant, and the charge is manslaughter. The last thing I'm going to let her talk about is the old days. Not to you, not to anybody."

She was holding my arm so tightly it hurt. I tried to shake her free, but she was very tenacious. Flint was beside me, running interference with people who surged around us trying to get Fay's ear, or mine, or to fill their own. I didn't know who they all were.

"What a zoo," Flint said.

"But the maneaters are all locked up for the night." The voice came from close behind me and I wheeled on it. My stomach sank when I saw who was there: Lester Rowland, FBI. "Maggie, how you doin'?"

"I've been better," I said.

Lester was J. Edgar Hoover–era FBI, one of the boss's pets—a shark with a political agenda. For years he had tailed Emily, tapped her telephones, bugged her bedroom, rifled her files, and otherwise harassed her. Getting her and her colleagues behind bars had been his mission, his obsession. Again and again, Emily and Fay had foiled him, though, using his own infractions against the laws of due process to scuttle his evidence. In my parents' house, Lester Rowland had been the anti-Christ.

"What are you doing here?" I asked. "You must be retired by now."

"This is my show," Rowland said. "I brought Aleda in."

"Pissant," Fay spat.

"Nice way to talk, Fay." Lester feigned offense. "You going to let our Maggie talk to Aleda? See if she needs anything?"

"Aleda has everything she needs," Fay fumed. "No one talks to her. That means you, Herr Rowland. I know your tactics. You even look at Aleda when I'm not present and I'll have your hairy Gestapo balls for breakfast."

"You'd like that, wouldn't you?" Rowland laughed.

"Fuck you." Fay stomped away, swearing under her breath.

"Same old Fay, huh, Maggie?" I didn't like the way Rowland kept looking at me, or his making familiar. This was the first time I had personally spoken to him. It was an experience I could have made it through the rest of my life without. Lucas had talked about the taint of radicalism clinging to Rod. Lester carried a different stain, one of backroom beatings, blackmail, and ugly covert manipulations—all under the color of authority. I saw in his face something dark and vaguely obscene. Certainly the way he looked at me, a visual strip search, gave a certain weight to that impression.

Lester's grin showed a lot of good dental work. "You still swimmin', Maggie?"

"When I get a chance."

"You sure were cute. Bet you don't remember when I came to watch you swim."

I remembered Emily with an FBI escort at my high school swim meet. I had only had eyes for Emily that day, and hadn't paid much attention to the two feds sitting behind her. Now I felt squeamish just thinking of this big, leering man watching me then, seeing me as a young teenager in my little Speedo swimsuit.

He made me think about the story Flint had told the desk officers, about young Señora Magdalena. Even if Flint had made it all up, their wiseass laughter and their assumptions about the woman had been real enough. Okay, so I had laughed, too. It still made me feel very uncomfortable. The smug look that crossed Rowland's face when he said I was "cute" told volumes. I *knew* he and his partner had had nasty things to say about my adolescent body. I felt violated in retrospect.

"Don't you remember me, Maggie?" Rowland asked again.

I shrugged. "You all looked the same to me."

A guard inside with Aleda looked out at the crowd. "Say goodnight, Gracie," he said loudly as he began to roll a steel shutter over the cage opening.

"What's he doing?" I asked Flint.

"Aleda's being booked. She wants a little privacy when they take her clothes away."

We were six feet from the cage and I called out, "Aleda!"

She looked up, confused at first. I did stand out from the suits, so she spotted me quickly. A smile lifted the deep creases in her face. I had always been the pesty little sister Emily's friends barely tolerated. For that reason, I didn't expect Aleda to be particularly happy to see me. But she obviously was. She moved to the metal grid and laced her fingers through it to block the shutter.

"Excuse me," the guard said and tried to move her aside.

"Maggot," Aleda cried. "Thank God, you've come."

Flint held Fay back and I ran. I reached for the grid and put my fingers over Aleda's.

Aleda's face pressed close. "Is Emily okay?"

"No," I said. "Who would do that to her?"

"Any of them."

"Tell me."

The guard had managed to pry ner hands away.

"Give us a minute," I begged him.

"Sorry, lady, but that's it for now. Wave bye-bye."

A second guard held Aleda by the waist. She struggled against him and pleaded with me: "Be careful, Maggot." I saw tears running down her face. "For Marc."

The shutter slid over the cage and locked into place.

Fay was beside me, looking defeated.

"You heard her," I said. "She wants to talk to me."

"I heard her," Fay sighed. "Please. Wait until tomorrow. Aleda hasn't had any sleep for seventy-two hours. She hasn't been well and she's exhausted. I need her rested for the arraignment tomorrow. You can see her in court at two. Go away now, and I promise, I'll get you together after the hearing. Fair enough?"

"Fair enough," I said. "I'll see you in court."

Flint had me by the elbow. "Come on," he said. "I'll take you home."

I leaned against him. "You offered me a drink earlier."

"Okay. Where do you want to go?"

"Emily's. I have to change for midnight mass."

Chapter 8

It was almost midnight when Flint and I drove up outside La Placita church. The sidewalk in front was like a carnival from hell. The usual neighborhood loonies, always joiners, were out in force. I saw sandwich boards promising everything from salvation to direct communication with our Martian cousins. There were a few mainstream groups represented as well: pro-life pickets marched in a tight circle with placards denouncing Emily's work in a family health clinic that provided abortions. I'd had too much input during the day to feel properly offended.

I thought I understood why Emily had made arrangements with Father Hermilio for a private memorial mass for Marc. Marc's funeral had been such a media fiasco that some of our family hadn't been able to get inside the church. There had been so many issues vying for attention—Emily's indictment, the death of young Tom Potts, the heated-up Peace Movement generally—that it seemed Marc had been forgotten about.

There was a second reason. Emily felt responsible for Marc's death. He had been fragged by his own men the day the international edition of *Time* with Emily's face on the cover hit the stands in Saigon. She had spent her life in atonement.

We parked in the Olvera Street lot across the street and made our way through the crowd. I carried a brown paper shopping bag, its contents requested by Uncle Max.

The sanctuary of La Placita church was ablaze with candles. Flowers and pine boughs banked the altar.

Above it all, stretched across the ancient domed ceiling, was a hand-painted paper banner: HERMANO Y HERMANA. Brother and sister, it meant. Emily had been infused into Marc's service; in fact, she had overpowered him again. The irony of the scene struck me. Whatever her intentions, Emily had managed to stage her own media fiasco.

Flint wedged us down the packed aisle toward the front. I passed many familiar faces, a *Who's Who* collection of activists and politicians—a former governor, the mayor, the left flank of the City council—and a goodly number of neighborhood folks. There was also a smattering of men wearing bits of military garb: cunt caps, field jackets, khaki shirts, buttons that proclaimed, VETERANS FOR PEACE. What I sensed among the assembled crowd was an air of expectation, more celebrity-watching than grief. I worried about their motives.

The church is very old and not very large. Ordinarily the place has a certain historic charm. But I wasn't seeing it. Everything about La Placita seemed heavy, the three-feet-thick adobe walls, dark oak beams, gaudy religious paintings, the overused air. It all began to press in around me. I tried to get a breath, but the smells repulsed me—flowers, burning wax, mold, people who live without plumbing.

Uncle Max and Lucas Slaughter were sitting together on the front pew whispering. They looked up when Flint and I approached. I gave Max the bag he had asked me to bring, and squeezed in between Lucas and Flint. My parents had declined to come, preferring to stay with Emily. I was thinking I should be with them instead of here among so many strangers.

When we were settled, Flint nudged my arm. "You okay?"

"Yes."

"Brought you something." Out of his coat pocket he pulled Mrs. Lim's starched napkin, the one I had blown my nose into earlier. He must have picked it up when we went back to Emily's apartment for me to change

into my red suit. He pressed the napkin into my hand.
"Just in case."

"Thanks." I was very touched. I folded the napkin and
held on to it. "It was nice of you to bring me."

He shrugged. "I would have come anyway. This way,
I get a front-row seat."

"You're some tough guy, Flint," I managed before I
started to choke up. I kept my eyes on my hands in my
lap, to avoid having to speak to anyone. I didn't look up
again until I saw Rod Peebles's freckled hand on my
knee.

"God bless you, Maggie," he said, bending over me
solicitously.

"Sit down, Assemblyman," Lucas whispered. "They've
all had time to see you."

Rod glared quickly at Lucas and made his way down
the front pew, giving everyone a back pat or a double-
fisted handshake. Very sincere. The change in the nature
of the service seemed to have changed his mind about
coming—more politically correct. I didn't see where he
finally sat.

Father Hermilio entered the chancel in his robes. He
offered prayers in both Spanish and English. I wasn't
listening very closely to what he said. Most of it was from
the ritual and I could respond by rote.

"In the name of the Father, and the Son, and the Holy
Spirit, Amen." He made the sign of the cross; then he
called on Uncle Max to join him. This was a surprise to
me, though Max seemed prepared. He opened the bag I
had brought and took out the khaki field jacket I had
brought home from the hospital among Emily's clothes.
It was Marc's jacket.

Max kissed me, hard, on the cheek as he rose. "I love
you, Margot," he whispered.

"Did Emily ask you to do this?" I asked.

He nodded. "We'll be okay, kid."

In the chancel, Father Hermilio embraced Max dramatically, then stepped to the side, leaving Max alone
facing the congregation.

With a showy flourish, Max put on the field jacket. He was only a few feet away. I could see DUCHAMPS on the patch over the left pocket. There were Marine insignia on the breast and sergeant's stripes on the collar. The jacket had been sent home from Vietnam with Marc's few personal possessions.

The jacket had old dark stains and new mud. Stiff brown blood starched one side of the collar. I imagined I could smell it, and I nearly gagged.

Max squared his shoulders, but Marc's jacket was still too big for him.

"This is my shroud," he said in his clear, baritone voice. "The shroud worn by every one of you who ever loved my nephew, Marc Duchamps, who ever cherished my niece, Dr. Emily Duchamps Orozco, who ever lost innocence before its time.

"Marc was kind and good, and full of the spirit of life. Through him, we dwelt in hope for the future. Yet, twenty-two years ago on this day, our Marc was taken from us. It was unfair; he had not spent half his share of youth. That light he had shared with us was interred with him, forever, in his oblivious grave.

"Today, in full remembrance of that young life lost, Marc's twin, our shining Emily, put on this jacket he had worn in that faraway Asian forest. She did this perhaps to feel closer to him, to lighten the shadow his loss cast across the remainder of her life.

"Wearing this shroud, Emily, also, was stolen from us.

"We have lost them both, *hermano y hermana*. Now the shadow on our hearts is double, a cold void in our arms where once we held them, at our table where we broke bread together, in the missing voices in the family chorus, in our plans for companionship in old age. To our sorrow, Emily and Marc will live only in our memory, forever brash and young. 'The good Lord pity and pardon and help for the future those God has still left us.' "

Max got to that point before he was overcome. Father Hermilio bowed his head in prayer, but Lucas Slaughter rose to the chancel to put his arms around Max. Lucas began singing "Amazing Grace." A good portion of the congregation joined him, a capella.

I, too, was overcome, so many warring emotions flooding in at once. Among them was a rising anger. Here was a funeral, though Emily was not dead. What was the rush? Where was the prayer for her safety?

The congregation was standing, singing anthems from the old Peace Movement days. Many had joined hands and were leaning against each other, swaying as they sang. It was a scene straight out of 1969, except the faces were older, the clothes were better. They were contentedly bereaved, so many together once again after so many years. I didn't like what I was feeling toward them.

I turned to Mike Flint and whispered, "Can we leave?"

He rose with me and we started down the aisle. Hands groped for me, tried to hold on to me or embrace me. It was frightening. They were for the most part strangers, yet they seemed to want from me some sort of absolution, or maybe intercession with the not-yet-departed, as if I were a conduit to Emily's grace. I hated the idea of the martyrdom of Emily, Saint Emily. Even worse, Emily wasn't going to her folk beatification alone: we were sending Marc in with her.

A man in a wheelchair with a Veterans for Peace button on his lapel pressed a crumpled American flag into my hand. "God bless you," he said.

Pregnant women in dark shawls, like the one I had encountered on Emily's front steps, reached out at me from the pews. They touched my clothes and placed in my hands religious medals or small silver *milagros*, miracle charms crudely shaped like eyes or women.

The crowd pressed so close they seemed to suck away all the air.

"Mike," I pleaded, gripping his arm with both my hands. "Get me out."

From out of the corner of my eye I caught a dark movement that rose from the crowd and came flying toward my head. I was hemmed in so closely I couldn't have ducked even if there had been time.

The first blow fell on the back of my neck, fists clenched into a hammer. I got my arms up and took the next hit on my wrist.

"She was a murderer!" I felt cold spit hit my face.

I fell back against the fluid mass of people as Mike released me to lunge into the attacker. When the flurry of arms and legs cleared, when the screaming stopped, the man was face down on the red tile with his hands cuffed behind him, pinned to the floor by Mike's knee.

I didn't recognize the man. He was older than middle-aged, better cared for than the local street loonies. He wore pressed Dockers, soft leather shoes, a clean windbreaker. Washed and ironed garb. Without the handcuffs, he would look like anyone's nextdoor neighbor. He raised his head and strained to look up at me, his broken glasses hanging from one ear.

"She was no hero," he sobbed. "Doesn't anyone remember? She was a killer."

"That's enough," Mike said, hauling the man to his feet.

"Who are you?" I demanded.

"Potts." The man dropped his head and began to sob with tragic anguish. "Emily Duchamps murdered my son."

Chapter 9

At 5:00 A.M. the desert sky was deep black, the stars hidden by a canopy of haze. I sped through the void between the black sky above and the black road below, trying to keep the speedometer of Uncle Max's Beemer from slipping past 100 mph. I didn't try very hard.

The trucks in the lanes to my right were a blur as I passed, or more likely I was their blur, sailing down the left lane as if it were a chute out of the abyss.

I had the beginnings of a hangover, house wine on an empty stomach, and my neck ached dully where I had been struck in church. I wanted a hot shower, fresh clothes, a toothbrush, a handful of aspirin. And the truth. I was depending on Jaime Orozco to have it all.

Jaime, as I remembered him, probably wouldn't be up and coherent for hours yet. I kept thinking about margins of time, about the hour I spent sitting on Emily's stoop, possibly the same hour during which she was shot. Had I taken an earlier flight, I might have found Emily on time, I might have made a difference in someone's decision to put a gun to her head. Everything was timing. I forgot about the highway patrol and let the car go.

The speed, the cold air streaming in the window, made my head feel a little better as, over and over on Max's tapedeck, I replayed the message tape Flint had taken from Emily's answering machine. I was thinking about Aleda, the fresh pain in her voice when she said Marc's name. Max had said that he half-expected Marc to show up with Emily.

It was a ridiculous idea, born I'm sure from the mating

of anxiety and a bottle of scotch. But it was a notion I grasped for, longed for, as I thought of Emily immobile in her hospital bed, slipping away from me just as Marc had.

What had pushed me toward the edge was the strange service at La Placita and the even stranger conversation in the Bonaventure bar afterward. Max, I think, had been well-lubricated, though eloquent, when he delivered his eulogy. Later, he had been plain old drunk.

In the bar, I took him to task for speaking of Emily as if she were dead. He had said, "Don't let it bother you. We buried Marc before he was ready, too."

I asked him to explain himself, but he only grew more incoherent. As Lucas was finally helping him upstairs, Max had turned to me and said, "Marc lives."

In a metaphysical sense, sure. Just the same, it was an idea I could not let go. Every time I learned something about Emily on the day she was shot, I tripped over Marc.

Driving Max's car, as far as Riverside, I had tried to convince myself that the voice of the mystery caller on the tape was Marc's. I aged it twenty-two years, made allowances for substandard fiber optic transmission, adjusted the pitch to account for stress. I gave him a cold.

Then somewhere after the 60 interchange, I decided it couldn't be Marc at all. By the time I passed Banning, I had waffled back and forth so often, I couldn't even recognize my own voice. The only thing I was sure of was that I felt no shame over the method I had used to liberate the tape from Flint's pocket. He's a cop; he should be more careful. He shouldn't get drunk with distraught women.

As I neared the Indio offramp, I saw the first red sliver of sunrise over the Cottonwood Mountains. The moment of desert dawn came in a hurry. When the sun broke the ridge, soft rose light washed across the black desert floor like spillwaters pouring down from the mountains.

During the long drive through the night, I had felt a strong sense of isolation, as if I were passing alone through a vast and desolate wilderness. But in the first light, the illusion vanished. Desert-pink condos, new strip malls with turquoise trim, and the rolling green lawns of freshly planted golf courses emerged in relief as the night receded.

The arrival of another day reminded me I had missed a night's sleep. I felt tired, but there was too much I had to do to waste time in bed. At least, I thought, remembering the goofy look on Flint's face when I left him, wasting time sleeping.

I exited the freeway at Washington Street and was stuck immediately in a bottleneck of construction traffic. On both sides of the wide street the skeletons of new, half-framed condos cast long shadows across what was left of the open, white desert sand.

Trapped behind an earthmover, I found the last few miles to Jaime Orozco's house excruciatingly slow going. Like everything I had been looking for, he was so close yet so unobtainable.

I hadn't seen Jaime since his divorce from Emily, probably eight or nine years ago. I couldn't remember exactly. They had planned to be a one-family medical mission to the Third World, a team, he the orthodontist/dentist, she the specialist in communicable diseases. But somewhere between the amoebic dysentery they brought home from Honduras and the malaria they contracted in Bangladesh, the plan had soured. And so had the marriage. It was too bad, too, because I always liked Jaime. I can only describe him as loose. He was good for Emily.

My hope was that during long, intimate nights in Honduras, or during delirious ramblings in Bangladesh, or maybe somewhere in between, Emily had said something to Jaime that would help me now.

As the sky grew brighter, it became easier to recognize the few remaining landmarks. After getting lost only twice, I managed to find Jaime's place along what was now the road to Lake Cahuilla.

Last time I visited Jaime, there hadn't been a paved road, or a lake, either. His acreage had become trapped in the contagion of resort development that crept steadily, inexorably, across the sand and into the date palm groves. I wondered how close Jaime would let the new stucco walls encroach before he fled. He loved mankind in concept, but not necessarily as neighbors.

Jaime's weathered adobe and tile house was set well back from the road, still surrounded by a buffer of grapefruit, tangerine, and palm trees. I pulled into the long gravel drive, looking for signs of life in either the house or the attached dental office. I didn't relish waking him. Especially waking him with the news I had to bear.

When I came through the trees I saw that the rear office lights were on. A round little woman in a white pantsuit stood on the porch steps watching a collie relieve himself on the trunk of a palm tree.

I parked beside a pickup truck and got out. The crisp air was tinged with sweet tangerine blossoms and pungent sage. I took a deep breath and stretched my stiff muscles.

"Forgot your lights," the woman called.

I reached back into the car and snapped them off. The collie sauntered over, sniffed my hand, nudged my crotch. I must have passed muster, because he stayed close beside me, licking at my hand and trying to get his nose between my legs, all the way across the gravel drive.

The woman came down the porch steps to meet me. "You have an emergency? Otherwise you need an appointment."

"I only want to speak with Dr. Orozco," I said. "I'm his sister-in-law."

"Jaime ain't married," she said, widening her stance.

"When he was married, I was his sister-in-law."

"I know," she said. "Max called and said you was coming."

"You know Max?"

"Sure. Don't you?" She outweighed me by a few stones, and had a lower center of gravity, but I decided that if push came to shove—and at that point, I almost hoped that it would—I had speed and reach on my side.

I tried once more. "May I please see Jaime?"

"Sure"—she shrugged—"why not?"

She led me through a small reception room and into Jaime's brightly lit examination room.

"What is it, Lupe?" Jaime had his back to the door, bent over a patient in his chair. From behind, he looked wonderful. Tall, slim, firm. There was more gray in his black hair than I expected, and his long ponytail was gone, but overall he wasn't much changed. In his 501 jeans and cowhide boots, he seemed more natural to the desert environment than the Polo-clad golfers I had seen waiting on the greens for enough daylight to tee off.

The dental chair was enormous and the patient in it very small. From where I stood, I couldn't see much of him except skinny elbows on the armrests and a stiff thatch of very straight, blue-black hair above Jaime's hands. Whatever Jaime was doing to him required all of his concentration. I moved into the small room and found a spot between the spit bowl and a magazine rack.

Lupe waited for Jaime to notice me by himself, then gave up and announced, "She's here." Then she left.

"Thanks, Lupe." Jaime glanced over at me. First he registered surprise, then pleasure. "Yep, she really is here. Heard you had a rough night, Maggot, took a pretty good shot."

"Max talks a lot," I said. "You're at it early."

"It's grapefruit season. I have to be available before these kids go out to pick in the morning. They won't give up a day's wages to see the dentist. Right, Rafael?" He grinned at the boy in his chair, showing off a good number of his own perfect teeth.

"Hey, Rafael," he said. "You know who this is? An honest-to-God TV star, Miss Margot Eugenie Duchamps MacGowen. You ever heard of her?"

The boy leaned around and took a long, very doubtful look at me. He had a beautiful face, smooth oak-colored skin, huge, liquid brown eyes. It was his mouth, however, that caught my attention; he had a bite like an alligator. His teeth, top and bottom, protruded at such acute angles that his lips wouldn't close over them.

"You really a TV star?" he said. He sounded as if he had a mouth full of straw.

"Dr. Orozco's teasing you." I took out the Dodgers cap I had stuffed in the raincoat pocket and put it on his head. "You have my permission to bite him."

Rafael laughed and made a few experimental nips at Jaime with his deformed choppers. Jaime picked up a plaster cast of those same teeth and nipped back. Then, manipulating the plaster teeth like a puppet, Jaime said, "Tell your mother we'll be ready to start putting the bands on your teeth Thursday, the day after Christmas."

"We're going south to pick lettuce."

"You come here before you leave. Promise?"

Rafael's smile faded.

"If you wait as long to come back as you did this time, your face will grow some more," Jaime said. "We'll have to start all over again, make new casts and everything."

Rafael, looking depressed, unclipped his paper bib and started to rise from the chair. Jaime leaned over him, putting his hands on the child's shoulders. "What do the kids call you now?"

Rafael said something that I think was Scissors Mouth.

"When your teeth are fixed, they will call you Rafael," Jaime said.

Rafael turned his soulful eyes on Jaime's rugged face. "Promise?"

"You bet. Give those braces two years and you'll be as cute as me."

Rafael shook his head, smiling his distorted smile. "Cuter."

"Don't push it." Jaime laughed. He gave Rafael a hand out of the chair. "You tell your mother to bring you here before you go south for lettuce. No matter what."

"I will."

"Good. Lupe's cooking chorizo. You better hurry and get some before this TV star goes in and eats it all."

Clutching the Dodgers hat to his head, Rafael paused

to give Jaime a quick, shy hug before he ran to find Lupe.

"You're such a softy," I said. "You fix their teeth, fill their bellies, feed their self-esteem. I hope you have a few paying customers."

"Not enough," he said. "You wouldn't happen to have ten thousand dollars, would you?"

"Not on me," I said. "Or anywhere else. I'm paying retail for Casey's braces."

"Casey," he sighed. "God, I haven't seen her for so long. How is she?"

"She's fine, Jaime. She's with her dad for the holidays," I said. "How are you?"

"How am I?" He went over to the sink and began lathering his hands. "At the moment, I feel old. Ever since Max called last night, I've been thinking about Emily, and the old days, the people we knew, the vision we had. I vowed I would always keep the flame alive.

"Max kept talking about old friends, old shit we'd gone through together. I finally had to say to him, 'Twenty-two years is a long time. Who can remember so far back?' Yesterday, I probably wrote December twentieth eight or nine times, before I made the connection. How could I forget what that date meant to us? It started me thinking. Time and again, Em and I risked so much, but I think I've forgotten that *thing* that was so damned important to us. Maggie, I think it's young people who are meant to fight the good fights. And I'm not young anymore."

"You're just tired."

"God bless you." He smiled. "If I had said all that to Emily, she would have diagnosed some hormonal skip and given me a chemical adjustment. But Maggie, the problem is in my heart. If you put your hand on my chest, you wouldn't find anything beating in there."

"Jaime," I said.

"More proof," he said, slowly drying his hands in a white towel. "Old men get morose. I'm morose."

"You're not old. You're not morose."

"What then?" he demanded.

"Simply, grief," I said. "How much did Max tell you?"

"What he knew—not enough. How is Em?"

"No change. I called the hospital from Max's car about an hour ago. Mom and Dad are with her."

"How are they?"

"Numb," I said. "Emily called them yesterday and told them she was bringing someone home for Christmas. Someone very special."

"Who?"

"She didn't say. They decided she was getting married again."

"Ouch," he said.

"Didn't she call you?" I asked. "She seems to have called everyone else."

"She called. I wasn't here—yesterday was my day up at the Tahquitz Reservation. She left a message with Lupe. I never got back to her."

"Did you try?"

He started piling used instruments on a tray and tidying up, and making a lot of noise doing it.

"Jaime?"

He sighed as he dropped the tray beside the small sink. "No. I didn't call her back."

"Still hurts, huh?"

"Bleeds," he said.

"Max said something bizarre last night."

"Not unusual for Max."

"He said Emily had been behaving so strangely that he wouldn't have been surprised if she had shown up with Marc."

Jaime grew very still. He looked at me the way a parent looks at an idiot child, baffled, worried, fond.

"How have things been with you, Maggie? You've had a pretty full dance card yourself lately: divorce, teenage kid to raise alone, big job, earthquake through your living room. Now Emily. Adds up to a lot of pressure."

"I'm fine, Doctor Freud."

"There's no way around it, Maggie. Marc died in Vietnam twenty-two years ago."

"Identification mistakes were made all the time. We both know deserters who came back to the States and disappeared into the underground."

"It's a tempting idea, Mag, but it won't wash," he said. "Marc knew we loved him unconditionally. Thinking from your head only," he said, "is it in any way possible that Marc is still alive, and in all that time he never contacted us?"

"I can't think from my head only right now," I said. "You may feel empty inside. But if you put your hand on my chest, you would certainly find the heart beating."

Jaime sighed and covered his face. He seemed to be overcome. Then I saw a slow smile curl around the edges of his lips.

"What?" I said.

"If I put my hand on your chest, my love, I wouldn't be looking for your heartbeat."

I laughed. "You're not old yet, Jaime."

"Maybe there's hope. Okay kid, either hop into the chair and let me look at your teeth, or come into the kitchen for some of Lupe's chorizo and eggs."

"How about just coffee, black."

"Not in Lupe's kitchen."

He took my hand and led me, and it felt very nice, very familiar. But nothing more.

Jaime had been my first adolescent crush. I was about fourteen when Emily had brought him home to meet the family. He had been a lot like her, a head taller than the crowd and full of fire. In comparison, the pimply-faced boys my own age seemed incredibly dull and immature. Jaime was unfair competition.

Seeing Jaime again after a space of time, I saw that he was attractive, but I didn't feel it. For one thing, he smelled like a dentist. I'm sure now that when I was fourteen, I fell for Jaime primarily because he was Emily's boyfriend. She had weaned me on competition.

Being with him again, I realized how much I had

missed Jaime, and how much Emily had lost out on. But you can never know what happens between two people. I know for a fact that there are many intelligent, discerning souls who still believe that my ex is a wonderful man, and that I am an idiot for cutting him loose. They may be right on both accounts. Doesn't make me wrong.

Lupe was just seeing Rafael out when we walked into the kitchen. She cleared the boy's dishes from the table before she set in front of us plates heaped with a mixture of scrambled eggs and fried chorizo sausage. It was a spicy, greasy-looking mass. My stomach was as iffy as my head, and there was no way I could eat the stuff. I took a hot tortilla from the basket on the table and used it to push the eggs around my plate.

Lupe watched to make sure we were eating, then picked up a broom and went out the back door.

Jaime swallowed his mouthful. "Lupe will know if you don't eat anything," he said.

"Could be." I put down the tortilla and looked up at him.

"So?" he asked.

"I saw Aleda last night."

"Max told me."

"What else did he tell you?" I asked.

"That he was worried about his car," he said. "If he'd been sober he wouldn't have given you the keys."

I smiled. "If I'd been sober, I wouldn't have asked for them."

He poured me fresh coffee. "How did Aleda look to you?"

"Ragged. Older."

"Too bad. She was such a doll. Everyone was in love with her."

I held the warm cup to my forehead, a small comfort. I had to push the plate far enough away so I couldn't smell it.

"Do you believe in coincidence?" I asked.

"Now and then."

"On December twentieth, Emily is shot and Aleda

Weston comes in out of the cold. Suggest anything to you?"

"Old wounds," he said. "If you keep picking at them, they never heal."

"Whose old wounds?"

"I wouldn't know where to start."

"Try," I said. "I asked Aleda who would hurt Emily. She said, 'Any of them.' Tell me who she meant."

"You were around, you remember all that."

"I wasn't *there,* I was in a convent, for chrissake."

"Any of them, huh?" He got up and started stacking dishes in a distracted way. "*Them* covers a lot of territory, unless she meant *them* as opposed to *us.* Think about 1969 and everything we were involved with: we made a trip to Hanoi, we organized a big peace demonstration in Berkeley, the death of Tom Potts, our indictment, then Marc. If *them* is anyone who opposed us, wanted to arrest us, was offended by us, you could have a list half as thick as a phone book."

"And *us*?"

"The core group. The seven of us indicted for conspiracy, inciting to riot, manslaughter, and whatever else was trumped up. You could throw in our families—at least some of them—attorneys, fellow-travelers of one stripe or another. That would net you the other half of the phone book."

"The seven of you were close, like a family?"

He laughed. "More like the Hatfields and the McCoys. We feuded all the time. About the moral extent of the use of violence, and political bedfellows, over whose turn it was to make the coffee, and whether Camus or de Beauvoir was more correct, what to watch on TV, and over rumors that one or more of us was on the FBI payroll. It was always a fractious group."

"But you stayed together," I said.

"We came together for a moment, for one cause that intersected all our ideologies on the same axis: a tiny point in time and space. By early 1970, we had split up."

"Just like that, you split up?" I helped him carry the

dishes to the sink and scrape the remains of eggs into a plastic bowl. "I don't hear the angst I expected."

"People change, evolve, have different destinies to pursue. Some of our group split off into other movements, became more radical, found Jesus, disappeared like Aleda. Whatever."

"That's it?" I asked. "You evolved away from the Movement? I'm looking for the source of a festering wound that may have led to murder. What you offer me is Jesus?"

Jaime chuckled softly. "Maybe Jesus has better answers than I do."

"Try again."

"You want old wounds?"

"Yes. As you said, open, bleeding wounds."

"Where to start? We all took some pretty good licks," he said. "Going to Hanoi was a big mistake. We got a glimpse of the real world over there, and came home damned scared, with a message to share that no one seemed to want to hear. We were tailed, bugged, harassed by the Feds. From the pulpit, Billy Graham called us Satan's children. There were death threats. Your parents' house was firebombed. We organized a demonstration at Berzerkly that got out of hand, and a perfectly innocent kid died as a result. We were indicted on charges that ranged from conspiracy all the way to murder. We did some jail time—jail time being the one essential rite of passage for an organizer. Police and National Guardsmen thumped us now and then. Is that enough?"

"What about the other side, *them*?"

"That's vast territory. Far and away the biggest hurt, as you know, was the death of Tom Potts. He was an only child, a grad student on a hardship fellowship. That's a lot of hope dashed." He became very thoughtful. "The rest seems petty in comparison. At least one of us was an FBI informant; there was some foundation to the rumors. I have my suspicions, but I don't know for a certainty who it was. If that came out even now, it could be damned embarrassing."

He poured himself the last of the coffee in the pot, tasted it, then dumped it into the sink. The bitter residue showed on his face.

"We weren't caught for everything we did that was illegal, or immoral," he said. "We slept with each other, did some drugs together, plotted mischief together, went to court *ensemble.* How serious it might be to have some of that old shit made public depends, I suppose, on one's career or position. Or, maybe, family."

"Starting at the beginning," I said, "I guess the big question is, whose idea was it to set the bomb that killed Tom Potts?"

"Oh, God," he moaned. He spent a lot of time putting dish soap in the sink, running water, getting out a fresh towel. He avoided looking at me.

"Are we picking at the old wounds yet?" I asked.

He looked at me sideways, almost smiling. "You were always the most persistent kid."

"Who made the bomb?"

"Hell, I don't know. Anyone can make a bomb."

"I can't," I said, feeling some heat.

"If you have the right cookbook you can." Jaime picked up the dish towel and wiped his hands as he headed out of the room. "Hold on a minute. Maybe I have something."

The collie waited until Jaime was out of sight, then came over and laid his head against my leg. I took the bowl of table scraps off the counter and sat down on the floor beside the dog. He was a clever creature; he refused the bits of chorizo I offered him, but eagerly ate clumps of egg and a few pieces of tortilla. I didn't know if doggie snacking was allowable, but it gave us both something to do while we waited for Jaime to come back. Besides, Lupe's feelings might be hurt if she saw how much of her breakfast had been rejected.

For me, there was some uncomfortable déjà vu involved in being left behind to wait for Jaime. Time does distort reality, but it seems to me that, as a kid, I was always being left behind by big people dashing off to do endlessly interesting and mysterious things. Em and Marc, because they were so much older than I was, and thus bigger, more competent, more independent, used to infuriate me. No matter how much I grew and matured, they always had a head start. Whenever I hit a milestone, they had already been there and were long gone. Especially Emily, primarily because we were the same sex. For instance, by the time I finally entered school, Emily already had a bra. When I got my first bra, Em had thrown hers away and was taking the Pill. I was doomed to always miss the good stuff.

I was certainly left out in 1969. I was shielded, given an expurgated version of everything because of my tender age. It made me mad. Even twenty-two years later, no one had told me the whole truth. Maybe that's why I was always so nosy—I just wanted to know what was going on. I still do.

The dog was a big help merely by being warm and available. He sighed contentedly and was just closing his eyes with his head in my lap when Jaime came back into the kitchen.

Jaime held a faded color snapshot in front of me. "You can have this."

The picture wasn't very clear. I took it from him and looked at it closely. It was the core group, plus Marc.

The group in the snapshot was casually posed, squeezed in together to fit into the frame. Marc looked sharp in a fresh Marine uniform. He was sandwiched between Emily in a wilted cotton sundress and Aleda in shorts and Madras shirt. Clustered around them were six others.

"Where was this?" I asked.

"Honolulu Airport. We were on our way to Hanoi. Marc had some R and R coming between tours of duty. We arranged to meet."

"You kept the picture?"

"So I'm sentimental. It's a sin I've paid for dearly," he said. "I loved Marc like a brother."

I didn't want to cry again; I didn't want the tears welling in Jaime's eyes to fall. I got up for a drink of water.

"You okay?" he asked.

"Yes. These people have changed so much."

"You've kept in touch?"

"No. I've seen almost all of them during the last twenty-four hours," I said. "All except Arthur Dodds and Celeste Baldwin."

"Arthur Fulham Dodds," he said, running his thumbnail under the earnest young face in the picture. "He blew himself up making bombs in a basement in New York City about a year after this was taken."

"Was he a bomb expert?" I asked.

"Obviously not very expert. Art's eternal address is the Mount Carmel Cemetery. The dumb shit."

"Was he?"

"He should have studied more chemistry before he tried cooking explosives," Jaime said, frowning. "Art went east after the acquittal, joined the Weather Underground. He always got his high from confrontation. We were just too tame for him."

I pointed to the skinny young boy with masses of kinky red hair framing his narrow face. "I can't believe that's Rod Peebles," I said.

Jaime laughed. "Every time he comes up for re-election, he hopes everyone forgets he was there. For most of us, that isn't too difficult, he was just a limpet. He was always around, but he never had much to contribute. Except money."

"Look at Lucas," I said. "He looks so young. I always thought he was ancient."

"Age is relative." Jaime smiled. "You used to think I was old, too."

"Yeah, I did. I thought you were gorgeous, though."

"Wish you had said so, somewhere along the way."

I stood up to pace a little, trying to force down the lump gathering in my throat again. Most of these people

had been so familiar to me, a sort of extended family. I
hadn't thought about most of them for a long time.

My parents' house is a short uphill walk from the UC,
Berkeley campus. My father teaches there. During the
Peace Movement, Emily had run their two guest bed-
rooms like a hostel for Movement organizers. A lot of
people, including everyone in Jaime's snapshot, had
found succor in those rooms at some point.

Mornings, when I still lived at home, I never knew
who I might find in the hall waiting for a turn at the
bathroom. I remember on more than one occasion taking
my place in line behind the Reverend Lucas Slaughter—
in the snapshot he was standing behind Aleda.

I used to wonder what Lucas slept in, because in the
bathroom line he never wore anything except a towel
sarong and a heavy crucifix, which lay in his thick mat
of chest hair like a tiny Jesus sunning in tall grass. He
taught me two verses of "Did My Savior Bleed" one
morning while we waited for Daniel Berrigan to shave:

> *Alas! and did my Savior bleed?*
> *And did my Sovereign die?*
> *Would he devote that sacred head*
> *For such a worm as I?*
>
> *Was it for crimes that I have done,*
> *He groaned upon the tree?*
> *Amazing pity! Grace unknown!*
> *And love beyond degree.*

I don't know whether our hymn singing made Berrigan
shave any faster, but he came out laughing.

There was only one surviving person in the snapshot I
hadn't spoken with.

"What do you hear from Celeste Baldwin?" I asked.

"Nothing. You know who she married?"

"Yes."

"So you know as much as I do," he said. "I told you,

I didn't keep up. You were the newsperson. You should still have the contacts to reach her."

"Possibly," I said. I studied the faces in the faded photograph. "All I have now is a list. Can't you tell me what I need to know? Were these people Emily's friends? Her rivals? Her enemies?"

"It was so long ago, Maggot." He turned the picture over. "Who remembers?"

I watched him for a moment. He was obviously uncomfortable and fighting my prodding. I didn't want to make him hurt. I just wanted some truth.

I stood and stretched. "You know what I remember most about that time?" I asked.

"What?"

"The passion," I said. "And not only passion for the cause. Remember Marcella, my mother's cleaning lady?"

"I think so."

"She hated the years of the Movement in Berkeley. You know why?"

"Tell me."

"Because of the love stains she had to bleach out of the sheets when Emily's house guests left town again. You would all come back from a rally or teach-in or march so fired up the house seemed to shake with the leftover passion. There was always a terrific racket: hot debates, loud music, enormous amounts of food, lots of grass. Then, two by two, people would peel from the group and slip up the stairs. Sleep was impossible with all the headboard banging during the night."

He smiled. "That was the best part."

"So you do remember?"

"Passion I remember."

"Passion can wear many faces."

"So?"

"So, it would take a lot of passion to put a gun to an old friend's head and pull the trigger."

Chapter 10

After breakfast, Jaime drove me in his pickup into downtown Indio for a change of clothes. It was just after nine and the only place open was a western store called Trader Sam's. I picked out some snug, button-front blue jeans, a white shirt, an Indian blanket-weave flannel jacket and a pair of natural cowhide boots, all from the marked-down shelves. When my MasterCard didn't clear, Jaime put the clothes on his account.

"Some TV star you are," he said, as we walked back out to his truck. "You broke?"

"Always," I said. "My gigs are publicly funded."

"Who's paying for the trip to Belfast?"

"I don't know and I won't ask. As long as I have content control, I don't care."

"You're serious?"

"I'm not as politically pure as Emily."

Jaime laughed. "That's okay by me. The way you look in those jeans, I'll forgive damn near anything."

I think I smiled before I left him to walk to the passenger side of the truck. He didn't mean anything by the remark, just flexing. It was sweet.

I climbed into the truck and closed the door. In the few seconds it took for him to walk from the store, a shadow had come over Jaime. I reached across the seat and touched his arm.

"What's on your mind?" I asked.

He sighed. "Life is fleeting."

"It is."

"Last time you and I really talked," he said, "you were

still a bratty little kid with freckles on your nose. You were so cute and so smart and I loved you to pieces. I no more than turn around, and here you are with a half-grown child of your own. Where is that little girl I knew?"

"Long gone, Jaime."

"I don't think so."

"You are a sentimental old thing, aren't you, Jaime?" I rolled down my window and leaned against the door-frame, letting the wind redo my hair as we drove back toward his house. "Soon as I get a check, I'll pay you back. Thanks for everything. My own brother couldn't have been more helpful."

"Brother, huh?" He sighed wistfully, and I appreciated that. One time I had asked Emily how Jaime kissed, and she had said, "You'll never find that out." Maybe it was the way she said it. In a purely academic sense, I still wondered what sort of kisser he might be. As long as Emily was where she was, I would never find out.

"You never remarried," I said.

He shook his head. "Emily is a tough act for any woman to follow."

"Do you get lonely, living by yourself out here?"

"Sometimes," he said. "I have friends. I'm busy. I feel useful. How about you?"

"I have Casey. I have a job."

"Kids and jobs don't warm the sheets at night."

I may have blushed—my face felt hot. "My sheets are warm enough."

"Yeah?"

I thought about it for a moment. "I went through the post-divorce crazies for a while."

"Is that still called dating?"

"You've been there, huh?" I laughed. "It's just one of the four phases of divorce. You know, denial, anger, slutting, celibacy."

"Where are you now?" he asked.

"Phase four," I said, trying to remember the last time

I had been to bed with someone interesting. "I have no prospects and no time to pursue any."

"I'm coming up to the Bay Area for a conference in the spring. Can I come see you?"

"As a member of the family, sure, come. We need to catch up. You're the only uncle Casey has. I'd like her to know you better."

There was sadness in his smile again. He pulled into his driveway, still not saying whatever it was that weighed on his mind. We got out of the truck and stood in a patch of thin sunlight, making toe patterns in the fine white desert sand while we talked.

"What are your plans for the rest of the day?" he asked.

"I want to talk to Celeste Baldwin."

"She won't see you."

"Sure she will. Celeste and Emily were very close."

"Were," he said. "Past tense. Celeste wants nothing to do with any of us from the old days. She's even worse than Rod Peebles. We carry the taint. Rod finds us politically embarrassing, Celeste finds us unclean," he said. "She must have gotten into some bad weed. She told Emily one night that she met God. He told her He was a Republican. She asked us to stay away from her."

"Just the same . . ."

Jaime shook his head. "She won't see you."

"I have my methods."

"You'll need them."

Lupe called from the porch, "Dr. Jaime, you have a patient waiting."

Jaime tucked my hand into his elbow and walked me inside. He was very pensive. He pulled me into his arms and I could feel him shaking.

"I really miss you," he said. "When Em and I broke up, it was too painful to see you and Casey, your mom and dad. I thought the best thing was to just sever the ties completely. I was wrong, but you do understand?"

"I think so," I said. I was leaning against him and he was so tall that I felt very small again. Very young. Very safe. I pulled away and looked up into his handsome face.

"You and Emily were such a good pair," I said. "What happened?"

"The usual sorts of things, I suppose." He took a deep breath. "No. That's not true. What came between us was Marc. Dead or alive, I couldn't compete with him."

"Neither could I."

Lupe came out of the examination room, impatient. "Didn't I tell you, you have a patient waiting, Jaime?"

"You told me." He smiled and gave me a final hug. "Good luck with Celeste. Call me later."

"Bye, Jaime."

I watched him walk away. His back was very straight. The athletic way he walked reminded me of Emily, and how striking she and Jaime had been together, both of them tall, broad-shouldered, narrow in the hips.

I ran after him and caught him by the arm.

"Emily had a boob job," I said.

He was taken aback at first. Given a moment to get used to the idea, he nodded. "Good for her. She talked about doing it for long enough. I'm glad she finally did it."

"Why now?"

He shrugged. "Maybe she finally passed into stage three."

Out of anger and on to slutting? I could not imagine my sister, Emily . . . But who can imagine a sibling in bed?

With Lupe looking over my shoulder, I used the kitchen telephone to try the obvious approach to Celeste Baldwin Smith first. It took a few calls, but I managed to wheedle Celeste's home phone number out of an old contact in the capitol. He seemed very nervous about giving it to me, and asked me three times not to snitch him off.

Celeste seemed to have a mania for privacy. Or someone else very much wanted to keep her out of the public eye.

Celeste's banker husband, T. Rexford Smith, had long

been part of the California power-brokering elite, a back room advisor. Smith had done a courtesy stint in the Reagan administration, but scuttlebutt was that he would never expose himself to the scrutiny that comes with a run for public office. It did not take much imagination, however, to picture him in a few years plugged into the ambassadorship of some plum nation, wearing knee britches and satin sashes. The pomp and circumstance would suit him.

About Celeste's career after she left the Movement, I knew nothing. As far as I could remember, her only foray into the public spotlight had been a plea for legislation to purge the contents of rock lyrics. Celeste had de-evolved a long way from the Free Speech Movement. Certainly a long way from the firebrand of easy virtue I remembered. There was never halfway with Celeste.

Emily and her friends were great discoursers on the meaning of life and other trivialities. One afternoon in my parents' backyard, during a heated debate about the political implications of existentialism, I had accused Celeste of mistranslating Camus to fit her arguments. I spoke with all the authority of a third-year high school student, while she was working on a master's in French lit. I was simply throwing barbs into the wind, but that one found home.

Humiliated, Celeste flashed out angrily at me. She threw a heavy paperback in the general direction of my head. The book's title wasn't lost on me: *The Complete Guide to Homemade Explosives*.

"I've read the book," she said. "Watch yourself."

I believe that was our last conversation, because Marc died shortly after. I was never afraid of Celeste, or so I thought. Still, I had to take a deep breath before I could dial her number in the Holmby Hills section of Los Angeles.

"Smith residence." The female voice was too crisp to be domestic help, which was a shame. So often an overworked maid will let through the odd annoying call just for the hell of it.

"This is Margot Duchamps MacGowen," I said. "May I speak with Mrs. Smith?"

"Mrs. Smith isn't taking calls."

"It's a matter of importance."

"Do you wish to leave a message?"

"Yes," I said. "Tell her Maggot called. Tell her I said, *'Aujourd'hui, Emily est morte.'* "

"I see." I wondered whether she had written down anything, or whether she had read Camus. She didn't ask me to repeat the opening line from *The Stranger*. "I will tell Mrs. Smith that you called."

"Thank you," I said.

I hung up and moved on to Plan B.

Jaime was still with his patient. I left a note for him on the kitchen table and drove off in Max's car toward Palm Springs.

I had told Jaime that I had connections in town. But they were old connections, left over from the three years I was evening news anchor at KMIR-TV, a local Palm Springs station with a network affiliation.

My best hope was Garth Underwood, my co-anchor then, station manager now. Garth and I had worked well together and had parted under friendly terms. We keep in touch the way old colleagues do: now and then, when favors are needed or a bottle of wine brings on a bout of nostalgia. I knew Garth would go to the ends of the earth for me, as long as there was the prospect of a good story in it for him.

I called the studio from the car and was told that Garth wasn't coming in until late. I headed for his house.

From Indio, where Jaime lived, Palm Springs is a forty-minute drive along the base of the San Jacinto mountains. Though rain clouds hovered along the crest of the peaks ahead, the sky was a clear, diluted, blue. I rolled down the car window and breathed in a mixture of the fresh-cut golf course and Mercedes exhaust that scented the air.

Garth still lived in the same condo on the ninth hole

of the Thunderbird Country Club. The same housekeeper let me in.

I walked through the house and found Garth on the
patio, brunching with an ornamental blonde: she was tall,
hard-bodied, big breasted. Her looks had a sharp edge
that her careful makeup couldn't dull. She had sharp
breasts, too, and they seemed to point daggerously
toward the green, where Bob Hope was sinking a birdie.
As soon as Hope's foursome drove off, her chest seemed
to deflate.

Garth was watching her with open glee. He may be an
incorrigible womanizer, but he's no fool.

"Good morning," I said.

My voice startled Garth. He turned, and when he got
over his initial surprise, he flashed me his on-camera smile.

"Maggie, honey, you look great." He got up from the
spread of bran muffins and sliced papaya to fold me in
his arms. He seemed a whole lot happier to see me than
she did.

"It's been too long," he said.

"You look good," I said. And he did, slim in his tennis
whites. He had trimmed and darkened his Afro since I
had seen him last. I had liked the gray.

"What brings you out here, baby?" he asked. "You in
trouble?"

"Worse than usual."

"So, you need some help from your old Garth." I saw
him signal the housekeeper, and a fresh round of Ramos
fizzes appeared on the tray. "I heard about Emily—terrible tragedy. I want you to know that I'll do anything,
anything. Have you had breakfast?"

"What I need, Garth, is access to Celeste Baldwin
Smith."

"Whatever for? I'm nicer. I'm cuter. And you can use
all the dirty words you want to when you sing in my ear."

"Can you help me?" I asked.

"Celeste Smith is a tough one to crack," he said. "I
may be able to get you access, but I can't make her talk
to you."

"Access is all I ask."

"All right, then," he said. "There's a little benefit party at the Century Plaza tonight. Celeste and His Nibs will be there."

"You can get me in?"

"Hell yes. You'll be my date. We'll get so bombed and obnoxious that unless Oprah goes on another diet, we'll headline *The Inquirer* for weeks."

"You're driving all the way into L.A. for this gig?"

"Why not?" He glanced at the blonde, caught her yawning. "Nothing doing around here."

"Black tie?"

"Always."

"What time?"

Garth reached out and smoothed the lapel of my jacket. "Can you spend the day? We'll relax a little, go out to the Orchard for lunch. Drive in later together."

"I wish I could, Garth. But there's so much I have to do. I'll meet you in town tonight, around eight, Emily's apartment. You remember where it is. Is that okay?"

"If it has to be," he said. "Anything I can do for you in the meantime?"

"Maybe. How complete is the film library at the station?"

"For local news, excellent. Anything beyond the Coachella Valley, I can get from the network. What do you want?"

"1969. Nightly news reports from early August until Christmas day."

"Sports and weather, I assume."

"The Peace Movement. War news."

He nodded. "Emily and Marc."

I handed him a list of the people indicted with Emily. "Anything you can find."

"Sure," he laughed. "What are friends for, except to abuse?"

"You take abuse so well," I said.

The blonde stood up and stretched to her full, and impressive, height.

"Are we going to play tennis or what?" she demanded.

"Let's 'or what' for a while." Garth grinned. "We can play tennis anytime."

"Forget it." She picked up her drink and carried it into the house.

"Sorry, Garth," I said. "I've interrupted things."

"Don't worry about it. I'll work on the news tapes this afternoon, bring what I have tonight."

"You really want to do this?"

"It's a privilege to be asked. I remember Emily Duchamps when she was taking a lot of flak. I believed in her then. I still do."

"I believe in her, too," I said. I sipped the Ramos fizz he handed me. It hit my empty stomach like a cold bolt, but it tasted good.

"Are you feeling sad, baby?" he asked.

"Yes. At the same time, I've met so many people who care deeply for Emily that I've begun to finally understand who she was. I feel some of her strength." I handed him the glass. "Garth, she's going to die. But she lived the life she wanted to. She left a mark. Who can ask for more?"

"Can't ask for nothin' more." He kissed the top of my head. "I'll see you tonight and we'll set the city on its butt."

Garth may sound like a patronizing son-of-a-bitch, but I love him. I can say anything to him and face no risk. That's a rare quality in a friend.

As I walked away from him, I was thinking also of Jaime, of how awful it is to leave people behind. I had moved frequently, following jobs. In my wake I had left many friends, a husband, a world of possibilities.

Garth held the front door for me. "What are you wearing tonight?"

"I'll come up with something."

"The station still has a contract with Desert Mode. You might give them a call, drop my name."

"Thanks," I said. "I will."

"Take care of yourself," Garth called after me.

"See you at eight."

"I'll count the minutes."

Something occurred to me as I unlocked the car. "We're going to a fundraiser for what?"

"Carrie Smith Clinic, drug rehab for teenagers."

"Who is Carrie Smith?"

"Celeste's daughter. She O.D.ed late last year," he said. "She was thirteen."

I got into Max's car and backed out into the street. I wasn't feeling at all like attending a gala fundraiser, especially one that promised to have sad undercurrents. But if it was the only way to see Celeste, then I would do it. I had been well-trained by Garth.

I called Desert Mode as Garth had suggested. The shop was a boutique on El Paseo in Palm Desert that had dressed me for my nightly newscasts way back when I still read the news. I had always hated the clothes they sent over—desert glitz—but the price was right: nothing more than a promotional plug. So I called them.

After I mentioned Garth's name, the shop owner was willing to honor the old arrangement one more time.

"Are you the same size?" she asked.

"Same size, yes. Just make adjustments for the effects of gravity," I said. "I need everything. Dress, shoes, underwear. It's black tie in Century City."

"I'll take care of you," she said. "Mention my name during the evening."

"Early and often. Can you send it to Garth Underwood's by five o'clock?"

"He's at the same address?"

"Yes."

"Don't worry about a thing, Maggie. You'll be magnificent."

"Passable is all I ask."

"Magnificent is what I'll deliver."

I envisioned sequins and shoulder pads. I really didn't care, as long as it got me through the door at the Century Plaza.

Chapter 11

Aleda Weston was scheduled for arraignment in federal court at two o'clock. I wanted to be there early to talk with Fay Cohen.

It was nearly eleven by the time I got back on the freeway headed for L.A. If traffic cooperated, and I drove like a bat out of hell, I figured I might also be able to squeeze in a few minutes with Emily and my parents at the hospital.

I made good time as far as Norco. Then I hit the weather front. There was a deluge. It so rarely rains in Southern California that people forget from one storm to the next how to drive on wet streets. That meant bumper cars the rest of the way in.

Every few minutes, I tried to call my mother at the hospital, to check in. But the weather played hell with the telephone cells, and I couldn't get through. Everything rolled together made me feel antsy. I've never mastered being in two places at once, or flying over obstructions, and that frustrates the hell out of me.

When I finally arrived downtown, I was out of time. If I skipped the hospital and drove straight to the federal courthouse where the hearing was scheduled, and if I lucked into a decent parking place, I knew a few minutes with Fay would be the most I could hope for. Mother would understand, that's her nature. But it's not mine. I was fuming.

I found parking in a public structure only a block and a half away. When I cleared the metal detectors at the courthouse entrance, I had maybe ten minutes, optimum, to find Fay and pound her ear. Still feeling juiced, I stopped at the information desk to ask for the department number and directions. What the desk officer told me stopped me like a full speed run at a block wall:

"There is no Weston arraignment scheduled in this court this afternoon," she said, unmoved by my persistence. "You might call the court clerk."

I called Metro Detention.

"Aleda Weston was arraigned at oh-nine-hundred hours and kicked," I was told.

"Could you interpret that?" I asked.

"She posted bail and left."

Not what I expected to hear. "Where is she now?" I demanded.

"I don't have that information."

I had such a weird feeling, like *coitus interruptus* I had said to Flint. That pretty much describes it. I had come expecting answers, some resolution. Suddenly, zip. Nothing. Christmas without Santa.

For a good minute, I stood in the cavernous court lobby trying to figure out which way I had come in and how and where I should go next, and whether or not I should just sit down on the marble floor and cry.

The handful of change I had dumped on the shelf under the telephone lay there like a rebuke. I could call around, but I didn't know where to start. Fay Cohen must have been staying in the city, but I had no idea where. I did try Max, but of course he wasn't in. I doubted whether Flint would even speak to me, and I had no idea what I would say to him: "How's the love bite on your neck?"

While waiting for inspiration, I plunked some coins into the slots and dialed Denver. I hoped I wasn't waking Linda from her afternoon nap. I prayed I wouldn't have to argue with Scotty about his complaint of the day, whatever it might be. I wanted only to speak with my daughter.

To my great relief, Casey herself answered the phone.

"How's it going?" I asked.

"Okay." The connection was scratchy. "Snowed last night and the powder on the slopes today was really good."

"You skied?"

"Uh huh. With Dad. How's Aunt Emily?"

"The same. Grandma and Grandpa are with her."

"Oh," was all she said.

"Have you thought any more about coming to Ireland with me?" I asked.

"Sure. It's cool." But she sounded cool.

"How's Linda feeling?"

"She throws up a lot."

"When is the baby due?"

"In June," Casey said. "It'll be strange to have a brother or sister. I mean, I don't have a lot of relatives."

"Good strange or bad strange?" I asked.

"Good, I guess. Babies are pretty cute." There was a pause; then her voice came back very low. "Dad's really happy."

"He should be. He makes great babies."

She made "Mom" sound like three syllables.

"Casey," I said. "I'm happy Dad's happy. You can enjoy yourself there and not be disloyal to me."

"I know that," she snapped.

"Good." I missed her more than I thought I would.

"Mom, when will we get back from Ireland?"

"I'm not sure. When the project is finished or the grant money runs out."

"By June?"

"Long before," I said. "Casey, you don't have to decide about Ireland for a while. Wait and see how you feel when you come home from Dad's after the holidays."

"Okay. Mom, I have to hang up. We're going to some kind of Christmas party."

" 'Bye. Have fun."

"Mom?"

"Yes?"

"I love you."

I said good-bye and hung up, because one more word

from her would have done me in. She was so far away and I really needed to hold her. Small uncomfortable insight here: I didn't think I could get through the Ireland project without her company. What must it be like for Scotty, I wondered, month after month with only phone calls to connect them? I hoped he had a nice baby.

I gathered what was left of the change and poured it into my pocket. When I turned to leave, I walked face first into the broad chest of Flint's partner, Detective Bronkowski. Surprised, I stumbled back and he caught me by the arm.

"Thought that was you I saw coming in," he said. "McGee, right?"

"MacGowen," I said.

"Right." He hung on to my arm above the elbow. "I hear you've been out looking for scalps."

"Just talking to old friends," I said, thinking this surprise encounter was no accident. "Have you found out anything useful?"

"This and that," he shrugged. "Case hasn't broken yet. But it will."

"Sure," I said.

"Are you still staying at Emily's?" he asked.

"At least through tonight."

He handed me his card with its gold-embossed detective shield. "If you move, or you have anything you want to talk about, give me a call. You can reach Flint at the same number."

"Thanks."

"Come on. I'll walk you out," he said. We were in a big, empty lobby. He filled up his share of it with physical bulk rather than idle chatter while we walked. I knew he had something he wanted to say. He was awfully slow getting around to it. Maybe it was his technique, I thought. When he finally opened up, I was expecting him to say something like keep your nose out, or don't track up the evidence. He surprised me again.

"Mike Flint's a decent guy," he said out of the side of his mouth, somewhere short of hostile.

"Yes," I said. "He seems to be."

"A good cop. I'd hate for him to get hurt."

"So would I."

"Uh huh." Bronkowski tapped his chest above the tie tack. "I worry he might take a direct one right here. You know, from someone who was just fooling around."

"You mean like a drive-by shooting?" I said.

"You know what I mean."

"Flint's a big boy. I suspect he can take care of himself."

"He can," Bronkowski said. "When he's playing in his own league."

I left Bronkowski in front of the courthouse. I turned once and saw him lumbering up the hill toward Parker Center, police headquarters. He had certainly given me something new to think about. I wasn't aware that all that much had passed between Mike Flint and me. Some kissing and touching. He had been rougher than I expected. And I had liked it more than I thought I would. It was all vaguely disturbing.

The clouds began to clear just as I drove out of the parking structure. The sky was God-speaks-to-Moses stuff, straight out of the film files of Cecil B. DeMille. I had a lot of time to admire it. Though official rush hour didn't begin for hours yet, traffic downtown already approached gridlock. I could have walked from the courthouse to French Hospital in the time it took me to drive.

It would have been nice to walk, I thought, to get a little fresh air to spur the thought processes. I simply couldn't afford to walk. The parking lot charged three dollars an hour and I was down to the last twenty I had borrowed from Max.

At the hospital, I followed the sound of music to Emily's room—Wagner played at top volume, the way it should be played. Emily used to argue with my father about Wagner. He insisted that one could appreciate Wagner without being a Nazi, no matter how Hitler had used his music. Emily disagreed noisily until Dad confiscated the keys to her VW bug, reminding her that the original bug was a product of the Third Reich. Even Emily had a price.

Because of the music, I expected to find my father inside. My mother was alone with Emily.

Lohengrin covered the sound of the door closing behind me. I paused for a moment and just watched her as she massaged lotion into Emily's hands. No matter what she did, there was always an air of elegance about my mother. Her gray hair was pinned into its usual bun, a loose arrangement that always looks as if it's ready to unravel, though it never does. She wore pleated gabardine trousers, loafers, a handknit sweater—a faculty wife's uniform.

Emily inherited her long legs from Mother. They're too thin and bony to look like much bare. But they do fabulous things for pants. Mother sat with one leg gracefully draped over the other, seeming very calm, considering the situation.

"Mother?" I said, reluctant to interrupt.

"Hello, dear." She turned down the volume of the tape player and raised her cheek for a kiss.

"How are you?" I asked.

"I'm not sure." She smiled. "I think I've had rather a lot of Valium. Dr. Song has been an angel about it. Once I get home, I'll probably sleep for two days. Ask me how I am once I've wakened again. The hysterics are doubtless waiting for a more chemically friendly atmosphere."

I laughed. "Is Dad stoned, too?"

"No, the poor dear. He and Max are out making preparations to fly Emily up to Palo Alto. The doctor thinks more can be done for her in a larger hospital. If she must move, we might as well have her closer to home. Don't you agree?"

"Yes," I said. "How is she?"

Mom touched Emily's cheek. "No change."

I went to the bed and leaned over Emily. The expression on her face was exactly as it had been the night before, her lips puckered into the same tight O. I felt discouraged. I sat down on the edge of the bed and patted her leg through the thin blanket.

"You look tired, Margot," Mom said.

"I had a long night."

"Have you learned anything useful?"

I shook my head. "I've collected more questions than answers. It's maddening."

"Aleda was very anxious to speak with you."

That snapped me to attention. "You spoke with her?"

"Very briefly. I always thought the world of that girl. So did Marc. I always hoped something would develop between them. Such a shame what she's going through."

"Start at the beginning, please," I said. "Where, when, who . . ."

"Let me think." Mother glanced at her watch. "She telephoned rather early. She had been very sick during the night, she said. She didn't sound well. The long trip across country and then incarceration just exhausted her. Jail always seemed to knock out Emily, too. The smell of the place, and all that racket, I suppose. I never much liked having a turn at bailing her out. Thank God you never put us through that."

"Mother?" I prodded. "Aleda?"

"As I said, she was awfully sick. Rod Peebles—remember him? Awkward sort of duck. Rod was able to pull some strings. Privileges of office, I suppose. Maybe it's not quite the fair thing, but now and then it is nice to have some influence on your side. Rod managed to get a judge out of bed for a quickie arraignment on compassionate grounds. Aleda was released into his custody. Nice of him. Odd, though. Of all that mob Em hung with, I never expected Rod to amount to much. Sometimes people surprise you."

"Where is Aleda now?"

"Seeing a doctor, I hope," she said with some force.

I called Rod's assembly district office downtown and got a recording telling me the offices were closed for the day. I must have shown my disappointment. Mother took my hand.

"Ask Lucas," she said. "He gave me his number. In Pasadena, I think he said. I wrote it down."

I picked up the notepad beside the bed and tried to decipher my mother's penciled scrawl. "Does this say St. Arnie's? Only Lucas would have a church called St. Arnie's."

Mother put on her glasses and took the pad from me. "St. Anne's. Says so very clearly. And Lucas doesn't have a church. He was defrocked ages ago. I don't know what this place is."

There was no area code written down—Pasadena is outside L.A.'s 213. The second numeral in the phone number Mother had written down could have been either a loopy seven or a half-formed nine. I tried nine, hoped it was local.

"Hotline." The answering voice sounded young, female.

"I'm looking for Lucas Slaughter," I said.

"I think he's around. I can't leave the phone to go look for him. He checks for messages."

"Are you at St. Anne's?"

"Yes."

"Where are you?"

"Pasadena Avenue at Lacy Street. Lincoln Heights."

The address was only ten minutes away.

I hung up and met my mother's tranquilized gaze.

"Do you need me?" I asked.

"Don't be offended, dear, but not at all. Go do what you have to do."

"I wish I knew exactly what that was." I bent to kiss her. "Call me when you get to Palo Alto. And Mom? Can I borrow some cash?"

"That's my girl." She handed me a wad and patted my arm. "Be careful."

"You, too." I went to the door. "Give my love to Dad."

"Margot, dear," she called. "Max is driving Emily's old Volvo. He has been patient about it, but he does seem concerned about his own car."

I laughed. "He should be."

St. Anne's turned out to be a 1920s-era woodframe bungalow with a sloppy paint job and wrought iron bars on the windows. A couple of blocks further up the street was the Florence Crittenton Home, a juvenile facility for young mothers and their infants.

The girl who answered the door at St. Anne's was about Casey's age, very thin and very pretty. She balanced a toddler on each hip. Somewhere deep inside the house, a baby cried.

"Is Lucas Slaughter here?" I asked the girl.

"Yes, he is," she said. She turned and yelled over her shoulder, "Luke! Visitor."

Lucas appeared out of the darkness behind her, drying his hands on a kitchen towel.

"Maggie," he said, grinning, as he ushered me inside. "Welcome."

"You live here?" I asked.

"Bite your tongue. The residents are all mothers under the age of eighteen. I don't come through that door without both a cast-iron jockstrap and a chaperone. How was your head this morning?"

"Leaden," I said.

"Mine still is. Can't drink the way I used to. Your detective friend seemed able to hold his own." Ever Lucas, he broke into a raucus hymn:

> *There is a fountain filled with blood,*
> *Drawn from Immanuel's veins;*
> *And sinners plunged beneath that flood,*
> *Lose all their guilty stains.*

Lucas took a breath. "Do you remember the second verse?"

"No," I said.

"I don't either." He shook his head. "Come into my office."

He led me through a living room crammed with mismatched furniture and into a small office with HEAD

SHRINK painted on the door. Among the cartoons and notices taped to the door was a counseling sign-in sheet with a pen imprinted Hotel Bonaventure dangling from a length of twine.

"The shrink?" I asked. "Is that you?"

"Yep. Counselor and general dog's body." He perched on the corner of a battered desk. "Good to see you, Maggot."

In spite of his hymn singing, he seemed unusually reserved. Could have been the influence of his place of work, or something else. I didn't have time to pursue it.

"Lucas, I very much want to see Aleda. But she keeps slipping away from me. Any idea where she is now?"

He frowned. "One of Rod's staffers was assigned to take care of her, make sure she got the right medical treatment, didn't take off again. Shit like that."

"The question was, where is she?"

"I don't know," he sighed. "I never had a chance to see her."

"You told me last night that Rod kept his distance from people in the Movement. Seems to me he's really stuck out his political neck by helping Aleda this way."

"Does seem uncharacteristically noble of old Rod," he smiled wryly. "Still, it's the best thing. Aleda's sick, Maggie. She needs a little space out of the public eye to tie up some loose ends. When she's ready, we'll all get together."

"I'm not the public."

"Don't get your back up. Remember, Aleda has been in hiding for half her lifetime. She survived by being cautious. You can't expect her to open up all at once. Give her time."

A soft knock on the door interrupted.

"Come," Lucas called.

A teenager with a little curly-haired boy clinging to her neck stepped into the room. She had tears running down her face.

"What is it, Nicole?"

"I forgot what you said about how long to cook the spaghetti." Nicole burst into sobs. "It's ruined."

"There's almost no way you can ruin spaghetti," he said with saintly calm. "Unless there are flames shooting from the pan. There aren't, are there?"

"What?" She wiped her nose on the child's shirttail.

"Flames."

She seemed confused, but she shook her head.

"Wait for me in the kitchen. I'll be right there." Lucas pulled a tissue from a jumbo-size box on the desk and handed it to her. "Be careful that Stevie doesn't get near the stove."

I started to follow Nicole, but Lucas caught me by the arm and held me back.

"Give her a minute to figure things out by herself," he said. "When she moves into a place of her own, she'll have more than spaghetti to worry about."

I didn't smell smoke, but I stepped into the hall and sniffed the air, anyway. I could see Nicole through the kitchen door. Lucas looked over my shoulder.

"Mother told me you had left the church, Lucas," I said. "Is this your church, the church of the here and now?"

He chuckled. "It's the only one that will have me. I like it just fine, too. Every time I take a pregnant twelve- or thirteen-year-old girl over to Planned Parenthood, I like it better. Damn it, Maggie, those old farts at the diocese in their dark suits and clerical collars don't have the least idea what the reality is for children like Nicole, babies raising babies. Or two babies or three babies. Let the collars pontificate. I'm making spaghetti."

"St. Anne's sounds religious Establishment to me."

"House used to be a nunnery, teachers at Sacred Heart High School lived here. Emily bought them out years ago."

"Emily?"

"She raised the financing, anyway. This is one of her pet projects."

"I didn't know that," I said. I should have. What I

was seeing at St. Anne's was totally consistent with Emily. Then I remembered a pro-choice sticker on an arrangement of flowers left for Emily at the hospital. And ugly graffiti on her apartment house wall. Controversy was Em's morning coffee.

Lucas nodded toward the kitchen. "Shall we check on chaos?"

"Sure." I walked with him. "Did Emily spend time here?"

"Oh yeah. We have a couple of projects in common. We're both on the board at Planned Parenthood."

With Stevie on her hip, Nicole was mopping up boiled-over pasta water. Lucas held out his hands and the boy reached up for him, happily transferring his grip from Nicole's neck to Lucas's.

Nicole had turned off the heat under the spaghetti pot. I tweezed a long piece out of the water. It was long past *al dente,* but edible. I found a collander by the sink and drained the pot into it. There was enough to feed a multitude.

"Can you stay for dinner?" Lucas asked.

"Another time. I'm going to see Celeste tonight."

"Hah!" he barked. "But good luck trying."

I smiled, but I felt a sudden torque. I counted off the people on the old indictment with Emily.

"Lucas," I said, interrupting a game of patty cake. "There's a great big world out there, with wrongs to right in every corner. How did so many of you end up in L.A.?"

" 'Sometimes, I think they'se poison in th' life in a big city. The flowers won't grow there . . .' "

"I'm supposed to recognize that, right? Bob Dylan or Pete Seeger, maybe."

"Mr. Dooley. 1892."

"If it was 1892, he wasn't talking about Los Angeles," I said. "What's the point?"

"It's simple. If you're going to make flowers grow, then go where the sun shines."

Chapter 12

Emily's apartment had a cold, unused feeling. First thing, I switched on all the lights and turned up the radiator. Mrs. Lim had tidied up from the night before.

For the services at La Placita, Max had taken the field jacket from the bag of clothes I had carried home from the hospital. The rest of the stuff, jeans, shirt, underwear, Mrs. Lim had rinsed out and hung up to dry. The sweats I had borrowed to wear while my own things dried were neatly folded on top of the dresser.

I took off the jeans I had worn all day and slipped into the sweats again. I was feeling the lack of sleep and had begun to notice that I hadn't eaten all day. Without much optimism, I headed for the kitchen to see what I could find.

Mrs. Lim, bless her, had considerately laid out tea-making things for me on the kitchen counter. Silently, I apologized for any less-than-kind thoughts I had ever entertained about her.

I turned on the fire under the kettle and looked in the refrigerator for something to eat, knowing how bleak the prospects were. Again, I had underestimated Mrs. Lim. Sitting next to a block of tofu, I found a beautiful, thick, chicken sandwich with sliced tomatoes on the side.

I took Vivaldi off the CD, put in Phil Collins, and turned up the volume. Sitting on the floor with my back against the sofa, I ate the sandwich and washed it down with hot tea. If the room had been warmer, I would have fallen asleep right where I sat, with crumbs on my lap and an empty cup in my hand.

But I was cold and grubby. I had a lot of repair work to do before I confronted Celeste Baldwin Smith at the Century Plaza.

I went into the bathroom, stripped, and stood under a hot shower for longer than is kosher in drought-stricken California. I shampooed my hair with Emily's shampoo, shaved my legs with her razor, wrapped myself in her terry robe when I got out. It felt very strange to be there, handling her things, without hearing Em rattling around in the next room or popping in and out to talk to me. I kept hearing noises that I knew existed only in my memory. It was spooky to be there alone, but it was also reassuring to be among her ordinary, private little essentials.

The many dramatic events of our lives had, I think, overshadowed my recollection of the texture of our everyday routines. I regretted that. Emily was more than the radical peacenik, more than the sainted doctor. She could be incredibly funny. She sang off-key in the shower and left wet towels and dirty clothes all over the bathroom. On the few occasions when I had come to stay with her, or her with me, she would come into the bathroom while I bathed, sit on the toilet lid and talk to me. Generally with a glass of wine in her hand.

Emily could be an incorrigible tease. She often made me furious. I thought about those times, too, because I needed to remember everything about her. I dabbed on some of her L'Air du Temps and breathed in her scent from my skin.

Emily was six feet tall. She had bought her robe at a men's big-and-tall shop, the only place she could find one to reach her ankles. I had put on her robe because it was all there was other than a skimpy bath towel. The robe was so big that I kept tripping over the hem while I blew my hair dry and used her makeup to correct a night without sleep. The thing was a nuisance. I was tired and my fuse was very short. By the time I had finished with the bathroom routine, I was plain old cranky.

I didn't expect Garth with my clothes from Desert

Mode for another couple of hours. So I went to the kitchen. opened Emily's bottle of celebratory chardonnay, and poured myself a glass. We had already shared so much, why not this?

I turned on the television and sat down on the sofa with my glass of wine to watch the evening news. The Ken and Barbie news team told me nothing that I didn't already know: Emily was being moved to Stanford, there was a new rainstorm on its way down the coast, Aleda had been bailed out and was in seclusion. The single new story was about the Vice President's official Christmas card going out in the mail with an embarrassing typo. I don't remember what the typo was, because I heard it just as I drifted off to sleep.

Someone banging on the apartment door interrupted a dream I was having about swimming in a pool with no water. It all made perfect sense, until I woke up. Disoriented, I staggered through the apartment in the direction of the knocking and opened the door.

"Jesus, Maggie," Garth said, looking me over. In his perfect silk tux, he looked like the ornament from the top of a wedding cake. "I thought we had a date."

I was a mess, hair and makeup undone, the nubbly weave of the couch upholstery pressed into one cheek. I took the garment bag Garth carried and waved him in.

"There's wine in the kitchen," I said. "I won't be long."

"Take your time, honey. Take your time. Party starts at eight. We don't want to get there too early or too sober."

"What time is it now?"

"Eight-fifteen."

"I don't want to miss Celeste. What if she decides to go home early?"

"She won't. It's her bash."

"Just the same." I tripped over the robe and he caught me by the elbow.

"How much of that wine have you had?" he asked, laughing.

"Obviously, not enough. Go away. I'll only be five minutes."

My hands were filled with the long garment bag, but I managed to gather up enough of the robe's hem to stumble into Em's walk-in closet. I spent some time repairing the hair and face, in essence girding my loins before I braved a look at the creation Desert Mode had sent me. At last, I pulled the zipper on the garment bag.

I had been right: sequins and shoulder pads. That is, one shoulder pad. The basic dress was a slinky, black-sequined tube that covered one arm to the wrist and left the other one bare, as well as a good part of the chest. A massive red-sequin poinsettia bloomed atop the single shoulder and leafed across the cleavage. The flower's stem was a spangley green-and-silver vine down the front of the dress, ending where the slit in the skirt began, about five inches below my crotch.

I didn't know whether I could walk in the thing, much less sit. This confection was almost funny to me, whose only after-five attire is a well-cut black-silk suit I bought on sale at Saks six years ago. The suit looks great and no one ever remembers it. If it didn't get wrinkled in a suitcase, it would be perfect.

There was a fur coat in the bag. I hung it up and intended to leave it behind. A paper sack in the bottom of the garment bag held the rest of the costume essentials: three-inch silver sandals, metallic silver hose, underwear, accessories. I started with the strapless bra. It was too small around the back, and too big up front, so I tossed it aside and did without a bra. Everything else fit beautifully, to use beautifully loosely.

The pièce de résistance was a pair of crystal earrings long enough to dust the top of my single bare shoulder.

When I was in full regalia, I took a long look in the mirror on the back of the closet door. As a whole, it was okay, certainly not to my taste, but what the hell? I have worn jungle fatigues in El Salvador, a chador in Iran, Laura Ashley in England, medium gray on Wall Street, all to blend into the environment. Reminding myself that this rig was only another form of camouflage, I opened the closet door and slinked out to dazzle Garth.

"Yo, baby," he grinned, twirling me around. "Why waste this gorgeous creature on some boring-as-shit fundraiser? Let's go dancing."

"Let's just get this over with. Are you ready?"

"Get your coat." He tilted his wine glass to drain it. When he saw me drape my camel coat over my arm, he froze. "Desert Mode should have sent over some fur."

"They did. But there's no way I'm going to take responsibility for a full-length mink. If some animal rights nut doused me with paint, I couldn't pay for the repairs."

"I'll be responsible for the coat," he said.

"It's useless to argue," I said, taking his arm. "How many times have you been able to change my mind?"

"I can remember a few little victories," he said, holding my camel coat for me. "But Pyrrhic victories, every one."

I kissed his cheek as I went past on my way out the door. "Have I told you how nice you look?"

"Not yet."

"You are elegant, Garth," I said, taking his arm as we walked down the hall. "A credit to your sex."

"Thank you." He kissed the hand that I had tucked into his arm. "I brought the videotapes you wanted. They're in the car."

"I don't have words to tell you how much I appreciate what you're doing for me."

He bumped my shoulder. "Try."

"I thought I just did." I laughed.

"You're a wordsmith. You can do better."

"I'll work on it," I said. "Sorry I'm such miserable company. The whole idea of going to this party, even if it's the only way I can get at Celeste, seems all wrong when I think about Emily. This dress makes me feel like an absolute ass."

"Emily would get a kick out of your efforts on her behalf. You're doing the right thing."

"Did I forget to tell you how nice it is to see you again, Garth?"

"For some messages, you don't need words."

Garth's latest car was a black Jaguar XJS with a buff-colored ragtop and chrome wire wheels. It little more than purred as he sliced through traffic along Sunset and down to Santa Monica Boulevard. "Thus Spake Zarathustra" blasted on quad speakers. I folded my coat across the gape-front of the dress, leaned into the smooth leather upholstery and tried to get into the spirit of things.

Garth pulled into the curved drive in front of the Century Plaza, taking his place in the line of limos and Rollses waiting to disgorge passengers. As we got out of the car, some paparazzi snuck past the attendants and took a few quick flash shots of us, just in case we were somebody. I wanted to tell him not to bother, but Spiro Agnew was walking in ahead of us, and his picture was taken, too. If he's news, then so am I.

I recognized many of the faces in the receiving line. Though there was an abundance of designer gowns and Versace tuxes, I saw early on that this was definitely a B list of political and entertainment figures. Then, who could expect Madonna to show up to help raise funds with a woman who called for the censorship of rock lyrics? Big names or not, there were certainly plenty of big bucks, all of them from the Right side of the political aisle.

Celeste stood just outside the ballroom, under a bower of decorated Christmas pines, greeting arriving guests. Her dress was strapless red taffeta, simple and tasteful to set off the handfuls of baroque rubies that circled her neck. The exposed skin of her face and shoulders was magnificent, like polished white alabaster—smooth, hard and cold.

Stories from the old days were legion about Celeste dropping onto her back and spreading her legs for anyone who asked nicely. Male or female, straight and quick or kinky as hell, she had been an equal opportunity lay.

Sex had been part of her politics, a rejection of traditional relationships that she said repressed women.

I looked at this latest incarnation of Celeste and could not imagine her fucking anyone or anything. Ever. She was the epitome of the frigid society matron. Never changing the degree of her smile, she greeted each guest by name, said something appropriately friendly, sent them along into the elaborately decorated ballroom.

I had been brazenly staring at her as we inched our way up the line, wondering what she would find to say to me. She had my hand in her light-as-a-butterfly grip before she realized who I was.

"Maggot!" she said, drawing back. "I had no idea you were coming."

"Good to see you, Celeste," I said. "I want to have a nice long chat."

"Yes?" For the first time her smile flagged.

Her hand fell away from mine, but just seemed to hang there in midair until Garth caught it.

"Wasn't it sweet of Maggie to come with me tonight?" he effused. "Couldn't keep her away. She's so involved with teens and drugs."

I don't know how Celeste read the remark, or how Garth intended it. She smiled a tight Bryn Mawr smile. "Lovely to see you, Maggot, so all grown up. We'll find a quiet moment later, to catch up."

"Until later, then," I said as the people behind me pressed forward.

"What do you think?" Garth whispered in my ear as we went inside.

"She looks stoned," I said. "I wonder what they had to give her before she could show up tonight."

"A little dope wouldn't have hurt you," he said. "Relax, Maggie. Emily wouldn't care if you had just a little bit of fun."

"I'm working up to it, Garth. Stick with me."

"Like glue."

He stayed tight beside me as we walked through the room. We greeted people as they surged toward us, but didn't merge with any of the little conversational clusters that beckoned us.

At the far end of the room, a full orchestra played waltzy music while half a dozen mirrored balls rotated over the crowded dance floor. The spangles on women's dresses and their fresh-from-the-vault jewels caught the light until it hurt my eyes to look at them. I could hardly look down at my dazzley self.

That is not to say that others didn't look at me. There was no way I could walk without showing a lot of thigh. Garth was loving it. As we walked toward the trays of Dom Pérignon, I watched women look at me, at my hand on him, then up at his face with greedy interest. I hoped this was some payback for the help he had given me.

We had to wait until the stream of newcomers dwindled before Celeste was approachable. I gulped my second glass of champagne and started for her. T. Rexford Smith, the husband, got to her first and led her onto the dance floor.

"Do something," I said to Garth.

We followed them. Shadowed them actually, trying to get close to our hosts. Garth took me in his arms and we wedged through the box-stepping crowd.

T. Rexford was an energetic if graceless dancer. We had to dodge some elbows, but Garth managed to get us inside, close enough to manipulate a partner swap. Since I was the one who wanted to speak with Celeste, I didn't know what the point was of getting me into T. Rexford's arms. I watched Garth float away with Celeste and hoped he remembered why we had come.

In my heels, I was three inches taller than T. Rex, making it difficult to follow his lead. He sweated a great deal, roamed with his hand down my back more than we were taught was acceptable at St. Catherine's.

"I'm Maggie MacGowen," I said, trying to keep my feet out from under his. "I've known your wife for a very long time."

"Have you?" His hand dipped to my ass. I pulled back and twirled him by the fingertips in a wide pirouette. He rebounded off the couple next to us, spun back and clutched me against his round, ruffle-fronted tummy.

He grinned at me. "How many of the men in this room have you slept with?"

"I don't know," I said. "I haven't had time to look around much."

"Lovely dress. When you walked across the room, I could see the entire inner curve of your thigh."

"Mr. Smith," I crooned. "You're an insufferable toad. If you don't move your hand, I will emasculate you with the zipper of that rented monkey suit. *Capiche*?"

"*Capiche*," he laughed. "I'm familiar with your films, Miss MacGowen. Brilliant work. I'm not sure I can agree with the liberal undercurrents, but I can't fault the craftsmanship."

"What do you know about filmmaking?"

"The two essentials: Profit and Loss. I know that a good, low-budget product with long-term potential is a far better investment in this economy than a blockbuster that's top-heavy with star salaries and perks. Good and cheap, that's what you deliver consistently, Maggie. Films that will accrue earnings into the millennium."

"I don't do theatrical films."

"You will," he said smugly, maneuvering me into a dip. "Come see me after the holidays."

"I'm going to Ireland after the holidays on a project."

"Oh? Another paean to the IRA?"

"Not this time. We're going to talk with young Irish women about coping with the chronic shortage of marriageable men. I think it will be fun."

In the same tone he might quiz a leper, he asked, "Are you a feminist?"

"Are you?"

Garth and Celeste were beside us. "May I?" Garth asked, and I simply danced into his arms before T. Rex could answer. T. Rex grasped Celeste around her tight waist and they glided away into the crowd.

"What a workout," I said, as Garth waltzed me off the dance floor. "Learn anything?"

"Celeste will meet you out on the terrace in five minutes. I'll stay outside the door and run interference for you."

"How did you manage it?" I asked.

"Easy. I told her I had been working on Emily's video obit and Celeste's face kept showing up in the file footage. She asked what it would take to be forgotten. I said she had to talk to you. I told her you were the boss on the project."

"You're a genius. Thanks. I'm going to the terrace now. Keep an eye on Celeste. Make sure no one slips her anything like cyanide or a nine-millimeter slug before she joins me."

"That isn't funny," Garth said. "You keep a sharp eye out for yourself. And a clear head."

My head was already a bit muzzy from the champagne. I knew better, but when I walked past a waiter bearing a full tray, I said to hell with it and took a glass. Sipping champagne along the way, I went out through a side door that led to a small balcony overlooking Avenue of the Stars.

I wasn't nearly drunk enough not to feel the cold. I was thinking about going back inside for my coat when Celeste came.

She stayed near the door, ready for flight. I could see that she was nervous about being with me.

"I received the message you left at my house this morning," she said. "You said, '*Aujourd'hui Emily est morte.*' But Emily didn't die today, did she?"

"No."

"Then why did you say she had?"

"To see if you remembered."

"Oh, yes, I remembered." She relaxed a little. "That's the opening line from *The Stranger*. I remember throwing Camus at your head once when you were being especially awful."

"It wasn't Camus you threw; it was a guide for making explosives."

"Was it?" She smiled. "Such a long time ago."

"I was sorry to hear about your daughter," I said. "I never met her, but I have a daughter of my own and I can't imagine going on with life if I lost her."

"Who says I've gone on with my life?" Her chin quivered slightly, the first show of genuine emotion I had seen from her. "Have you ever lived with an addict?"

"No."

"Then you have no idea." She came further out onto the balcony, the movement of her feet hidden by the long red dress so that she seemed to float toward the rail at the edge. She seemed weightless, so otherworldly that I wondered how gravity managed to keep its hold on her. If there hadn't been a Plexiglas windscreen behind the rail, I would have worried about her blowing away. Or jumping. She had a scary, desperate quality about her.

"Do you have other children?" I asked, holding us to this world.

"Yes, two." She looked at me over her shoulder. "Paix graduates this June from Princeton, and young Rex is a freshman in prep school."

"Paix," I repeated. "The name means peace, doesn't it? He must be graduating young."

She laughed softly. "You always were nosy, Maggot. In June, he will be twenty-two. What does that suggest to you?"

"Suppose you tell me."

"My eldest was born exactly nine months after I saw your brother, Marc, for the last time."

"Are you saying my brother was the father?"

She gave me a small sardonic smile. "Check the calendar. Could have been Marc. Could have been Ho Chi Minh, or maybe a redcap at the Honolulu Airport. You would have to look at Paix and decide that for yourself."

"I'd like that. Tomorrow morning all right?"

She sagged against the balcony rail. "Oh, Maggie, never mind."

"If he is Marc's son, he's my nephew. And I mind very much."

"No point. Rexford accepted him, and that's all that

matters to me. Paix grew up, and I grew up along with him. Everything that happened before was nothing more than youthful folly."

"It was a great deal more than folly," I said. "People died."

"Tom Potts," she sighed as she reached for what was left of my glass of champagne. "I've worked so hard to put all that behind me. Won't it ever end?"

"You brought it up."

"Emily called me yesterday," she said. "Such a surprise. I hadn't spoken with her for years. She wanted to see me. When I heard what happened to her . . ."

"Did she say why she wanted to see you?"

"A reunion, she said. And a memorial service for Marc. I couldn't possibly go. Not with this bash happening tonight." A sudden breeze made her shiver. "The whole idea gave me the creeps. We're only entitled to one funeral per customer. I always thought Emily's attachment to Marc was a bit perverse."

"Perverse?"

"Poor Jaime. Can you imagine what it must have been like to go to bed with a woman who was fixated on her dead brother?"

"Watch yourself, Celeste. Don't forget who I am."

"None of this ever occurred to you? My God, poor Marc had to go to Vietnam to get away from Emily. And still she followed him. She killed him, you know. The trip to Hanoi, the Berkeley demonstration, all the publicity."

"You were with her through it all. Does this mean you share some blame?"

"No," she snapped. "Emily choreographed every step we took. She and Aleda. They insisted we stop over in Honolulu to see Marc on the way to Hanoi. I thought it was a waste. Who did Emily think she was, anyway, dragging us along behind her? Queen Emily. Queen Bee Emily."

"You're so bitter."

"Perhaps I have a right. Maggie, have you any conception what that little epoch cost me?"

"Suppose you tell me."

"It cost me my life."

"You hardly seem deprived," I said, noting the way her rubies seemed to sparkle even in the near-dark. "You've married a rich and powerful man; you have access to the movers and shakers."

She was shaking her head. "I didn't marry a rich and powerful man, I made one. I bought him access to the movers and shakers. But it means that Rex is having the life that should have been mine. Don't tell me not to be bitter."

"I don't understand," I said. "What was to stop you from doing anything you wanted?"

"Surely you're not so naive. It happened to all of us, Maggie."

"What did?"

"The dirty suggestions," she seethed. "We would apply for jobs and someone would show up to plant the seeds, show copies of our FBI files to the right people, make vague threats. We were blocked from the work we wanted to do, should have been doing.

"They even did it to my son, Paix," she said. "I was raising him alone. I enrolled him in a good preschool, but when we showed up for the first day, suddenly there were no openings."

"Maybe there were no openings, Celeste," I said. "Look at Emily's career. How can you say anyone interfered with her success."

"Success? Innoculating illegal immigrants is hardly the path she had in mind. She and Jaime were going to spearhead health reform throughout the Third World. But there wasn't an international health organization that would touch them. Or a federally funded American research institution that would hire her. Look at Jaime. What sort of practice does he have?"

"He seems happy."

"Then you should look again. And while you're at it, look at your own career."

"You're nuts," I said. "I was just a kid during all that. It had nothing to do with me."

"Do you remember an offer for a Capitol correspondent job that evaporated as soon as you resigned from your old anchor position? Where was that? Atlanta?"

"But surely . . ."

"And then a long dry spell, no job offers came, did they? Some of your husband's clients drifted away, too. And where did you end up? PBS. Was that the goal you had in mind?"

"Sounds so paranoid. Why would anyone bother with me?"

"To get at Emily."

"Why?" I demanded.

"To pay old debts," she said. "It's still happening, Maggie. I told you my son is graduating in June. Ask him about what happens after job interviews."

"You're saying *they* are the FBI?"

"I wish it were, because then I would know how to fight back. I only know that this has been a very personal vendetta from the beginning. Whoever it is has access to the single most powerful tool that exists in our political system."

"What?"

"Information. Information for blackmail."

Chapter 13

"Celeste is full of shit," Garth said. "This nonsense she fed you about spooks in her woodpile is just a new form of terrorism for her. Did Emily ever say anything about harassment to you? Or did Max or Jaime? Anyone you ever worked with just drop a few hints that they were being warned off? I'm old enough to remember the days of the blacklist. It didn't operate in secret. It couldn't. You know what gossips people in our industry are."

"Maybe." I leaned against the door frame and looked back into the darkness of Emily's apartment. What Celeste said had really shaken me, especially when she brought me into this Grand Plot she described. I had other, valid, explanations for what had happened in my own life.

The Washington correspondent job offer came, and vanished, the year I turned thirty. Scotty was still drinking heavily then and our life together was falling apart. Maybe I didn't look stable enough, young enough, sexy enough, girl-next-door enough to the new network management that came aboard just after the contracts were signed. In the end, the network bought out my contract. I got a lot of money and felt very little grief.

I have been in television most of my working life. I think I understand, by now, the way it operates. Crow's feet seems to me to be more likely grounds for dismissal of on-camera staff than blackmail does. But still . . . Celeste had done a fair job of planting her own seeds.

"Have you ever used the Freedom of Information Act to search for FBI files on yourself?" I asked.

"No. If there are files on me, I don't give a shit what they say. Would you think I was less cute if you found out I was a Commie mole?"

"Gee, Garth," I said. "You just couldn't be more cute than you already are."

"Well, that's true. Forget what Celeste said. Anyway, if anyone, FBI, XYZ, LSMFT, came to you and tried to warn you off a co-worker, using some frigging old files, what would you do first?"

"Call a news conference."

"I rest my case." He leaned over me and peered into the apartment. "You going to invite me in, or are you going to make me drive all the way home tonight?"

"I'll make hotel reservations for you," I said. "Garth, I'm rotten company."

"I might disagree with that." He kissed me on the forehead and buttoned up his overcoat. "I'll call you tomorrow."

"Thanks for everything. You're a good cheerleader."

"That's my curse." He had set a good size carton of news videos he had compiled just inside the door. He nudged the carton with the toe of his patent pump. "Let me know if you find anything interesting on those."

"I will. Good night." For something to do with my hands, I was fingering the scraps of junk in my coat pockets as I watched him walk away. I pulled out a BART ticket that still had five cents on it, and a gum wrapper. Garth turned at the stairs and started back.

"Maggie, this is nuts. You shouldn't be here alone. I don't believe Celeste for a minute, but something rough is going on. At least come home with me."

"I'm fine. There are big locks on the doors and Mrs. Lim is on the lookout downstairs. I'm fine," I insisted. "Drive carefully."

"I'll call you," he said again and, after some hesitation, went away.

I waited in the open door until I heard him going downstairs. I had by then found in my pocket a ticket stub for *The Return of the Jedi,* reminding me how old the coat was, some used Kleenex, and a small wad of white paper.

As I went inside and closed the door I was trying to open the wad. It looked as if it had been wet when it was rolled up. Then I remembered the tract that a transient had handed me on the street in front of Lee's Bakery the night before. I was about to toss it into the bathroom trashcan, when I saw that it wasn't a commercially printed sheet. It was handwritten. And it was handwritten on one of Emily's prescription forms.

"I am Caesar," the man had said when he handed the paper to me. "Here is the message and the truth."

The ink was a little smeared, but "the message and the truth" was clear enough to read: "Maggot, Sorry I couldn't wait for you. Max is at the Bonaventure. Meet us there. ASAP. Em."

There was nothing essentially new in the message. The puzzle was, how did Emily get it into the hands of Caesar, and from his to mine? And when had she written it?

Obviously, all the answers rested with Caesar. I pulled the apartment door closed after me and ran down the stairs and out onto the street. At some point I thought I should have taken time to change into more practical clothes, but I planned only to go down Hill Street as far as Lee's Bakery, where I had seen Caesar before. If I didn't find him, someone might know where he was. I thought I would be out five, maybe ten minutes at the most.

It was almost eleven and all the choice covered doorways were filled with overnight guests. I stopped at the first recumbent figure.

"Excuse me," I said. "May I have a word with you?"

"Hey man." A fuzzy head appeared out of a tangle of bedding. "I'm tryin' to sleep here, man."

"Sorry," I said. "I'm looking for a man named Caesar. Do you know him? He has a dog."

"I don' want no dog, man. I just want to sleep. Don' you shout at me no mo'."

"Sorry," I said again, and walked on. I found an apparently conscious man sitting upright in his blankets in the recessed entry of the *Quong Fook Tong* Benevolent Association.

"Excuse me," I said, already tired of the routine. "I'm looking for a man named Caesar. He has a dog with him."

"Who do you want? The man or the dog?"

"The man."

"You can have me, you sweet thing. And you didn't have to get all dressed up."

"Do you know Caesar?"

"Sure." He started to rise. "He's cooping in this alley back here. Let me show you."

I could see the mouth of the alley, and there was no way I was going in there, alone or escorted by a platoon of marines, much less with this character.

"You don't know Caesar, do you?"

"Know thyself, that's my motto."

"Thanks anyway."

I tried two more sleepers, with similar results. Lee's Bakery was still open, so I went in. Mr. Lee was working behind the counter in crisp white overalls and a tall white cap. He looked up at me and bowed.

"May I have some coffee, Mr. Lee?" I asked.

"You sit," he said, gesturing toward the tables by the front window. "I bring."

I drew my coat closer around me and sat down. I hadn't realized how cold I was until I came inside where it was warm. The sky had begun to cloud over again and there was a very brisk wind.

Mr. Lee put a mug of coffee and a plate of pork cookies in front of me.

"Dr. Emily, she be okay?" he asked.

"I hope so, Mr. Lee. I hope so."

He bowed twice and started to walk away.

"Mr. Lee," I called. "Do you happen to know a man named Caesar? I met him outside your bakery last night."

"Man have dog?"

"Yes." I stood up. "Have you any idea where he might be?"

He scratched his head. Then he scratched his shoulder. "Possible. Come with me."

He headed out the front door, with me close on his heels. We waited for traffic, then crossed the street to a Chevron station on the corner. The station was closed for the night, but there was a light showing from somewhere inside. Mr. Lee rapped on the front window.

An inside door opened, and I saw the dark shape of a man. He seemed to be very cautious. He looked us over before he came out into the station's office and turned on the overhead lights.

"That you, Mr. Lee?" The man didn't have any front teeth, but he seemed well-scrubbed and he wore fresh blue overalls with a Chevron logo on the sleeve. He unlocked the door and talked to us through a narrow crack. "What do you want?"

"You know Caesar?" Mr. Lee asked.

"He's not here, honest. I told the boss I won't let Caesar in here no more at night, and I meant it. He never hurt nothing. I mean, I take good care of the place. I wouldn't let no one touch nothing he wasn't suppose' to."

A dog sauntered in from the back room and growled at us from behind the man's legs.

"Is that Caesar's dog?" I asked.

"The boss never said nothing about no dog. 'Sides, a watchdog's good company, don't you think? I don't like being in here all alone all night. A good dog's good company."

"Where is Caesar?" I asked.

"Said he was goin' over to the Weingart for dinner, see if he could find him a bed. On account of, they won't give him a bed if he has a dog."

"Thank you so much," I said, slipping him a five from the wad of bills my mother had given me. I walked Mr. Lee back to his store, tried in vain, again, to pay for the coffee, thanked him twice, bowed a few times, then ran to the curb where I had parked Max's car.

The Henry Weingart Center is the best financed, most efficiently run shelter and soup kitchen on Los Angeles's Skid Row. I couldn't remember exactly where it was. I drove south from the civic center, tracking the density and general direction of the migration of street people until they maxed out on San Pedro Street. Weingart was in the block after Fifth Street. I parked in a loading zone out front and walked in the front door.

Weingart was better established, certainly, than Grace House, though the clientele was essentially the same. The place itself was large and clean and well-staffed.

It had begun to drizzle again. Just inside the door, two staff members were handing out silver survival ponchos. There was a long queue waiting for the ponchos. I walked up to the man who seemed to be in charge.

"Excuse me," I said.

I was roughly nudged aside by a man draped with so many Glad Bag bundles he looked like a kid's Halloween version of a bunch of grapes.

"You gotta wait," he said, crossly. "Can't just walk into a line like that. Ain't right. You gotta wait your turn."

"Do you know a man named Caesar?" I asked him. "He was coming here for dinner."

"Dinner?" He turned to the people behind him in line to affirm how stupid my question was. "If he's looking for dinner, he done missed it. It's damn near breakfast time, lady. And you still have to wait in line like everyone else."

I moved to the woman behind him. "How about you? Do you know a man named Caesar, usually has a dog with him?"

"Everyone knows Caesar." She flipped a hank of gray hair over her shoulder, rearranged her army blanket toga, and recited: " 'Cowards die many times before their deaths; the valiant never taste of death but once. Of all the wonders that I yet have heard, it seems to me most strange that men should fear seeing death. A necessary end, will come when it will come.' " She bowed with a flourish.

"What you say?" the grape man demanded.

"Shakespeare," she said. "Julius Caesar, act two, scene two."

"Who's he? He here tonight?"

"*He* is always with us," the woman sighed. She looked over at me. "The man, Caesar, about whom you inquire, was turned away tonight. He was quite in his cups, you know. The staff here will not admit one in that state. If he's sleeping in the neighborhood tonight, then he makes the cobbles of the street his pillow."

"You're sure he isn't in the dormitory?" I asked.

She rolled her eyes. "I just told you, bitch. They gave the sot the heave-ho."

"Thanks for your help," I said. I went back out to the street. It was a mob scene, something like the streets of Pasadena the night before the Rose Parade—all done in a silver motif. Poncho-clad people lined the sidewalks two and three deep. A canopy of ponchos strung together sheltered a noisy crowd partying to the accompaniment of huge boom boxes. They shared bottles, jostled each other, or just roamed. Lying here and there around the entire area were the silver-wrapped mounds of bodies at rest. Or bodies, period.

In the grassy verges behind the sidewalk, in the driveways of boarded-up warehouses, people clustered around K-Mart barbecues for warmth. Some of them lounged in plastic lawn chairs, their feet resting on ice chests. Whatever they were doing, everyone faced the street as if waiting for something—I don't know what, a marching band, a fight, someone to mug, Armageddon.

A pair of overweight, underage hookers plied the crowd, seeking to exchange a little quick pleasure for a hit of crack. They didn't seem to be having much success.

I beckoned them over as they moved off the sidewalk in front of the center and into the street.

"I'm looking for a man," I said.

"Who ain't?" The taller of the girls laughed behind her hand, modestly covering the gaps among her front teeth. She probably was no more than fifteen, but it was difficult to tell.

"His name is Caesar. Do you know him?" I asked, slipping her a five.

"What'd he do to you?" The money disappeared into the top of her black satin shorts.

"I just want to talk to him."

"Maybe I know him, maybe I don't. No one tells me his name, just what he wants. What does this dude look like?"

I looked at the men walking by, or sitting at the curb stoned. Caesar looked like all of them.

"I don't know," I said. I didn't have another five, so I gave her a ten. "Ask around. If you find him, leave a message at the Weingart for Maggie. There'll be another twenty in it for you if you do. I'll be back later."

"Listen," the girl said, grabbing my arm as I walked away. "You look more like Hollywood Boulevard than San Pedro Street. They don't pay so good down here. If you find this Caesar guy, better ask him to pay in advance."

"Good advice," I said. I slid into the Beemer, tucking in my sequin train.

I locked the car doors and turned on the engine and the cellular phone. I needed some help. There was no way in hell I was going to move more than six feet down San Pedro Street alone.

From the car, I called the Bonaventure and asked for Uncle Max. He was out. So were Rod and Lucas. After a few minutes of quiet swearing, I took out the card Detective Bronkowski had handed me at the courthouse.

I placed a call to Parker Center.

"Robbery-Homicide, Arce speaking."

"Hello," I said. "I'm looking for Detective Bronkowski. Can you page him for me?"

"He's out on a call."

"How about Mike Flint?"

"He's off his beeper. Maybe I can help you."

I thought about it. I didn't want to start at the beginning, try to explain everything to Detective Arce. Actually, that isn't true. I needed help, and this detective would certainly know what to do. The sticking point was Flint. I had been surprised at how disappointed I felt when Arce said Flint wasn't available, another little pinch to the already bruised conscience.

So things between Flint and I had gotten out of hand the night before. I hadn't made a graceful exit. Bronkowski had let me know that Flint wasn't feeling so good himself. I wanted to patch things up with Flint. I needed to find Caesar. Seemed they could dovetail.

"Listen," I said to Arce, in a pitiful little voice. "I really need to find Mike Flint. Bronk told me to call him if Mike hadn't shown up by now."

"Shown up where?"

"My house. I hate to bother you, but we had this big fight last night, and I think he's afraid to come home. I really want to find him."

"You're the squeeze, huh?" he said.

"I guess."

"It's Saturday night before Christmas. You try the lounge at the academy?"

"Not yet."

"Give them a call. Bartender's name is Verna. She'll know if he's there. If you don't find Mike, I'll be through here around midnight. Give me a call."

"Thanks," I said. I hung up and shifted into drive. The L.A. Police Academy was only a few minutes away.

I had been to the academy some years ago to watch a boxing demonstration given by women police officers. We had celebrated the victory of an amazon brunette named Officer Bambi by getting blind drunk in the academy's lounge. I don't remember how I got home from there, but I knew I could easily find the academy again; it sits at the far edge of the Dodger Stadium parking lot, in the hills of Elysian Park.

The sky opened up. I turned on the windshield wipers,

put my foot on the accelerator, and headed straight north out of downtown, just following the signs to Dodger Stadium.

The Police Academy looks more like a rustic lodge than an urban-combat training facility. Built of natural river rock and heavy timbers, it is nestled into a canyon filled with lacy eucalyptus. The view of downtown, when the sky is clear, is magnificent.

The parking lot that curved up the hill past the rifle range was full. So I went back down front and found a space between two black-and-white units in the lot below the gift shop. The stone walkways were uneven and slick with rain. I managed to make it up the stairs to the lounge without permanent injury.

Inside the door, there was a coat rack. I decided it would be prudent not only to keep my coat on, but also to keep it buttoned.

I was working my way toward the bar when I was intercepted by an officer in motorcycle boots, jodhpurs, and a plain black sweatshirt. His boots creaked as he walked.

"Looking for a friend?" he asked, parking a foot on the rung of a stool and striking a John Wayne pose.

"I'm looking for Mike Flint," I said. "Have you seen him?"

He leaned into me. "Never heard of him."

"He's a detective from Major Crimes Section."

He shook his head. "What does he look like?"

"A squint. Gray suit, gray hair."

"Lot of suits here. What does he have that I can't offer you?"

I extended my index finger stiffly in front of his nose. "Can you make a woman scream for mercy six times in a row without ever . . ." I let my index finger droop, slowly.

He laughed and put his foot down. "Mike's inside. I think you deserve each other."

"Thanks." I walked on in and searched through the crowd.

The near end of the lounge is a big horseshoe-shaped standing bar; the far end is clusters of small tables, a dinky dance floor, and big doors that lead out to the rock garden. A lot of love blooms in the rock garden at night, I remembered Officer Bambi telling me. Tonight it was wet outside, and the doors were closed.

This was a noisy group. Not exactly the same mob I had seen earlier at the Century Plaza. Working people at the end of their work day. No one was in full uniform, there were no badges showing, but the body language separated police from civilian guests—a certain swagger, men and women both, an air of authority, a watchfulness, a bulge at the waist about the size of a 9mm automatic. Scattered among them, like flower garnishes in a field of navy blue and medium gray, were young women with heavy makeup, short skirts, lots of moussed hair.

I spotted Mike Flint at a table near the rock garden doors. The sweet young thing with him was sipping something pink with paper umbrellas stuck on the rim of the glass. I couldn't tell whether he was trying to get lucky or babysitting.

He didn't seem overly happy to see me, but I walked over and put my hand on his shoulder, anyway.

"Hi, Mike," I said, drawing it out. "How've you been?"

"Where's my tape?" he said.

"That's all you have to say to me after last night?"

The girl with him sucked the pink stuff through her straw as if she was on a timer.

"Will you excuse us?" I said to her.

She looked at Flint for a cue.

"Be right back, sweetie," he said. "This won't take long."

Flint picked up the beer he'd been nursing and led me to a corner table. He pointedly sat down on the far side. Nothing really had happened between us after drinks at the Bonaventure, nothing serious. Just fooling around. Once when my hand was on his chest, I felt the tape he had taken from Emily's answering machine in his pocket. Somehow, the tape had ended up in my own pocket. It was a tacky thing to do. I wasn't altogether sober, and I was desperate to hear the tape again, carefully. Cheesy excuse, but the best I had.

"I'm sorry," I said.

"Sorry? That's it? You get me all fired up just so you can pick my pocket. You steal evidence, you get me in trouble, then you come sniffing around here looking like Garbo in heat. Where did you get that dress?"

"Garbo?" I said. "How old are you, anyway?"

"You know what I mean. Jeez, look at that dress."

The coat was buttoned up under my neck, but there was a lot of sparkle and leg left over below it. "You weren't such a prude last night," I said.

He leaned forward and put his face near mine. "If you have any class, you won't bring up last night."

"Mike, I had to listen to the tape. Anyway, it just sort of fell into my hand. I'm sorry you're upset," I said. "You can have the tape back. It's out in the car."

"Damn right, I can have it back. A lot of good that does now. It's tainted. How do I know you didn't alter it? No court will accept that tape now."

"I said I'm sorry. I'm sorry your feelings are hurt. If I could kiss it and make it better, I would. Except that's how we got here, isn't it? So, maybe I have something for you that's better than the tape. A peace offering." I handed him the note from Emily. "What do you think?"

He read the note. "Where'd this come from?"

"A bum, a man named Caesar, gave it to me last night."

"And you're just getting around to showing it to me?"

"I just read it. I didn't pay any attention to it last night."

"Okay, so?" He wasn't going to let me off easy.

"I traced the bum to Skid Row, but I need some help locating him."

He put the note into his shirt pocket and folded his arms across his chest.

"Please, Mike, will you help me find Caesar?"

"I can't take you into an area like that. Thanks for the information. Now go home and let the police handle it."

"You won't know if you find the right man. I have to go with you."

"Forget it. I said, this is a police situation. The police will handle it. Got it?" He stood up and headed for the bar. I followed.

He ordered another beer.

"Please, Mike," I said, standing beside him.

"Do it, Flint," I heard behind me. "Or move over and let me do it for you."

Flint didn't acknowledge the comment. He was watching a gaggle of young latinas who had just come in the door, all dressed up, looking for a good time.

"Mike?" I said.

"I've said all I have to say to you." He picked up his beer. "I'm on my own time now. I've been waiting for the El Sereno bus all night. Now it's here. I'm a busy man. Catch you later." His step was none too steady as he walked over to greet the new material.

A glass of wine appeared on the bar in front of me. I turned and looked at the owner of the hand attached to it. He was tall, maybe forty, with nice eyes and a starched collar.

"You look like white wine to me," he said. "Fine white wine. Sorry this is the best I can offer you."

"Thanks," I said.

"Jack Riley," he said, touching the tip of my finger. "Known Flint long?"

"Since yesterday." I noticed Mike was watching me. Riley rested a foot on the brass rail under the bar. I put the toe of my shoe next to his, letting the coat and the skirt fall away from my leg. Riley was too close to see anything, but I knew Mike did. He turned his back.

"Thanks for the wine, Jack," I said. "I have to go."

"Sorry to hear that," he said. He smiled. "Merry Christmas."

"Merry Christmas to you," I said, smiling back as I

stepped away from the bar. "Your white wine line is a good one. Keep it."

He laughed and gave me a thumbs up. On my way out the door, I turned and saw him giving the same glass to a young woman officer who was sitting all alone by the rock garden doors.

Flint had quickly involved himself with a pair from the El Sereno bus. There was nothing more I could say to him—he had made that clear.

I felt bad, I felt cheap. I just opened the door and walked out.

The rain had let up some, but the wind whipped it into a stinging mist that hit me in the face, made me even more miserable. I struggled against the wind as I picked my way back down to Max's car. Before I did anything else, I planned to stop at Emily's and change. And I vowed that I would never again wear sequins.

I ducked into Max's car, but the wind pulled against the open door and I had to get out to pull it shut. I was just getting back in when Mike Flint reached out through the dark and grabbed the door.

"Slide over," he said, and pushed his way inside.

"Slide over" is also a great line, or was before bucket seats. I didn't slide over, I clambered over the console and cellular phone apparatus. It was a less than graceful progress. After some tugging and pulling, I managed to rearrange myself in the passenger seat.

I ejected the tape in the tapedeck and handed it to Mike. He sat looking at it and not at me.

"Last night," I said, "things may have gotten out of hand when we went back to the Bonaventure. I was terribly upset and I got a little drunk. You had been very nice about everything, Mike. Very sympathetic. I want you to know the reason I went along with you later. The only reason."

"Yeah?"

I put my hand on his arm. "I wanted to."

Finally, he looked at me. He had a sheepish grin. "The

only reason I got so pissed when you took the tape was, I really liked being with you."

"Good." I touched the soft little hairs at the back of his neck and kissed his cheek. "Will you take me back to Emily's so I can get out of these clothes?"

"You don't waste much time with the preliminaries, do you?"

I laughed. "I have to change before we go down to Skid Row."

"That again? Maggie, it's just a plain old bad idea for you to go down there. I have a loaded Roscoe and two extra clips on my belt, but I'm not sure that would be enough if something went down."

"It's late. Everyone I saw on San Pedro Street was either asleep or bombed, or otherwise out of his mind. How much harm can they do us when they can hardly walk?"

"Plenty. You wouldn't go down there alone, would you?"

"I may be a pain in the ass, but I'm not stupid," I said. "Mike, I know this man, Caesar, went to the Weingart Center tonight. He was turned away because he was drunk. So he's probably still in the neighborhood. Please. I'm so afraid we'll lose him if we don't move fast."

Mike rubbed the stubble on his cheek. "He seems to be a local. Be easier to find him in the morning."

"I had a date with my sister at four o'clock yesterday afternoon, and she didn't make it. I'd hate for something to happen to Caesar before we could talk to him."

"Okay," he sighed. He opened the door and started to get out. "You win. Let's go."

"Go where? It's too wet to walk."

"I told you, this is police business. If we're going, we're going in my car."

Chapter 14

"I don't know what you were afraid of, Mike," I said. It was just after midnight and we were walking around Skid Row, looking for our contact, a hooker named Latonya. "Everyone's so gosh darn friendly."

"Sure, you're with The Man," he chuckled. "But you never know. Things can turn ugly in a hurry."

"Evenin', officer." A passing loony tipped his hat. A fifty-one-fifty Flint would have called him, mental incompetent. "Evenin', ma'am."

"See," I said to Mike. "Nice as pie."

"Uh huh." He nudged a body sprawled across the sidewalk. When the body roused, Mike gave him another nudge and ordered, "Get to steppin'."

The body scuttled away.

"What would you have done if that man hadn't gotten up?" I asked.

"Called the coroner to bring the scoop."

"Assuming that the man was dead."

Mike swaggered just a little. "The only reason he wouldn't have gotten up was if he was dead."

"You're some tough guy, Flint." I laughed.

"So you keep telling me. But down here, I'm the only law west of the Pecos."

He made me laugh again. We had walked about three blocks through scuzz that made the Inferno look like the Home Show. Looking for Latonya. Flint told me she was an old friend of his. I didn't want to ask how close a friend, or anything else about her. She had left word for me at the Weingart that she knew where Caesar was cooped for the night and had heard there was twenty dollars in it.

Seventh Street and Wall was her home corner, according to Mike. She seemed to be away on business when we came calling. So we were just moseying around, staying visible until she came back.

As we walked, Flint, The Man, the *po*lice, cut a wide swath. No one molested us or panhandled us with very much conviction. I had this great sensation of power just being with him. Besides, he was great company, one outrageous war story after another.

As we turned off Wall Street, a monstrously obese woman barreled down upon us. She had YO BABY YO spray-painted on her short-cropped hair.

"Officer, officer," she wailed. "He's stealin' all my stuff."

"Who is?"

"My boyfriend. See him? He's takin' all my stuff."

Indeed, a youngish man was snatching dark-looking garments out of a shopping cart that had been spilled onto the weedy verge. Flint just shook his head. "Why is he taking your stuff?"

"He's gonna sell it. He says I owe him money."

"Do you owe him money?"

"No way."

"Yes she do." The boyfriend joined the fray, tattered clothes spilling over his arms, tangling around his feet as he tried to walk. "She done took my weed. Thirty dollars worth."

"Do you have his weed?" Flint asked, bland as a schoolmaster.

"No, I don't," she said, indignant.

"Yes you do," the boyfriend screamed.

"I ain't got it," she screamed back. "I done smoked it."

I thought the boyfriend would weep.

Flint, who had listened to all of this stone-faced, raised his hand and they both shut up. He pointed down the sidewalk to the left and spoke to the boyfriend:

"Drop all of her stuff right now and get yourself movin' down the street in the direction I'm pointing. It's over, understand? If I hear of you coming back and trying something, you know what I'll do. Right?"

"Yes, officer."

"Then be on your way."

Meekly, the boyfriend dumped the clothes and headed off. But the woman still had some unspent fight in her.

"Officer," she said. "He done got everything all wet, dumpin' it that way."

Flint pointed down the street to the right. "You heard me. It's all over. Pick up your stuff and beat it."

She muttered, but she did as he said.

We walked on.

"I'm impressed," I said. "Solon couldn't have handled that better."

"Who's Solon?"

"Never mind."

We walked back up to Latonya's corner. There was a woman strutting up and down the street in a silver Weingart poncho, flashing passing cars, snuggling up to the derelicts who walked by her. She was skinny. No, she was bones in a push-up bra. There was so little flesh on her legs, I couldn't see how she stayed atop her spindly, rundown heels. The weather was still a little drizzly, and no one seemed interested in stopping. She yelled obscenities at every car or bum that spurned her advances and passed on by.

"A fifty-one-fifty?" I asked.

Flint grinned at me as he impelled me by the elbow. "That's our girl."

"Latonya?" *Po*lice or not, I didn't think Flint was enough protection to keep me safe from this creature. She looked contagious.

"Hey, Latonya," he called.

She wheeled, saw us, completely disregarded me, thank God, and came running up to Flint.

"Mikey, Mikey," she squealed as she rubbed herself against him. I hung back. Mike turned and grinned nastily at me. I thrust my hands deep into my pockets and just glared back.

"What brings you down to this 'hood, Mikey?" she crooned. "You come to see me?"

"You left word at the Weingart that you knew where to find Caesar."

"Maybe I do," she said coyly. "And maybe I don't."

Mike handed Latonya a brown paper bag with a bottle in it. "Brought you something for your trouble," he said.

She tucked the bottle away in her clothes somewhere without looking at it. "My favorite, Mikey. You're so nice to your lady."

"You taking us to Caesar?" he asked.

"What did I hear about a twenty-dollar bill?"

"The usual terms, baby," he said. "Payment on delivery."

"You just come with me, sugar."

It was all I could do to walk behind them. I couldn't stand it that he let her get so close. I was six feet away and I could smell the dimestore cologne and *eau de* Thunderbird that enveloped her. All the way down the block, Latonya cuddled Mike's arm and wiggled against him. I couldn't hear what she was whispering to him, but he was laughing a lot.

Latonya gave me a malevolent glance, and I flipped her off. Ordinarily, I would have recognized the bile at the back of my throat as jealousy. I just didn't want to admit it to myself, and I hated myself for being such a twit.

She turned down Sixth Street and pointed out a dumpster behind a sweatshop.

"There he is," she said.

"Show me," Flint said.

When she started to go behind the dumpster, I shied back further and scoped out an escape route. It was really dark behind there. Flint hung in with her, so I swallowed my better judgment and went along with them. I didn't want to look like a wimp after all the hard talking

I had done to get Flint to bring me along. Besides, I thought he needed some looking after.

The wind whipping down the street was bitter. Behind the dumpster, there was some shelter. We came upon a silver poncho–wrapped bundle lying on the pavement. Latonya toed the bundle.

"That's him," she said.

"You're sure?" I asked.

"Damn sure," she huffed, offended. "Fool say, 'Do me now, I pay you tomorrow.' This whore ain't takin' none of that shit. Uh uh. That's Caesar, you be sure. He smells like dog."

Mike slipped her something and patted her back. She strutted off down Sixth Street toward San Pedro, her poncho flapping open to display her fleshless wares.

"Friend of yours, huh?" I said.

"Be nice," he admonished. "She gave you what you wanted."

"Are you sure?"

"We'll see." Flint squatted down and gave the bundle a good shake. "Caesar, we want to talk to you."

Caesar's voice was muffled by the stuff covering his head. "Go 'way, man."

"I said, we want to talk to you."

"What I say? Go 'way."

Flint chuckled and gave him a rough push. "Did I forget to say, this is the police? Get out of there, and get out of there, now. You know how we are."

Caesar's face appeared out of the silver poncho. I could not have described him to anyone, though I recognized him as soon as I saw him again. He looked up, first at Mike, then at me.

"Am I dreamin'?" he asked.

"You're asking me?" Mike laughed.

Caesar grinned. "Hello, pretty lady. Nice to see you again."

"Hello, Caesar," I said. I knelt down beside Mike. Latonya had been right; the man reeked of dog, among other things. And Mike now reeked of Latonya.

Caesar wiped his nose on the edge of his blanket. "What you doin' down in this 'hood?"

"I came to talk to you," I said. "Last night you gave me a note."

"Yes I did. Doc give the note to me, say here's a message."

"Do you remember where you saw her, and about what time that was?"

"I don't have me no watch," he shrugged. "It were still daylight. I'm startin' to think about dinner."

"Where did you see the doc?" Flint asked.

"I'm hangin' by the wishin' well, you know? Down there in Chinatown?" He spoke in a fast and steady stream. "Sometimes I can hook me some coin, get me somethin' to eat. So I'm standin' there, an' I see the doc a comin'. She runnin' a little, you know? Then all of a sudden she stop, like she forget somethin'. She start to go back the way she come. Then she see me. She call me over, she write me this paper. She say, 'This is a message for my sister, go pin it on the door up at my house.' I say, 'Yes, ma'am.' She give me a dinner ticket for the Center here. Then she go on her way."

"Where did she go?" I asked.

"Nowhere. She just hang there, by the wishin' well."

"Dr. Duchamps gave you the note and paid you," Flint said. "But you didn't put the note on her door."

"I mean to, officer. But see, this dude I know, he see what go down, an' he say, 'Give you a dollar for that dinner ticket.' I figure on eatin' at the mission anyhow, so I say, what you say, man? We trade, dollar for dinner. I was goin' up to the doc's house, like she say. But first I stop, get me a short dog to tide me over. Then I guess I forget 'bout the note for a while. I don't remember 'bout it 'til I hear the doc gets herself shot up. I think to myself, maybe the note mean somethin'. And I don't want it in my pocket no mo'. Like I say, I'm goin' up to her house, when I runs into you, pretty lady. An' I gives you the message, the true words, don' I? Anyway, I figure that's way better than pinnin' it on no door. Man, it be rainin' hard."

"Yes it was," I said. "How did you recognize me? I don't remember ever meeting you."

He smiled. "The doc, she puts on the TV at the mission all the time, and she say, 'See her, she's my baby sister.' I know you real well. You ever try makin' some comedy? You show some sad shit on that TV, man."

Flint laughed.

"Something to think about," I said. I doubted whether I could get funding for anything funnier than war or famine.

"After the doc gave you the note," Flint said, "did you happen to see her again, maybe down the street or inside a shop?"

"No, officer, that were the very last time," Caesar said, shaking his head sadly. "I go back to the wishin' well later, lookin' to hook me some coin, like I say. She be gone."

"How much later?" I asked.

Caesar shrugged. "Long's it takes to have me a short one."

"Ten minutes?" Flint asked. "Twenty minutes?"

"More like a half hour," Caesar said.

Caesar had filled in some of Emily's last minutes for us, but it wasn't nearly enough. At the time Emily walked down to the wishing well for her mysterious rendezvous, I was probably either on my way from the airport or sitting on her front stoop. I couldn't help wondering how differently things might have gone down if Caesar had just delivered his note on time.

Caesar emerged from his silver cocoon to sit cross-legged beside us, putting his face on a level with ours. His breath was indescribable. Flint's eyes watered and I had to turn my head to get some fresh air. It took a strong stomach, but I hung in there.

"When you saw her," I asked, "was she alone?"

"Mos'ly. People come by say, hey Doc. But it start rainin', so not many people were around."

Flint held a handkerchief over his face. "Did you hear anything like a gunshot that afternoon, see anything out of the ordinary?"

"Might be," Caesar smiled. "I don' hear nothin'. But someone else be lookin' for the doc 'bout then."

"When?" I asked.

"Back then. That same day."

"Who was it?"

"Some dude."

"Some dude, huh?" Flint squeezed my hand. "When you saw this man, could it have been around four o'clock?"

" 'Bout then. Before dinner time."

"This was when you went to the wishing well the second time. After the doc was gone."

"Like I say."

I was excited. "The four o'clock date," I said, to Flint.

"Could be." Flint literally held me down. "Let's hear him out."

Flint turned from me, back to Caesar. "Did you know the man? Someone from the neighborhood, maybe?"

"Coulda' been," Caesar said. There was a crafty look on his grizzled face. "That was some time ago. I can't exac'ly remember."

"It was only yesterday," I said.

Flint held out a five-dollar bill. "Maybe a dollar-and-a-dime will help your memory."

"Dollar-an'-a-dime, ease my mind." Two fingers came out of the blanket and hooked the money. "Like I say, I never seen him before."

"Describe him," Flint said.

Caesar thought for a moment. "Like the doc. You know, tall dude. Skinny nose."

"Dark or fair?"

"It's rainin'. He wear a hat. But he no brother."

"How old do you think he was?"

He shrugged. He smiled. "Old enough to be out walkin' by hisself."

"Okay," Flint sighed. "Anything else you can tell us?"

"Maybe it's worth somethin'?" Caesar asked slyly.

Flint shook his head. "I already gave you enough for a dollar-and-a-dime and a forty ouncer to chase it. If you want to try for a few dummy bumps, keep at it."

Caesar rubbed his head and grinned up at Flint. "I already got me enough dummy bumps, officer."

"Then tell me what you know."

"I tell you this. This tall dude, he come up to me an' he say, do I know the doc? I say she done left already. Nex' thing, some lady come around, kinda' hang there by the wishin' well, lookin' at him like maybe he want a date. The dude, he walk up to her, real cautious. He call her by some number. He jus' say, 'M.' Like a question, you know, 'M?' Like that."

"What did she do?"

"She say a little prayer. She say, 'Dear Lord, it's true.' Then she take off runnin'."

"Where did she run to?" Flint asked.

"I don' know. None of my business. I jus' ke'p on walkin'."

"What did she look like?"

"She have on a raincoat with a hat on it. Can't see much."

"You sure it was a woman?"

"Yeah." Caesar ran his long, pink tongue over his lips. "She walk the walk. You know."

I looked up at Flint. "Who do you think?"

He shook his head. "We'll talk about it later."

Flint stood up and brought me with him. He reached into his pocket, found some change, then dropped a quarter and his card onto the sidewalk in front of Caesar's nest.

"You put that coin in your pocket with my number," he said to Caesar, heavy menace in his voice. "That's for the telephone. If you start remembering things, or if you hear something, you call me. I already gave you enough money to buy yourself some comfort for the night. If I find out—and you know I will—that you held out because you used that pissy little quarter to buy a pull on someone's bottle, I'm going to come back and pull your chitlins out of your ears. Got it?"

Caesar cringed, but there was still a simpery smile on his face. "Yes, officer."

Mike held tightly onto my arm. "Another thing. Better find another place to sleep tonight. If we found you, whoever shot the doc might find you, too."

"But I didn' see nothin'," Caesar protested.

"The shooter doesn't know that," I said.

Caesar was on his feet, gathering his meager possessions about him.

"Come with us," Flint said. "We'll drop you off in Chinatown. Maybe I can persuade your friend at the Chevron to let you in."

Away from the dumpster, the night was bitter cold. Trailing his blankets and his poncho, Caesar followed us back to Mike's car on San Pedro. It took some persuading—he said the last time he was in a police car he was being booked on a fifty-one-fifty charge that got him seventy hours of detention—but he finally climbed into the back seat.

We left him at the Chevron station, amid a slobbery reunion with his dog, and drove up Hill Street to Emily's apartment with all the car windows rolled down, in spite of the cold.

"Are you coming in?" I asked.

Flint looked up at the three-story building. "Why do you ask?"

"Let me think," I said. I crossed my arms and slouched down into the seat. "How about, Oh, Mike, I'm so scared to go up there all alone. Will you come and turn on the lights for me?"

"Looks to me like the lights are already on."

"If you're going to be difficult, then how about, my friend dropped off some video news footage from the sixties. Maybe you can help me evaluate it."

"Maybe I can." He took the keys out of the ignition. "How long do you think it will take?"

I shrugged as I groped for the door handle. "What time is sunrise?"

Chapter 15

Little arrangements of flowers had made a reappearance on the stoop. There were a few votive candles among them, and some burning incense. Mrs. Lim had scrubbed at the spray-painted message on the wall until the beige stucco had lost nearly all of its texture bumps. For all of her effort, she had only managed to fade the heavy black lines: DIE FAST, BITCH was still easily readable from the street.

"I called someone to take care of that," Flint said. "Mrs. Lim shouldn't have to deal with it."

"Nice of you," I said. I unlocked the front door and held it for him. "I was going to get some paint in the morning."

"Good idea, if that filth is still there." We were walking past Mrs. Lim's door, so he whispered, "How are you getting along with Mrs. Lim?"

"Fine, I think. I never see her. When I'm out, she comes in and cleans up, leaves food for me. She's a rare treasure. I'm sure she was indispensable to Emily. Maybe Em could solve health problems of global significance. But sometimes she had trouble crossing the street in heavy traffic all by herself."

"I know." He smiled. "Like the absent-minded professor. People were always watching out for her, making sure she didn't get herself lost."

The building was quiet. I found myself walking on tiptoes up the carpeted stairs to the third-floor landing. Sneaking in past the landlady, trying not to waken the other tenants.

Mike held onto my arm.

I turned to him at the top of the stairs. "What's a dummy bump?"

"A lump left on your head after a good thumping. Why?"

"So that was a threat, when you offered Caesar some dummy bumps."

"It was not," he said, quick, sharp denial. He could get his back up in a hurry. "He was trying to hold us up. I let him know we weren't going for it. That's all."

"I see." I liked having him on the defensive, for a change. In the downdraft, Flint still smelled of Latonya and I still felt the bile in the back of my throat. I wasn't about to let up on him. "How many people in town have to comb their hair around dummy bumps you administered?"

"You trying to get me to cop to something?" He pulled at my jacket. "You have a wire in there?"

"No wires. Just me. It's very interesting, this whole police culture of thumping and leaving scars. Tell me, what was the most satisfying beating you ever administered?"

He looked down at me through narrowed eyes. "I do not go around beating people."

"Maybe not now that you're a detective. What about when you were patrolling the mean streets?" I spoke softly to spare the sleeping tenants. "Go ahead, tell me about the best."

"The best?" He smiled and wrapped his arm around me. "I can't answer that. My career isn't over yet."

I snuggled against him, trying to ignore the cheap, second-hand cologne.

"These tapes we're going to see," he said, "what are you looking for?"

"Answers to some questions, like, who was the man with the skinny nose? Who was the woman who walked the walk?"

"Good questions," he said.

I stopped under the chandelier at the head of the stairs

to sort Emily's door key from the collection on her ring. Flint was looking around, as he always does, ever observant, waiting for me.

Mrs. Lim's building is long, with narrow frontage on the street. Emily's apartment was at the far end of the hall, the only flat that overlooked the street. From the stairs, the area around her door seemed very dark and a long way down. Some of the ceiling lights were out.

At nearly the same moment that I realized there was too much light escaping past Emily's doorjamb, I heard the crunch of glass underfoot. The thin, frosted glass of smashed lightbulbs.

Flint took out his automatic and pressed me against the wall with his free arm the way my mother, in the car, used to shoot out her arm whenever she had to brake real fast.

We slithered along toward Emily's apartment with our backs brushing against the bamboo-print wallpaper. I could see that Emily's door hung ajar. The building is old and hardly high-security. I kept thinking about the hate in the spray-painted scrawl on the wall outside, and how close below us that was. And how close we were to the alley on Gin Ling Way where Emily had been shot.

When we were a few feet from the door, Flint put his finger to his lips and motioned for me to stay put. I didn't argue—he had the gun.

Standing like statues in the hall, listening for noises inside the apartment, I imagined a wild variety of possibilities for what had happened, for what still might be happening in there. It was a full range, from Mrs. Lim wiping out the shower to the revivified Symbionese Liberation Army lying in wait with cocked grenade launchers. Quickly, I eliminated the most unlikely scenario; Mrs. Lim would never leave the door open.

I could only see the back of Flint's gray head as he listened. I put my hand on his shoulder, and he motioned again for me to stay back. He gave the silence a full minute before he booted the door. The door flew inward, banged against a table or something. Then there was silence again.

Motioning for me to wait, Flint slipped inside behind his automatic. No grenades burst through the gap, but the scene I imagined became more involved and more gruesome with each quiet second that passed. I waited, truly breathless, ready to flee down the stairs as soon as Flint cued me. Or to call for reinforcements if he didn't come out soon. I was worried about him alone in there. I could have followed him. I didn't want to get in his way.

All was stillness from Em's apartment for several minutes. I had just decided to give him until the count of ten before I banged on the neighbor's door to call for help, when I heard Mike's footsteps on the hardwood floor, walking, not running. And only one set of steps. I began to relax.

When Flint came back out, he had his gun holstered. The expression on his face was befuddlement.

"What happened?" I asked.

"Did you say Mrs. Lim tidied up today?"

"Yes."

"Better come in and have a look."

Staying close, I followed him inside. The hinges on the front door had been sprung, so it wouldn't shut all the way.

Most of the mayhem had occurred in Emily's office, though mayhem is an exaggeration. This burglar had been fairly tidy. And quite directed in his search.

Every one of Em's file drawers hung open. The floor around the cabinets was piled with hastily made stacks of manila folders. Some of the files looked as if someone had fanned through them. A few had spilled across the rug.

Em's desk had been similarly, systematically, rifled. Her computer, Grandmother Duchamps's heirloom inkwell, and Em's pretty-good wristwatch were all on the desk and undisturbed.

"Wonder if he found what he was looking for," Flint said.

"Is it all right to go in?" I asked.

"No. Let the fingerprint people do their thing first."

"You're going to report this?"

"I already have." He was looking around. "What was he after?"

"I don't know." I went on to the sitting room door and peered in. 'The room was so spare, so barren of ornamentation, that there was nothing for a burglar to take. But he had been there. The sofa cushions were just a little bit askew. The lamp in the corner cast its shadow at a slightly different angle than before.

At my feet was the box of videotapes that Garth had left. I hadn't had a chance to go through them. They might have been rearranged. Some might have been missing. I couldn't tell.

The bathroom was as I had left it—makeup on the sink, hairdryer on the back of the toilet, damp towels on the single rack. The contents of the medicine cabinet were at least tidy. I had never looked inside; I had no idea what should have been there.

Flint had been following me while I made this circuit.

"What do you think?" he asked.

"Too weird," I said.

"How so?"

"I don't know whether he found what he was looking for in the files or in the desk. But I can only see one thing that's missing."

"What's that?"

"It's too strange," I said.

"So, tell me what it is."

"A framed photograph of my brother, Marc."

Chapter 16

" 'Up against the wall, motherfucker?' " Flint put down his beer and paused Emily's VCR. "They let those long-hair peckerwoods say 'motherfucker' on the six o'clock news? Where was I? I don't remember language like that."

"Such a prude you are," I tsk'ed. "This is just raw, unedited footage. All the 'motherfuckers' and tit shots get purged before any of this hits the air."

"I know that," he said. "Just checking to see if you're awake."

"I'm awake. Barely. These tapes are so boring."

"Ditto," he said. "Anything for dessert?"

"Tofu."

"I pass."

The Corona beer we had picked up at Chico's all-night market on Broadway was warm. I gathered up the greasy wrappers of takeout tacos that littered the couch between us and wadded them into a bag I set on the floor next to the last two beers in the sixpack. My knees were stiff when I got up to put another tape from Garth's box into the VCR.

I needed to move around a little to stay awake. We had made it to the end of the first two tapes without finding enlightenment. The raw footage was damn tedious to watch. Most of it was just people milling around or mugging for the cameras, peace demonstration organizers looking for people to organize. There was an incredible amount of T and A. Young, nubile women had a magnetic attraction either for the zoom function of the camera lens or for the cameramen. I used the fast-forward button a lot. If I skipped past any young female material that looked especially choice, Flint rewound the tape and replayed it, sometimes a couple of times. He was a tease.

"What is this we're watching now?" Flint asked.

I picked up the tape cover and read to him from the label, "Demonstration against war-related research on campus, University of California, Berkeley, November 19, 1969."

"How long is this one?"

"Two hours, fourteen minutes, twenty-eight seconds."

"Hmm." He unsnapped his belt holster, took it off, and tucked his automatic under the sofa. After some stretching, he settled down into the sofa cushions and put his feet up on Em's coffee table. His socks smeared a few of the black graphite smudges the fingerprint man had left on every surface in the apartment. The place was a mess and I thought about poor Mrs. Lim tackling it alone. If I hadn't been so exhausted, and so beer-mellow, I would have gone in search of a rag and some cleanser.

Instead, I reached for the VCR remote and fast-forwarded the tape until something seemed to be happening.

The demonstration was in Berkeley, on a lovely, clear fall day. The camera was set up at the end of Telegraph Avenue near the Satter Gate. This was my hometown. I enjoyed watching people walk by, seeing again the familiar street scene just off-campus. It was something like watching home movies.

On the screen, a couple of cars pulled up, followed by a flatbed truck festooned with banners, HELL NO, WE WON'T GO, and variations on that theme. The truck parked in front of the Bear's Lair, a popular student hangout. The truck was positioned so that its bed was a stage facing down Telegraph. Two men in bright tie-dyed shirts and bellbottom jeans hooked up a P.A. system. I recognized one of them—young, thin, red-haired Rod Peebles.

The carloads of people who were dropped off next seemed to be a vanguard, the setup crew. A pudgy young woman in baggy jeans unfolded a card table on the sidewalk and taped a poster, LEGAL TEAM, to the front. I suspected this was Fay Cohen though I couldn't see her well enough to be sure. She was off at the side, down Bancroft, and not what the cameraman was looking for.

Cartons of pamphlets were hefted onto the flatbed, opened, and distributed to passersby. In the background, someone was singing Beatle songs, with a guitar accompanying him. Some things never seem to change. Street musicians in Berkeley are still playing Beatles music.

The camera panned left, and I thought I saw Emily standing in a cluster of kids passing a joint. The pale, shiny hair was the same, and the person was very tall. When she started to turn, the long hair swept across her face like a sheaf of wheat blowing in the wind. I was already standing close to the TV. I leaned forward anyway, to see better. The hair I was watching fell into place and uncovered the wrong face. I took a moment to accept this; I really wanted it to be Emily. The kid with the long, shiny hair also had a full beard and mustache, a hippie, dippy guy. I punched fast-forward.

Flint stifled a yawn. "Exactly what are you looking for?"

"I'll know when I see it."

"Hmm," he said again. His eyes were on the screen, but half-closed. "All that hair. Didn't any of their parents ever take them to the barbershop?"

I laughed. "Do you have kids, Mike?"

"One. He's fifteen."

"How does he wear his hair?"

He pointed to a young man on the screen who had a two-foot-long ponytail hanging over his shoulder. He might have been all of eighteen. "I'd never let my boy out of the house looking like that."

"So you say." I nudged him. "You want another beer?"

"No thanks." He seemed to rouse himself. He sat up and stretched.

"Maggie, where are you going to stay tonight?"

"Right here."

"I think that's a real bad idea until we get the door fixed."

"Exactly why I have to stay," I said. "I'm not leaving the apartment unattended. Not when someone's already broken in. Anyway, there isn't much night left."

"Could we argue that once around again, or is that final?"

"I'm staying right here," I said.

He sighed. "Then I'm staying with you."

"Do you have a note from home?"

"Yeah," he smiled. "I sign my own notes."

"Okay, then." I fast-forwarded a dead section of tape, watching the TV to avoid making eye contact with Flint, give away something before I was ready. I was glad I wouldn't be in the apartment alone. I could have had worse company than Mike with whom to see the night through. A whole lot worse.

I had long ago concluded that his resurrected-hawk routine was exactly that, a routine, cop talk. While I suspected he didn't pay dues to the ACLU, he wasn't as reactionary as he tried to make out. Flint, I was learning, was a provocateur. He would say anything to get a rise out of me. I didn't mind. I like a good argument now and then.

The scene on the TV began to take on some energy. Two army-green buses pulled up in front of the Bear's Lair and four or five dozen national guardsmen in riot gear spilled out. They jogged into position around the campus gate and formed phalanxes on both sides of the flatbed. With bayonets affixed, they held their rifles at the ready.

A couple of men in business suits arrived in a plain brown Plymouth and strutted over to the flatbed. I recognized a younger, thinner version of Lester Rowland. Something about him, his attitude or his carriage, set my teeth on edge. Plainclothes in Berkeley is not J. C. Penney's suits. Never was. If these two agents had had signs on their backs, KICK ME, I'M FBI, their identity could not have been plainer.

Rod Peebles stuck close to them. He looked over their shoulders when they took leaflets out of one of the boxes on the truck. Lester Rowland said something to Rod, and Rod raised a fist in reaction. Just as the exchange seemed about to escalate into something interesting, a young woman carrying an armload of daisies entered frame right and seduced the cameraman's focus away.

The woman was energetic and fresh-looking, with a curly mass of Renaissance-red hair that was held away from her face by a leather band. Her batik sundress was long. Its thin fabric billowed around her legs and fell away from her slender, suntanned arm when she raised a hand to sweep back a shiny lock of hair. Love beads swung from her neck in rhythm with the graceful step of her bare feet.

The cameraman must have been besotted. He stayed with her, giving us a full side angle as she broke off daisy stems from her bouquet and, ever careful of the bayonets, inserted a yellow daisy into the barrel of each guardsman's rifle.

The guardsmen, who seemed to be about the same age as the woman, held their positions. But when she smiled, they smiled, dimples and healthy white teeth showing under flak helmets. As the camera moved in for a closeup, one of the guardsmen picked up a flower that had fallen to the pavement. He smelled it before he tucked it into his helmet.

The confrontation between Rod and the suits had been cast into oblivion. The girl and the guardsmen were better footage.

I sat down again beside Flint.

"She's pretty cute," he said, watching her make her charming way to the end of the ranks.

" 'Cute' is the right word," I said. "Do you recognize her?"

"Should I?"

"Maybe. That's Celeste Baldwin, Mrs. T. Rexford Smith."

"No shit?"

"No shit. I wonder what she had under her daisies."

"Little bitty titties, from the looks of 'em."

"Be serious." I punched his arm.

"Serious about what?"

"What she just did looks either incredibly stupid or just naive. Celeste was neither." I pushed rewind and watched the daisy routine in reverse, backing up to the place just before the bus arrived. Then I pushed play.

"Tell me about what you see," I said.

"What? A bunch of hippies thinking they're starting a revolution."

"Do they look dangerous?" I asked.

"Hardly. What are you getting at?"

The buses arrived, in rerun, and the guardsmen piled off with their weapons. "Now what do you see?"

"The cavalry."

I froze the frame. "To this point, you have maybe a dozen long-haired kids, none of them looking overly competent or threatening. The guardsmen outnumber them about four to one. A few idealistic youth versus a line of bayonets and helmets. If this picture were on the news, it would look like stormtroopers against Everyman's baby boy. For the people in the Movement, that's good."

I let the tape run. "Watch this—media image sabotage. Celeste waltzes in with her daisies. She gets the bayonets to smile at her. Suddenly, we no longer have a line of bayonets, we have a second bunch of baby boys. See the dimples in close up?"

"You think she knew what she was doing?"

"She wrote the book."

On the TV, Celeste continued her daisy walk. She moved from the last guardsman over to the two men in suits, Lester Rowland and his partner. Celeste guided a perfect little flower through Rowland's lapel, playing up to the lecherous grin on his face. Then she got into a waiting VW Bug and was driven away.

If she had seduced no one else, she had certainly made a conquest of the man behind the camera: he followed her every move. The scene had charm, visual and social contrast, a palatable political message. I wondered whether the cameraman was thinking Pulitzer possibilities or simply admiring her hard young ass under the flimsy Indian cotton of her dress.

"What do you think?" Flint asked.

"Celeste's forte was arson, but she may have had other talents. I wish I had Emily here to translate for me."

"I was thinking about Emily, too." He gathered the food wrappers from the floor and got up. "Want anything from the kitchen?"

"No thanks."

Flint found the trash can in the kitchen, then made a trip to the bathroom while I watched the tape, waiting for Emily to tell me something.

Finally, the demonstrators we had been waiting for marched into view. At first sight, they were a slow wave rolling up Telegraph Avenue, covering both lanes of the street. Square picket signs rode above their heads like sails on a rough sea. There were probably several hundred marchers, maybe more. They engulfed the relative order of the street scene we had been watching, swallowed up into their mass the by-now familiar figures on the screen.

In 1969, video cameras were still fairly bulky. The cameraman didn't run along beside his prey. He staked out a strategic position and waited for the action to come to him. And the demonstrators did come. As they neared the camera position, what had been a sea of people became individuals.

As always, the leaders were in the front with their arms linked. They were chanting, "One, two, three, four, we don't want your fuckin' war." It sounded like a football cheer. Most of the demonstrators were college students.

Emily and Jaime were on the left flank of the front row, arms linked with Lucas Slaughter and Aleda Weston on either side of them.

So maybe, according to their credo, the world had gone to hell. That didn't mean they couldn't have fun righting it. They were all smiles as they chanted. Emily brushed her cheek against Jaime's shoulder and he turned and beamed into her face. She kissed him lightly, then picked up the chant again.

Jaime boosted Emily onto the bed of the truck. She reached down and gave him a hand up. He seemed to stumble a little and fell into her. It was a transparent ploy to be in her arms, but she was laughing as she caught him, held him longer than was necessary for him to get his feet under him.

I couldn't take my eyes off Jaime and Emily. They were so young, so very beautiful together. And painfully in love. I wanted to warn them to steer clear of the monsters swimming just beyond the horizon. What they had together seemed to me to be worth a bigger struggle than I think they gave it. I don't know where it came from, but I suddenly got a big, painful flash of Scotty and his pregnant new wife.

I heard water run in the bathroom, and Flint came out. He was yawning and digging sleepily at his ear with his knuckle. He got a look at me and stopped in his tracks.

"Not again," he said. I didn't know what he meant. He ducked back into the bathroom, which suggested a variety of possibilities, but he came right out again carrying a box of tissues. He dropped the tissues into my lap as he sat down.

"I can't leave you for a minute or you start bawling all over again."

I blew my nose. "Shut up."

"That's better than 'fuck you,' I guess. Come here." He pulled me over against him so I could sob into his shoulder. It felt good. I wasn't bawling, really, just tearing a little. I missed Emily terribly. Seeing her so happy only made me feel worse. So I pressed my face against his shirt and listened to Emily's voice on the TV:

"Henry Kissinger tells us our goal in Vietnam is peace with honor. I ask Mr. Kissinger, and his boss, Richard Nixon, how many more young American lives, how many more Vietnamese youth, must be sacrificed before Washington is satisfied that honor cannot be achieved except by our complete, unconditional withdrawal from this immoral and decidedly dishonorable war?" The crowd roared, like a Chautauqua tent revival: "Amen." "Right on." "No more war."

Emily's strong voice continued. "President Nixon says this is a war for peace. I say, fuck this war, Mr. President, and give peace a chance."

A chant was picked up by the crowd: "Give peace a chance. Just do it, Mr. President, do it, do it."

I closed my eyes to hear them better. "Do it. Do it."

Over the roar of the crowd, I found Emily's clear voice: "Do it, do it. Do it, Maggot, do it."

I sat up with a start.

"Were you asleep?" Flint asked.

"I don't know. What did they just say?"

"I wasn't listening. Want to rewind it?"

I shook my head. "Maybe later."

"Emily was quite a girl," he said. Then he chuckled. "Just don't tell her I called her a girl, okay?"

"I won't." Tears welled in my eyes again. I could say anything to Emily now and she wouldn't react. I hated it. My nose started to run.

"Come back here," Flint said. He put his arms around me and rocked me. It was too sweet.

With my face mashed against his chest, I said, "Don't start singing lullabies, okay?"

"Okay." He yawned.

When he started humming, I looked up at him. He kissed me. At first it was just a brush of his mustache across my lips. When I didn't move away, he kissed me again, this time with a little more assurance, a little tongue. He tasted faintly of beer and tacos. His hesita-

couldn't get very excited about it. I knew the real story about children was sitting on the banquette next to me.

"What's the schedule tomorrow, Maggie?" Guido asked.

"The Florence Crittenton Home for unwed mothers in the morning, then Pop Warner cheerleader practice out in Orange County in the afternoon. Think you can get us to Yorba Linda?"

He curled his lip. "I'd rather go to Natchitoches."

"Maybe next time," I said.

The waitress set pastrami sandwiches in front of us that were at least five inches high, no exaggeration. As she set a squeeze bottle of yellow mustard in the middle of the table, she smiled maternally. "Can I get you anything else?"

"Yes, please," Pisces said with a smile. "A doggie bag."

The waitress drew back, disapproving. "You haven't eaten anything yet, honey. You pile into that sandwich, and when you're finished we'll talk about a doggie bag."

I started to laugh at the nerviness of the waitress, but stopped when I saw that Pisces was not amused. I guessed she might have later plans for her meal. The way she had devoured her salad, I knew she was hungry. In her position I would have mouthed off to the waitress. But Pisces docilely followed instructions and began to eat. At first, she only nibbled at the edges of the sandwich. In the end, there was nothing on her plate except a few strips of gristle. I couldn't even finish half of my serving, and neither could Guido.

When the waitress came back with the check, she picked up Pisces' plate first. I could have smacked the smug look off her powdered face. She said, "Well, young lady, I guess you were hungry after all."

"I guess so." Pisces seemed subdued. She seemed to have a lot on her mind. Maybe the end of dinner meant the beginning of whatever came next. I could not imagine seeing this child go back out onto the street. I was also powerless to stop her if that's what she decided to do.

I handed up my plate to the waitress with its half sandwich. "May I have a doggie bag? Guido needs one, too."

As the waitress walked away again, Pisces said, "If

you take the bread off the meat before you put the sandwich away, it won't get all soggy."

"Thanks for the advice," I said. "It's a lot of food. You know, Guido and I probably won't have a chance to get to it tomorrow. We'll be out all day. Be a shame to let it go to waste. Would you like to take the bags home with you?"

"Yes, thank you." She looked into her lap when her chin quivered. "Thank you for dinner. It was very good."

"Pisces." I touched her hand, and saw her tense up. "Please let me take you to a shelter?"

She shook her head. "I'm all right. I have an okay place to sleep."

"What does 'okay' mean?" Guido challenged. "You have an apartment, a room, what?"

"This shelter," she said, raising her face. "They don't ask a lot of questions?"

"As long as you're fourteen, there are no questions," I assured her.

"What if you're nine?" she asked.

Guido snapped to. "You're nine?"

"No. I told you, I'm fourteen. But what happens to a kid who's only nine?"

"If she's that young," I said, "Child Protective Services has to be called. A kid that young shouldn't even be crossing the street alone. Not that you should, either."

The waitress came back with change and two doggie bags. "Thank you." She smiled. "Have a nice evening."

Pisces wiped her hands on her napkin and sat forward on the seat, ready to go. She seemed resigned.

"What about the shelter?" I asked.

She shook her head and turned. "There's someone I have to look after."

The implications of her soft statement were not lost on Guido. When he looked up at me with dew in his eyes, I knew he also was doomed where this girl was concerned.

"I just thought of another place you might go," I said as we slid out of the booth. "A good friend of mine. You'd like her. You wouldn't have to say anything to her that you didn't want to."

Guido looked more hopeful than Pisces. "Really? Who?"

"Let me call her first, just to make sure it's okay."

Guido fished out two dimes again. There was a telephone booth in the back by the rest rooms. I walked back alone and placed the call to Sister Agnes Peter, an old friend, a professional easy touch.

"Pete," I said. "It's Maggie MacGowen."

"How nice to hear from you." Her voice was hearty, like a PE teacher's. "Are you in town?"

"Yes. I'm working on a film, and I've run into a situation with one of my subjects. I need your help."

She laughed. "Dare I ask?"

"Do you have a couple of extra beds for the night?"

"Certainly. You know the address. The front light is on."

"Good. We'll be there within the hour."

I walked back to Guido and Pisces, smiled at their expectant faces. "All set."

The girl wasn't ready to accept anything yet. "Your friend said we could come?"

"Yes. She's waiting. I told her there will be two of you."

Pisces' chin began to quiver. I put my arm around her and this time she did not flinch.

"Did you tell her who I am?" she asked.

"I don't know who you are," I said.

She pulled at her tight skirt self-consciously, and sniffled a couple of times. "I mean, what I do."

"You can tell her anything you want her to know. Or tell her nothing. She'll like you, don't worry. That's what her job is."

Pisces was working on the possibilities when I explained. "She's a nun."

"What about this other kid?" Guido asked. "Where is she?"

"He," Pisces corrected. She turned toward the glass front door and pointed outside. "He's right there."

I followed where she was pointing, but I didn't see anything except the straggly shrubbery lining the sidewalk. He must have been crouching there behind the low planter. When we opened the door, he stood and revealed himself. When he turned toward us, the light from the full moon hit his small face the way high beams catch roadkill.

tion was touching, considering what had gone on between us the night before.

"That was nice, Mike," I said. I pulled my hand free so I could stroke the back of his neck.

"That's nice, too," he said.

I felt so warm and comfortable cuddled against him, I could easily have fallen asleep. Until Mike moved his hand to cup my breast. I was lying over his lap, and I could feel him growing underneath me.

I looked up into his gray eyes and smiled. I said, "She felt the cold, hard steel of his snub-nosed .38 under his belt and whispered into his juglike ear, 'I love it when you hold me tight, baby, but that rod you're packing is digging into me.' "

Mike laughed. "I ain't packin' no rod."

Chapter 17

We were at a most delicious point of love making. I was hardly on this planet, so I don't know why I noticed the shadow pass across the gape in the broken door. Before we made up the sofa bed, Mike and I had shoved a heavy dresser against the door. It wasn't tall enough to fill all of the space between the jamb and the edge of the door, and it certainly wasn't heavy enough to have kept out a determined intruder. All we asked of it was to be sufficient barrier against entry to give Mike time to find his gun on the floor and cover our naked backsides. Trust me, Mike's backside was definitely worth protecting.

Anyway, a few moments after first seeing the shadow pass, I saw it move across the open space again. Mike was nuzzling at the side of my neck, or I wouldn't have been facing the door at all. I liked what he was doing under the sheets. I didn't want to say anything that might interrupt him. Until the shadow made a third pass.

I found Mike's ear, couldn't resist nibbling at the lobe a bit before I whispered, "There's someone lurking outside the apartment."

He raised himself enough to look. "Just another tenant going to work."

"Emily has the only apartment at this end of the hall."

Mike sighed. "You want me to go look?"

"I don't want you to go anywhere." I ran my hand over his freckled quads. "Tell whoever is there to disappear."

He raised himself again and cleared his throat. "Who's there?"

A man's voice responded from the other side. "Who's *there*?"

"No fair, I asked first," Mike called out. He got up from the bed and pulled on the trousers we'd left lying in a heap on the floor. He was grinning when he leaned over to kiss my knee. "You know who it is, don't you?"

I nodded. "Uncle Max."

"Shall we let him in?"

"Yes," I said, groping around for my own pants. "Once he's in, we'll shove the dresser back across the door so he won't get away again. I haven't been able to catch up with him for the last twenty-four hours."

Mike zipped himself up as he clambered over the sofa cushions piled around the bed. I had managed to get a shirt on and to comb my fingers through my hair before Mike had moved the dresser aside far enough for Max to squeeze inside.

"Maggie?" Max said, raising his heavy dark brows at me. He looked from Mike's bare chest to my bare feet, then to the tangle of sheets on and around the bed. He chuckled. "So, kid, what's new?"

"It's too early in the morning for a quick retort. Ask me later," I said.

In the pale light of morning, and through Max's proprietary eyes, it was just beginning to hit me what had occurred among the tangled sheets during the night. And with whom. Nothing I hadn't enjoyed tremendously and probably needed in more ways than one. Just the same, looking at Mike set off some nervous quavers that fell short of remorse but still well within the range of Oh Shit. What, after all, did I know about this man besides freckled quads and good hands? And that, the morning after, all rumpled and bristle-faced, he still looked damn good.

Max was grinning at me evilly.

"Did you happen to bring coffee?" I asked him.

"Nope," Max said. "But I'll be happy to go get some. How long would you like me to take?"

"You stay put. We have to talk." I tossed a cushion

aside. "Mike, I'm going to go call Mrs. Lim. If Max makes a move for the door, hog-tie him, okay?"

"Sure thing." Mike had found his shirt and buttoned it up. He extended his hand to Max. "How's it going, counselor?"

"You tell me," Max said, leering, cocksure.

I left them while I called Mrs. Lim from the study, to ask her to please bring up some hot coffee. In the few minutes consumed by the phone call, Mike had the sofa bed made. He also had the television on and a tape playing in the VCR. Max was watching Celeste gambol backward with her daisies.

She gave a terrifically dear performance. So dear that I thought I would be physically sick if I had to watch her prance through it one more time. I went over and perched on the arm of the sofa beside Mike.

"Mind if I take a quick shower?" I asked.

"Go ahead," he said, patting my thigh. "Is Mrs. Lim bringing coffee?"

"Yes," I said. "Max, take notes. When I get back, there will be a quiz."

He merely waved me away, never taking his eyes from Celeste. He sighed, "Damn, I forgot how lovely that bitch was."

I walked out on them. I borrowed clean underwear and a starched Polo shirt from Em and shut myself in the bathroom for no more than twenty minutes. When I rejoined Mike and Max, they were pouring coffee and passing back and forth a basket of croissants.

I sat crosslegged on the floor, facing them across the low table.

"Message from Mrs. Lim," Mike said, handing me a steaming mug.

"What is it?"

"I don't know. It was delivered in Chinese. I think it had something to do with the way pigs live."

"I'll straighten up the place later." I sipped the coffee gratefully. We had had maybe four hours of sleep. It was four hours more than I'd had the night before, but I still felt grainy behind the eyes. I drained the mug and refilled it from the pot, took a croissant from the basket, broke it in half and devoured it.

Max's eyes were riveted on the TV. Mike was watching Uncle Max with similar concentration.

"What do you think, Max?" I asked.

"Tell you what, kid, it hurts." He glanced over at me. "I watch Em and Jaime, and I see what I missed out on. I was in law school through all this, a real grind. Free love, peace, rock and roll—that whole scene just passed me by. I might as well be a Martian looking at these tapes."

"You lie," I said. "You know every person on that truck."

"I met them." He had his chin down on his starchy white shirtfront. "That's not quite the same thing as knowing them."

"I don't get you," Mike said.

"I used to spend holidays at my brother's house. Emily ran the place like a two-bit hotel. I never knew who I'd be sharing my room with; the most bizarre collection of unshaven radicals passed across my sheets," he said. "It was an old house. There weren't enough bathrooms. I knew these people because we all spent a lot of time together in the hall, waiting our turn at the loo. Here's the scoop on the exalted inner circle: Lucas took a shit after breakfast, so you had to get your shower before, or suffer. Emily and Jaime showered together and took three times as long as anyone else. While you waited, Celeste would lay down and spread her legs for you if asked real nice, even though she hated it. I doubt whether Rod Peebles did any of the above, shit, fuck or shower. He wasn't a loner by choice."

"Bathroom habits is all you learned?" I said, hoping my mouthful of croissant didn't mask the skeptical tone I was trying for.

Max grew serious. At least, he knit his brows.

I reached across the table and touched his knee. "So?"

"Private stuff, kid. We should respect the secrets of the heart."

"Jesus, Max," I groaned. "So profound."

"I'm not real big on hearts and flowers, counselor," Mike said. "Especially when there's attempted murder involved. Anyway, if you can't trust your own niece, what's the point of anything?"

Max glared at him.

"Come on, Max," I said. "You can at least tell us whose secrets you're talking about."

Max took a breath. "Aleda and Marc."

"This is news? For the last two days, I've been hearing that something was going on between Marc and Aleda," I said. "So what. Name two people in the group who weren't getting laid on a regular basis."

Max sighed. "Me and Rod."

I looked askance at him. "Remember the long walks we all used to take up Cyclotron Road? Everyone talking and getting stoned?"

"Sure."

"One afternoon," I said, "I think it was after Thanksgiving dinner, we set off on the usual hike, the usual people, the usual arguments. I got really bored. No one was paying the right kind of attention to me. Celeste was teasing me. When I saw you head for home, I followed you. I saw Aleda go into the house. I saw you go into the house. I went up to her room to talk to her, but she wasn't there."

"So?" Max said.

"So, your bedroom door was locked."

"You always were a snoop."

"Marc was in Vietnam," I said. "Tell me about Marc and Aleda."

The tape of the November demonstration was still running in the VCR. Now and then I caught something out of the side of my eye—more speeches, some singing. The sound was low, but I could hear what was happening.

The only response Max had given me was to pour me another cup of coffee.

"Max?" I said. "Tell me about Aleda."

"I'm a lawyer. I deal in facts and evidence."

"And?"

"I only know what Aleda told me. She thought she was pregnant."

"Yours?" I asked.

"Don't I wish." Max started to say something more, but a *whummp* from the television made us all turn.

The speakers on the flatbed truck, Emily and Jaime, Lucas and Aleda, et al., stood frozen.

Mike picked up the remote and rewound the tape.

When he hit play again, some man I didn't recognize was standing next to Lucas and pontificating about the genocide rained on the unsuspecting Vietnamese by chemicals and weapons developed in university laboratories. He wasn't a very good speaker, rather nasal and whiney. He was tremendously intense. Just as he arrived at his climax about children being incinerated by the liquid fire of napalm falling from American military helicopters, we heard it again: *whummp!*

"What happened?" I asked.

Max had blanched. "Lab explosion. If I'm right, what you heard was young Tom Potts shaking hands with his maker."

"Damn," Mike sighed. He reached for my hand across the table. I went over and sat beside him.

We watched at least a full minute of confusion. No one seemed to know either what had happened or what to do next. Even the leaders on the flatbed scurried around, impotently searching for an answer. There was some panic among the crowd. Someone knocked against the cameraman and we were treated to a dizzying panoramic sweep of the sky until he righted himself and his equipment. In the background, we heard approaching sirens, many of them.

The tape was twenty-two years old, but it still had the power to evoke vivid memories, painful emotions intact. I was thinking, as I watched the screen, that after Tom Potts was burned, both he and Marc had another whole month to live. Tom had spent that month in unspeakable pain, dying a little every day. Marc had had a full share of robust health and a quick, relatively painless death. Or, at least, that was the official version. I wished I knew how Marc had spent the last of his share. What really hurt was not having him around to ask.

I glanced over at Max. "What do you remember about Tom Potts?"

"I never met him. I understand he was a grind, like me." Max thought for a moment. "I did some work for Em and Jaime on the civil suit the Potts family filed against them. It was the summer I crammed for the California bar exam."

This was a new bit. "Why did the Pottses sue Jaime and Emily?"

"For depriving Tom of his civil rights. His parents filed against everyone who spoke at the demonstration, the city of Berkeley for issuing a parade permit, the regents of the university, Tom's research director for keeping him tied to his lab. None of it came to anything. There was no way to know who had set the fire. Nothing came of it: the Potts family didn't have the wherewithal to pursue the suit."

I was watching the people on the truck, Emily, Jaime, Lucas, Aleda, the speaker I didn't recognize, and, at the rear, Rod Peebles. Rod was very quiet, considering the level of turmoil around him. Finally, Celeste appeared and climbed up onto the truck bed with the others.

"So where did Celeste go?" I asked. "From the time we heard the explosion, do you think she had time to run from the labs on North Campus to the demonstration on Telegraph?"

Mike squeezed my hand. "Unless the arsonist was suicidal, he would have used a timer device on a charge of that magnitude. Could have been any of them. Or none of them."

"Enough," I said. I went over and turned off the VCR and the television.

Mike looked at his watch. "I hate to walk out on you, but I have to go to work."

"What time is it?" I asked.

"Almost nine. I'm only two hours late." He stood up and stretched. "I'll call you later, Maggie. Where will you be?"

"I don't know. Max?"

"What?" he said. "I only came over here looking for my car."

I had a sudden sinking feeling; for a moment I couldn't remember where I had left his Beemer. The expression on my face must have cued Mike.

"We left the car up at the Police Academy last night. Come with me, counselor. I'll drop you."

Max turned a dark glare on me. "You left my car where?"

"What could be safer?" I said. "Who would break into a car at the Police Academy?"

"How many love-besotted drunks rolled out of that lot past my car last night? Maggie, I swear, if anything has happened to my car . . ."

"Max," I said, "get a grip on yourself. It is only a fucking car."

"The things that come out of your mouth." Mike laughed. He kissed me. "I'll call you. Counselor? Are you coming?"

Max sighed heavily. "Maggot, this is L.A. Without a car, how will you get around town?"

"Emily's Volvo."

"That heap is a menace."

"So if it will make you feel better, I'll hang on to your Beemer. But I need a gas company card. The tank is empty, and I'm broke."

"Shit," he grumped, reaching for his wallet. "You damn kids always wrapped me around your fingers."

I took the Arco card he held out, and the five twenties. "I love you, Uncle Max."

"You hear that, Detective? I'm doomed." Max grabbed me and held me in a bear hug. "You will call me before you leave town, won't you, Maggie? Let me know where to send the wreckers for my car?"

"Count on it. Hang on for a minute, will you? I want to talk to you. Let me walk Mike out."

I helped Mike push the dresser back into Em's dressing room. Then I walked with him to the stairs.

Mike put his arms around my waist and pulled me against him. "Last night was incredible."

I wanted to keep things light, at least until I got them sorted through. "You're sweet," I said.

"Sweet? I can put a choke hold on a man until he's dancing like Howdy Doody, and you call me sweet?"

I didn't have anything to say, so I just kissed him. His mouth was warm from the coffee, all the way down as far as my tongue could reach. Mike knew how to kiss. I could have stripped right there and taken him on the stairs.

He drew back and pulled in a deep breath. "That's no way to say good-bye."

I laughed. "I like to leave them with their eyes rolled back in their heads."

"God, I guess you do. Call me."

"Yes."

I waited on the landing until I heard the front door close behind him. I think my own eyes were still rolled back in my head when I went back inside. At least, Max gave me a very long look.

"He's a cop, Maggie," Max said.

"So what? John Kennedy was a bootlegger's son. You have a point to make?"

"At least Kennedy was a democrat."

"Don't worry about me, Max." I tugged on his coat sleeve. "Come give me a hand."

He followed me into Emily's study and stood in the middle of the room looking at the stacks of files and the drawers hanging open, clucking his tongue. "What were you looking for?"

"Not me," I said. "It was Em's burglar."

"Goddamn sonofabitch," he stormed.

"Don't get started with that crap," I said. "Are you going to help me or are you going to have a tantrum?"

He stooped to pick up a stack of files. "What do you want me to do?"

"Just feed me some truth, Max. What did Emily tell you to get you to come down to L.A.?"

"Not much. She called the day before, demanded that I fly down. Said she had some legal problems I would enjoy. That's about it."

Max was on the floor, gathering together bundles of papers and handing them up to me. I took a stack from him and laid it in the top drawer.

"I talked to Lester Rowland at the jail two nights ago," I said. "He helped bring in Aleda."

"Rowland is, and was, a horse's twat."

"Is and was." I reached for more papers. "He's a scary character. He has a special beef, I think, with rich kids who knocked the system and who got away with murder. He's like something feral, stalking them after all this time, waiting for his moment of payback."

"It's been a long time, kiddo. How much payback can he expect? Even if he could somehow prove who set the bomb, other than the Potts family, who really gives a fuck anymore? There's nothing that he can do."

"Not legally, maybe. But he could spread more than a little grief with a well-placed accusation."

"Rowland or anyone else could." Max was on his hands and knees, gathering in the last of the papers, sorting to the side personal documents and putting them into logical groups: taxes, insurance, rent receipts, and so on. And dumping the esoterica randomly into folders and handing them up to me. We were nearly finished. It hadn't been much of a job, though it seemed to have fatigued him.

He stood and picked rug lint from his dark trousers. "Wonder if your burglar found what he was looking for."

"Wish I knew. As far as I can tell, a picture of Marc is all that's missing."

"No shit?" Max's brows met in the center when he

frowned really deeply. At that moment, his brows
seemed to overlap. He handed me an empty manila
folder.

"I've been rooting around for something to put in
there, but there's nothing left. Take a look," he said.
The label on the tab read, "Marc Duchamps. Birth Cer-
tificate and School Records. 1970–1987."

Chapter 18

"I clean now," Mrs. Lim said, struggling behind a cart stocked with enough cleaning equipment to put any hotel maid to shame. "You don't look so good. You go rest."

"Thanks," I said. "I think I will."

I had a lot to think about. Somewhere in the back of my mind, it was all beginning to gel—old mayhem, fresh mayhem. The possible connections between what had happened to Emily and events from twenty-something years before were both legion and intriguing. I could think of a variety of reasons why someone might want to keep those connections buried. Many of us live, work, on a keen edge that can be easily shattered, each of us perhaps with a different vulnerability.

I was thinking about what Celeste had said. If rumor got out that I was a drunk, perverse, belonged to the KKK, had AIDS, I would have major trouble getting project funding—a big chunk of arts donations comes from rich folks who are politically and socially sensitive themselves. If the charge is set in the right place it doesn't take much to blast most of us out of the water.

Some people are better survivors than others. My father had avoided being blacklisted during the fifties only by waiting out the craziness by taking a research position with a European university. Many of his colleagues hadn't been as prescient and had disappeared from academia.

I thought I was getting closer to the answer, but there were still many missing pieces.

I called my mother, but got the answering machine.

The message, typical of Mother's efficiency, said, "Emily tolerated the move to Palo Alto very well. Her condition remains stable. The rest of the family is fine. We hold our friends so dear and thank you for caring." That was that.

Another call netted me the information that Rod Peebles was hosting a holiday open house for his major supporters in his district offices later in the morning. I was told he was due to show in an hour or so, the variable there depending, I suspected, on how late his night before had been. For at least an hour, then, I was a bit at loose ends. So, while Mrs. Lim attacked what was left of the fingerprint technician's spotty mess, I turned on the television and tried to get through a few more of the videotapes.

It was tough going, watching Emily and her group perform at demonstrations around the county: at a massed rally on the steps of the Lincoln Memorial, marches on college campuses, speeches given in auditoriums, in city parks, in front of various federal buildings and induction centers.

I heard their cant over and over, heard their blueprint for a perfect world. It sounded so young, so impossibly utopian. It was a beautiful dream, the world they were fighting to create. Peace and love, equality for all, government of the people and by the people. It was also a seductive dream, and I suspect that's what made the message seem so dangerous. Someone in high places was afraid of them: the official response to their challenge was generally armed troops or squads of itchy-looking police.

Emily and her comrades preached passive resistance, but they were not creampuffs. As often as not, the demonstrations ended in violent routs. Sometimes before they even got underway they were cut off by a furious storm of nightsticks and rifle butts. I watched, with the ache of fear and dread, my knees pulled up to my chest and my hands clenched, as men in riot gear poured into the crowds of unarmed protesters.

Sometimes the men with batons swung their sticks like machetes to cut through the mass of demonstrators. Other times, they seemed to pick a target, always a long-haired kid. They would swarm over the kid, hold on to his arms so he couldn't cover his head, and beat him, their sticks swinging again and again like spokes on a broken windmill. I don't understand how anyone survived. When it was over, the men in uniform, smiling, spent, would drag the longhair away. Sometimes there would be a closeup of a bloody face, a semi-conscious kid suspended between two men in uniform, blood pouring into his beard.

On several tapes, I saw Jaime go down into that windmill. Once, Lucas was pulled off a park bandstand and submerged into the netherworld of batons and combat boots. He came up flashing a peace sign with bloodied fingers.

When Garth put together the tapes for me, he had intercut the scenes of violence at peace demonstrations with bits of Vietnam war footage, other young men being brutalized in a very different way. It was a matter of news chronology, I knew, and not an artistic or political device. But juxtaposed in this way, the two parts of those war years—the homefront and the war zone—looked strangely similar. Where *was* the war? It was a lot to absorb.

My parents, when I lived at home, used to restrict my television watching. And at school, we were allowed access only on the weekends. I grumbled about it as a matter of form. After seeing Emily take some good licks, I began to see their wisdom. As a teenager, I doubt I would have been able to handle the scope of both her struggle and her fame.

Though her message was fairly consistent, Emily's backdrop changed as she traveled back and forth across the country and to Hanoi, Paris, London, Frankfurt. I wondered who covered her travel expenses: Emily was a full-time student, and my parents couldn't have helped her—they struggled along on a professor's salary. She must have had enormous debts, financial and otherwise.

As I watched her and her comrades, what began to emerge were patterns, certain consistencies in the interaction of the core group and the crowds, the FBI, the police, the camera. And certainly, with each other.

I was reminded of dummy bumps. My own head hurt. The apartment was stuffy, and too small for Mrs. Lim, me, the TV, and the vacuum at the same time. I gave up and piled all the tapes back into the carton.

I got up to search Emily's medicine cabinet for some aspirin. She had a shitload of prescription drugs and pharmaceutical samples, but nothing that looked like ordinary aspirin. My days of chemical experimentation are long over, so I passed on it all.

I put on my jacket and went to tell Mrs. Lim that I was going out. When I found her, she had her head in the oven.

"I'm going over to Broadway," I said. "Need anything?"

Mrs. Lim sat back on her haunches and wiped her face on her sleeve. "I make noodle for dinner. You just put in oven, ten minute, maybe fifteen minute."

"Thank you. You've been so wonderful. I could not have gotten through the last two days without you."

She dismissed the schmaltz with a wave of her hand and picked up her cleaning rag again. "You be one for dinner tonight, or two?"

"Excuse me?" I said.

"Michael Flint leaves his tie under living room chair," she said, and winked lewdly. "I press, you give it back to him."

"I'll do that," I said.

She smiled up at me, showing the gaps among her front teeth. The smile was absolutely salacious. "Noodle for two?"

"That would be perfect. I'll get out of your way now."

It was pretty funny, thinking about Mrs. Lim taking

someone to her bony breast. But at some point, she must have. The image was damned disconcerting.

On my way out, I found Mike's tie folded over a hanger by the front door. I ran the red and blue silk through my fingers and thought about Mike and wondered how he was. I really had nothing new to tell him— Mrs. Lim found your tie?

I went into Emily's study, anyway, and dialed the number on the card he had given me.

"Robbery-Homicide. Pellegrino speaking."

"Is Detective Flint in?" I asked.

"Sorry, he's out in the field. Can I take a message?"

"Just tell him Maggie called."

"Will do."

I felt vaguely disappointed, and I puzzled over why I felt as I did all the way downstairs and out across Hill Street. The sky was clearing, deep blue holes burned through gray clouds. It was still windy. My short jacket, the one Jaime had paid for, didn't offer much warmth. But after the closeness of the apartment, the brisk air was a welcome slap.

I cut through Gin Ling Way, giving Hop Louie's wide berth, and headed for the shops on Broadway. There were at least a dozen Chinese apothecaries in the long block, but no occidental drugstores. Seeking at most directions to the nearest Thrifty, Jr., I stepped into Hong's, an apothecary I had once visited with Emily.

Hong's had been around long enough for the oak cabinets that lined the walls to have acquired a soft, burnished patina. The cabinets had hundreds of tiny drawers, each drawer no more than six inches square on the front. It was the contents of the drawers that gave the place its delicious air of mystery—the ingredients of ancient folk remedies: magic cures for impotence, rashes on the liver, a runny nose. Emily told me that Mr. Hong once offered to mix her a tea that would attract a husband. She had turned him down.

The shop was narrow. Much of the floor space was taken up by barrels and wooden crates filled with dried yellow fish and squid, cuttlebone, a variety of dessicated roots, herbs, preserved seaweed, and aromatic teas. Most of it looked fairly disgusting to the uninitiated eye. But the smell was wonderful, a combination of sharp spice and dry earth.

Mr. Hong, in a white pharmacy coat, stood behind the long glass counter. He was mixing a potion for an ancient man who sat on a high stool at the far end.

I walked over to watch, fascinated. Maybe a little magic was what I needed, too.

Suspended by a cord from Mr. Hong's forefinger was a scale, a salad-plate-size copper disk. He opened drawers and measured out ingredients, weighed each carefully on his scale, then poured it all into a stone mortar: white beetle carapaces, a length of dry snakeskin, thick black threads of something, a thumb-size bit of a hairy red root. All of this he ground in the mortar. Finally, he poured the powder onto a square of pink paper and twisted the corners.

The old man waiting for this concoction had no teeth and one eye had a milky cloud. He put some money on the counter, tucked the twist of pink paper into his shirt pocket, and shuffled with difficulty toward the door. I hoped the powder had the right magic. I hoped he lived long enough to get home and brew it up. Or whatever he was supposed to do with it.

Mr. Hong smiled at me. "May I help you?"

"I don't know," I said. "I have a headache."

He bowed, reached under the counter and brought out two large glass bottles filled with white tablets. "Bayer or Tylenol?" he asked.

"Bayer, please," I said, smiling to myself.

As I searched my pockets for money, he poured me a glass of water and opened the aspirin. He counted two onto a square of the pink paper and put the paper in front of me.

"It is the change in the weather that makes your head hurt," he said.

"Is it?" I swallowed the tablets and decided against

countering his theory with my own: too many late nights, a bit of booze, a good thumping, hours of old videotapes. Emily. I put the water glass down on the paper and set a dollar next to it. "Thank you."

He counted out some change and bowed when he handed it to me. "Have a nice day."

I walked out laughing. Even in Chinatown, weren't we to be spared? The prospects for the day I faced could hardly qualify for "nice."

My head began to clear a little. The back of my neck still felt stiff from the blow I had taken at La Placita church, but it was better, too. Maybe "nice" was relative.

I decided to take the bus downtown rather than hassle with Max's car in traffic. I could get the car anytime. I went down to the Dash stop across from Saigon Plaza and waited in the queue.

Caesar came shambling down the street and saw me before I could decide whether I wanted to speak with him or not.

"Hey, pretty lady," he said. "How you doin' this fine day?"

"Okay," I said. "How are you?"

"Not so good, but thanks for asking. You find that dude you was lookin' for?"

"Not yet."

"I'll keep my eyes open."

"I appreciate it." That should have been good-bye, but he just stood there.

"So?" I said.

"Like I say, I'm not doin' so good. Don' know how long I can keep my eyes open."

I found a couple of singles in my pocket. "Maybe a little pick-me-up would help?"

"Thank you, pretty lady." He scooted off at a good clip, going a whole lot faster than he had come.

I caught the Dash and took it to Sixth Street, then walked the two and a half blocks down Flower to Rod Peebles's district office in the Broadway Plaza. When I had called earlier, I hadn't asked if I could join the party nor even left my name. I thought surprise might be the best approach.

Rod was an enigma to me. After spending a good part of the last twelve hours watching Emily's core group in action, I still hadn't figured out how, where, perhaps if, Rod Peebles fit in. He wasn't quite what he seemed to be.

At every demonstration I had seen on Garth's tapes, Rod arrived early with the vanguard of people who set up the platform and sound system, got out the propaganda, tacked up the banners, piled picket signs, set up the legal table. They were a very efficient group: each had a task and performed it. But Rod was a floater. He hung around the sound man, though I never saw tools or electrical tape in his hands. He hovered near the boxes of printed matter while others took handfuls and headed off to enlighten passersby. Rod never picked up a flyer, tacked up a banner, touched a picket sign. During speeches, he stood on the platform with the others, but always at the rear. Rod was background noise; he didn't give speeches.

As far as I could see, Rod's single function was to keep track of the suits—FBI, campus administration types, I don't know who else. Lester Rowland seemed to be around a lot. And Rod was always at his elbow.

Within the core group, there was an obvious power elite—Emily, Jaime, Aleda. The others were satellites whose focus was primarily on the Big Three rather than each other. Taken as a whole, they all seemed to be good and affectionate friends, more extended family than comrades in arms. There was always a lot of hugging, supportive cheering, appreciative feedback. Rod was never in the clinches. I never saw him take a lick.

Though they appeared very cohesive in public, I had overheard many bitter arguments among the core group at my parents' house. I could not remember ever hearing Rod's voice amid the shouting.

What had Max said about Rod? He didn't seem to

shit, shower, or fuck. He wasn't a loner by choice. What was his function?

Rod Peebles might have been a walk-on player during the sixties, but in his own seventeenth floor office in the Broadway Towers, he was a star. Billboard art left over from his last campaign plastered an entire wall of the reception area: RE-ELECT ROD PEEBLES, and an eight-foot high air-brushed impression of his face. I don't know how his staffers could have worked everyday under the gaze of his hand-painted azure eyes.

Except for the poster, the furnishings were very subdued, if a bit posh for a government office. There was a Christmas tree in one corner, a menorah in another; all bases covered. A caterer was setting out trays of pastries and fruit on fold-up tables covered with neutral-colored cloths. I could smell coffee brewing in the big silver urns. The four or five staffers helping with last-minute preparations for the open house were young, well-trimmed and neatly turned out. Rod, at their age, would never have fit in among them.

A bright-looking young man in shirtsleeves and a modified Kennedy haircut walked over to greet me.

"Hi," he said. "We aren't quite ready, but welcome."

"I'm not here for the party," I said. "I want to speak with the Assemblyman for a moment."

"Rod's expecting you?"

"My name is Maggie MacGowen."

The blank expression behind his smile was filled in by a rush of recognition. "Emily Duchamps?"

"Yes. My sister."

As I said, he was bright-looking. He took my hand and held it perhaps longer than was necessary, maybe mulling through some possibilities.

"May I see the Assemblyman?" I asked again.

"Have a seat," he said. "I'll check."

The young man went through the heavy mahogany doors that led to the inner office.

Rod Peebles came right out, flushed, showing a lot of capped teeth.

"Maggie," he crooned, smothering me in an embrace. "Gosh, what a nice surprise."

"Can we talk somewhere?" I asked.

"Come on inside."

He ushered me through to an impressive office with a magnificent view of the city. I was hoping for someplace private, but I seemed to have interrupted a meeting. There were half a dozen men and women in intense discussion around the massive granite conference table. They didn't look like a party crowd. No one even looked up as we walked in. I counted six chairs pulled up to the table, all of them occupied. Rod and I went to a leather sofa against the near wall and found space to sit among a clutter of crossword puzzles and sunflower seed shells.

"What can I do for you, Maggie?" he asked.

"Where is Aleda?"

He threw up his hands. "Damned if I know. I walked on water to get her out—in my custody—but she took off for parts unknown."

"Am I supposed to believe you?"

"What choice do you have?" he laughed. "What choice do any of us have? Aleda has always done exactly what she wanted, and the rest of us be damned. My neck is really on the chopping block on this, Maggot. She's called in a couple of times, but she won't say where she is."

"Maybe that's smart, after what happened to Emily," I said. "But I really want to talk to her."

"Next time she calls, I'll tell her."

The discussion at the conference table grew very loud, seemed to crescendo; then there was a thoughtful silence. Rod seemed oblivious to it. One of the conferees, a tall, thirtyish woman with a well-cut, East Coast suit picked up a thick appointment book and walked over to us.

"Yes, ma'am?" Rod said, looking up at her.

"You up for one more assembly run before we try state senate?"

"You tell me. Am I?"

She grimaced. "That's the consensus. We'll make the

announcement in April, when you get back from Washington."

"When do I go to Washington?"

"Rod, did you look over the calendar I gave you?" She could have been speaking to an idiot child. She held her hand out to me.

"Lena Hilgard," she said. "I did my master's thesis at Columbia on Emily Duchamps and the political ramifications of the Peace Movement."

"Did you really?" I said. "Why does that make me feel old?"

She finally smiled. "It's nice to meet you, Miss Mac-Gowen. I admire your films."

"Thank you," I said. "I've thought for a long time that it would be interesting to do something about political staffers, what their function is within the system."

"Good idea," Rod said brightly. "Lena, see if you can work something out with Maggie to coincide with the campaign."

Lena gave Rod a dubious glance. "Trust me, Miss MacGowen. There are some aspects of politics the public would rather not know about."

I glanced at Rod and thought she might be right.

"Nice to meet you, Miss MacGowen," she said, offering her hand again. "Sorry to interrupt."

Rod passed me a bowl of sunflower seeds. "I have a good team," he said. "Top credentials, everyone."

I refrained from asking him why they hadn't saved a seat at the table for him.

"I've taken enough of your time," I said. "If Aleda should call, tell her how much I want to talk to her. I'll probably be out the rest of the day, but tell her I expect to be at Emily's all evening."

"If she calls, I'll tell her." He stood up with me and walked me to the door. He stretched. "It's about lunch time. Want to go out with me for a bite?"

"What about your party?"

"I forgot," he chuckled. "They won't miss me."

"Maybe another time," I said. "I left Max's Beemer

up at the Police Academy last night and I need to go fetch it."

"Police Academy?" he repeated, as if he hadn't a clue. Then suddenly he flashed me his poster smile and squeezed my hand. "Always good to see you. Drop in again."

"Thanks for your time." Thinking again that Rod wasn't a loner by choice, I turned and walked out, leaving him to his sunflower seeds and crossword puzzles.

I was in the hall, waiting for the elevator down, when Lena Hilgard slid out of Rod's office. The edgy way she kept looking over her shoulder toward the office, I knew she had something to tell me. When the elevator came, I held the door for her, ignoring the collective glares of the people inside who were thus forced to wait.

"Looking for me?" I asked.

She nodded, checked the hall a last time, and ducked into the elevator in front of me. There were maybe eight or nine people going down with us. She kept her eyes forward, and her mouth shut, until we came out in the basement shopping mall.

When the other passengers had moved along, she finally spoke: "Don't worry about Aleda. She's with friends. When it's safe, she'll call you."

I was dumbstruck for a moment. "Did Rod send you?"

"Good Lord, no."

Lena was maybe twenty-five or twenty-six. Too young to have known Aleda before she went underground, and too mainstream to have known her after.

I took her by the arm and quick-stepped her into a vacant public telephone alcove. "You talked to Aleda?"

"Not directly. Only to an old friend of hers."

"Who?"

"I can't say."

"I think you'd better."

"I can't take that responsibility." She looked around nervously. "I know it seems melodramatic, but honestly, it's too dangerous to say anything. My only motive was to reassure you."

"Okay." I leaned against the cold wall and took a few deep breaths. When I felt calmer, I tried again.

"How do you know this friend?" I asked.

"We became acquainted during the course of my research on Emily Duchamps and the Peace Movement. We've stayed in touch. This friend helped me get my job with Rod. And I returned the favor by using Rod's office to arrange for Aleda's release."

"*You* did?" I asked, leery. "Not Rod?"

She chuckled sardonically. "Rod couldn't release a fly from a glass of lemonade unless he had a committee to vote on it."

"You keep saying Aleda's friend. If this is someone from the old movement, someone with enough pull to get you a job, he or she should be Rod's friend, too?"

"Think about this," Lena said. "If Rod Peebles was such a close associate of Emily Duchamps, why is it that when I requested his federal dossier under the Freedom of Information Act, there wasn't a single document relating to him on file? No surveillance logs, no booking slips, no indictments, not one scrap of political writing?"

"You're the scholar," I said. "You tell me."

"I just did." She had said her piece and was edging away from me, back toward the elevator. I walked with her.

"Why do you work for Rod if he's such scum?" I asked.

"Ongoing research." She punched the elevator call button. "Rod *is* one of the political ramifications of the Peace Movement."

"Thanks, Lena," I said. "Call if I can ever do anything for you."

I waited until she was gone; then I walked back up into the light of day.

If Lena had been telling the truth, the only old friend I could eliminate was Rod Peebles. I thought it wouldn't be too difficult to track down Aleda when I was ready. I had a more pressing agenda to work on first: I needed something from Celeste.

Celeste lived on the far west side of town, in the posh Holmby Hills area bordering UCLA. I had to retrieve Max's car to get out there.

First things first. There was a rank of public telephones across Flower Street. I waited for the light, then walked over and waited my turn in line for a phone. I didn't have any heavy gold chains, or shopping bags, or even a baby in a stroller. I felt awfully out of place.

Mr. T's jeweler was behind me, waiting impatiently for the phone. I turned my back on him, dropped in two dimes and dialed Mike's office.

"Robbery-Homicide. Pellegrino speaking."

"Is Mike Flint back yet?" I asked.

"This Maggie again?" Pellegrino asked.

"Yes."

"He's in. Hold on." I heard him call out, "Hey Flint, call for you on the *love* line."

Mike snapped, "Get a life, Elmer," before he picked up the phone.

"Flint here," he said. "Don't pay any attention to these juveniles. You'd think they didn't have anything better to do than butt into other people's private affairs. Hi, Maggie."

"Hi, Mike. You left your tie under the chair."

He laughed. "Is that where it was? I had to stop and buy one on my way in. Found exactly what I wanted in the newsstand downstairs. Hand-painted hula dancer. Best one in the place. The only one, too."

"Are the big boys giving you a hard time?"

"Just something for them to do. How are you?"

"I dropped in on Rod Peebles at his office. Very interesting."

"Oh."

"That's all?" I asked. "Oh?"

"I hoped you were going to say something like, last night was fantastic and what am I doing after work."

"Mrs. Lim is making noodles for dinner. Enough for two."

"Is she?" he said, drawing it out.

"What time are you off?"

"Three," he said.

"I thought it might be a good idea to go hang out by the wishing well around four, the time Emily was supposed to be there, see who walks by. Maybe you could meet me there."

"You're all business, aren't you?"

"Not *all* business."

"In that case, I'll meet you by the wishing well at four. What are your plans for the rest of the day?"

"Not much. Get Max's car. Visit a few old friends."

"Maggie," he said, suddenly all seriousness. "Take care of yourself."

"I'll see you at four," I said.

After I hung up, I caught the Dash bus and took it back up through town. I got off at the end of the line on Bernard Street, just north of Chinatown. The Police Academy was maybe a little over a mile further, straight uphill. As long as it wasn't raining, I thought it would feel good to walk. I crossed under the freeway and found Stadium Way.

The neighborhood below the stadium was interesting, just about all that's left of old Chavez Ravine. I walked up a steep, curving road, past woodframe and stone houses, heard a few backyard chickens. The storm the night before had given everything a good scouring, washing away the usual coat of dust and smog residue. The houses were pretty rundown, but the air smelled fresh and everything looked bright and shiny. Leftover rainwater dripped from huge trees onto weedy lawns. A rare morning.

There was no sidewalk, so I walked at the side of the street. People greeted me; a toddler honked his trike horn for me. The neighborhood was so peaceful it could only exist in some space warp light years from L.A.

I heard a car approach behind me, so I stepped onto someone's lawn to give it more room to pass me. The driver went very slow. I hardly looked at the car, an old green Volvo, because, as any woman will tell you, you make eye contact with an asshole who is looking for a pickup and you have a nuisance on your hands. So I only glanced to make sure he wasn't going to run me down.

A little Toyota truck sped up the hill behind the Volvo and honked impatiently. The Volvo accelerated and passed me with gears grinding. I glanced at his rear as he drove on, noticed that the driver sat low and wore a baseball cap. That is a generic "he." The hat is all I saw of the driver.

When I came out at the top of the hill, the entire city was fanned out below me. As I skirted Dodger Stadium, the view below was so clear that I could see the ocean, a streak of silver on the horizon where the sun broke through the clouds. I had to stop for a moment to take it all in.

The entire trip had taken less than twenty minutes, but at the end, I felt better than if I'd had a full night's sleep.

I saw Max's car ahead in the Police Academy lot, just where I had left it. And in the same pristine condition. Actually better; the rain had washed away the sand and windshield bug kill I had picked up in the desert the day before. The BMW shone.

There were joggers in the hills above the academy. I could hear the police shooting range at a distance, shots fired in pairs—*crack crack*—followed by a third, single shot. Not quite dancing rhythm, but regular.

Police bodybuilders hung around the weight room above the training field. There was plenty of activity, but overall it was very quiet. I felt mellow.

I took out Max's keys and set off across Academy Road to the parking lot.

There are a lot of medium green Volvos in this world. Emily drove one. I thought little of the one that had passed me on the way up. Except that it put me in mind of Emily. I started thinking hard about the car when I saw it again, creeping toward me.

As I had before, at first I was thinking only that here was a horny bastard looking for a woman to give a little grief to. Nothing else was logical—I was walking into the

Police Academy parking lot. Everything may have seemed quiet, but there were police all around. A guy would have to be insane to bother me there.

In a few seconds, I thought, I would be in Max's car, and out of there. I knew the acceleration of the Beemer could humiliate an old Volvo with no effort. Still, the situation gave me the creeps—I was glad I had on long pants and a jacket, little flesh showing.

I was still thinking about Emily. Em was shot at close range. With a 9mm automatic of the sort used on Emily, a marksman can regularly hit a target within about fifty yards if he's good; within seventy yards if he's lucky. When the distance between me and the Volvo was somewhere between the range of good and lucky, I started to run, flat out, between the rows of parked cars.

Just as I reached the driver's side of Max's BMW, I heard the first shot. I ducked. A reflex.

I heard the Volvo rev its motor, as much as a station wagon can rev its motor. I couldn't tell if the driver was speeding in for the kill or making a fast retreat.

Staying low, I put the key in Max's lock, turned it, and opened the gates of hell. That's what it felt like.

A fiery blast rocketed me into the air, flipped me over a couple of times, then slammed me against a stone retaining wall. As I slid to the ground, I felt the stones and mortar peel the skin from my palms. I landed on my butt, dazed and deafened for the moment. I had enough presence left to cover my head against the flaming debris raining down around me.

When the rain of fire stopped, I took a sort of inventory. My right shoulder had taken the brunt of the impact. Though it throbbed, it functioned. The sleeve of my jacket was now a tattered wristlet, and bare skin showed through the knees of my jeans. I wondered about the blood running down my face, but what really bothered me was that I had no idea where I was or what had happened.

An incredible example of female beefcake vaulted the wall behind me and landed hardly rippling the muscles of her Schwarzenegger thighs. She was an Amazon goddess with LAPD 1989 WEIGHTLIFTING CHAMPS stretched across her remarkable chest. I thought I must be hallucinating. She crouched down beside me.

"You okay, ma'am?" she asked in a sweet, concerned soprano voice.

"I think so." I could hardly hear her, but my own voice boomed in my ears.

"Think you can get up?" the Amazon asked.

"Sure," I said, but I spoke too soon. I couldn't find solid ground.

She took my arm and gently assisted. She was a lot to lean against.

"Sure you're okay?" she asked again.

Being upright made me feel a little queasy, but I nodded. I was glad that she kept a grip on my arm because the ground still felt like pudding underfoot.

I managed to brush myself off. Then I looked out at the parking lot. Billowing black smoke poured into the clean air. The green Volvo was reduced to a smoking chassis at the bottom of a crater. The first row of cars in the lot were completely engulfed in flame.

And so was Uncle Max's Beemer.

Chapter 19

"Crackhead named Theophilus came after me with a steak knife." Officer Paula, the Amazon goddess, pulled up her trouser leg to show me the five-inch zipper in the skin of her muscular left calf. "He pulled out a boot gun. My partner got him, right in the ten ring. What a mess."

I turned over my wrist to show her the faint-white half-moon gouge in the skin. "My pony, Sugar, balked at a jump and threw me into a sprinkler head. I was ten."

We were in the emergency room of French Hospital, comparing scars. Paula was winning. She had shown me the war trophies on only one of her legs. I had nothing left to offer, except an episiotomy and the head gash Dr. Song was closing up.

"All finished." Dr. Song made a few snips and laid his scissors and a roll of tape on the stainless steel tray Paula held for him.

"Nice job," she said, leaning in for a close look. "You'll have to part your hair on the other side, Mag, but the scar won't be too noticeable, given time."

"Good to know," I said. "Thanks, Dr. Song."

"You may need a little painkiller tonight," he said. "How are you with codeine?"

"It makes me throw up."

He pursed his lips thoughtfully. "I'll see what I can find. Go ahead and get your things together. I'll be right back."

I got up from the table and tried not to look as wobbly as I felt. Paula didn't seem so imposing when she had her muscles covered with street clothes. She was very nice, and very funny, but not what anyone would call sweet. I didn't want to pass out on her. She had given up part of her afternoon off to bring me in for repairs. I didn't want her to think it was effort wasted on a *wuss*—her word.

I went to the mirror over the doctor's wash basin to look at my new stitches. There wasn't much to see. The hair he hadn't shaved off he had braided over his handiwork as a sort of home-grown bandage. The whole mess was covered with light gauze and taped down. I thanked God for giving us Novocain.

Dr. Song came back and handed me a small sealed envelope. "This is pretty mild stuff," he said. "Take two when you get home. If your head starts to hurt after about four hours, take two more. Keep ice over the area. And don't wash it for a couple of days."

"But it's gross now," I protested.

"Sorry. The end of next week, have your own doctor look at it." He held my arm and walked me toward the exit. Paula followed with the remains of my jacket rolled under her arm.

Outside, Dr. Song put a tentative arm around my shoulders. "I've been waiting for you to come in and say hello. I'm sorry it was under these circumstances."

"This isn't an easy place for me to come for a social call," I said.

"I understand," he said. "I spoke with Stanford this morning. Emily is hanging in."

"Did they say anything about her prospects?"

He shook his head. "I hope this officer takes good care of you, Miss MacGowen. First Emily, now you . . ."

I reached for my jacket from Paula. "Thanks for everything, Dr. Song. If you send the bill to Emily's address, Mrs. Lim will forward it."

He raised his hands. "This hospital does not bill a Duchamps."

"Good-bye," I said.

"Dang, you rate," Paula said as we walked toward her 4-by-4 truck. "Where can I drop you?"

"What time is it?" I asked.

She checked her watch. "Two-fifteen."

"Do you have plans for the next hour or so?"

"Nothing special."

"You saw what happened to my car. I have no wheels. I really want to pay a quick visit to an old friend in Holmby Hills. She won't come to the phone. Can I talk you into driving me?"

"After what just happened, you want to go see a friend? If you want to go visiting, let's drop in on the coroner and see if he's IDed the driver of the Volvo yet."

"I'd rather go to Holmby Hills."

"Must be some pretty good friend," Paula said, sounding a lot like Mike. "Who is it?"

"Mrs. T. Rexford Smith."

"Oh yeah?" Her expression told me I had just found a driver. "She's some bitch."

"Do you know her?"

"Just stories." We had reached her shiny red truck.

"I have a few stories of my own," I said. "You go first."

Paula's little truck was as cute as it could be, the ultimate in road toys. Sensaround CD, Posturepedic seats, tinted glass, whatever. It was still a truck. I felt every pothole like a knife through my head. Paula was a fearless driver and a great storyteller.

"Swear to God?" I said, as Paula came to the end of a long, lurid tale about Celeste.

"My partner rolled on the call," she said. "I trust it. This guy, the banker, had sucked his revolver. Brains everywhere. My partner read the note he left. The banker said he couldn't take the pressure anymore. He'd covered some of Mr. Smith's dirty dealings in exchange for a weekly blow job from Mrs. Smith. They'd got him into a deep hole, and when he asked them for a hand up, they threw him in a shovel. Symbolic end for the guy, don't you think, his gun in his mouth?"

"Was this story in the papers?"

"Not the part about Mrs. Smith. I've heard other stories, how she invited a rookie cop up to the mansion and screwed her way out of a DUI rap, and how she got drug charges against her daughter dropped after an hour in private consultation in judge's chambers."

"You're making this up," I said.

"*I'm* not making it up. It's what I heard. She's a slut. A rich and powerful slut."

The mansions of Holmby Hills may not be as showy as those in Bel-Air or Brentwood, but the wealth is there. The difference is old money versus Hollywood.

The Smith house was nice. About the size of a small European hotel. Vines clung to the faux stone facade. In the gathering afternoon, tiny white Christmas lights outlined the bow-front windows and the hipped roof and twined among the shrubs that lined the circular drive. The effect was antique doll house.

Paula pulled her truck into the porte cochere, and we walked around to the front.

"She's expecting you?" Paula asked.

"No. I doubt whether she would even open the door if she knew I was coming."

"If we're lucky, we'll catch her in the sack, see what she's got."

Paula pounded on the front door. When it was opened by a uniformed maid, Paula whipped out her police ID.

"Like to talk to Mrs. Smith," Paula said.

"Come in, please." The maid bowed. "I will see if Mrs. Smith is in."

The maid left us in a foyer festooned with garlands of fresh cedar and holly tied with mammoth red-velvet bows and braided gold cord. The foyer was an oval, with a staircase curving up one side, and tall polished oak doors opening off the other. There was good art on the walls, old architectural prints, and an exceptional oil portrait of the Smith family: Celeste, T. Rex, the deceased Carrie, Rex, Jr., and Paix. The overall effect was intentionally subdued; a lot of money, it said, doesn't have to advertise.

"Holy shit," Paula said after making a circuit. "My apartment isn't as big as this entry."

"We can leave now," I said.

"We haven't even seen the lady of the house yet," Paula protested.

I reached for the door. "We don't have to. I've learned everything I need to know."

It was just past three-thirty when we got back to Chinatown. Mike had already staked out the wishing well. When we drove up, we saw him pacing around the plaza that fronted Broadway. I watched him stop an elderly housewife and try to question her. She did a lot of bowing, backward. She left in such a hurry that the parcels in her arms took a good bouncing.

Paula parked in the red zone in front of Sun Yat-sen's statue.

"Won't you get a ticket?" I asked.

"Who gives a fuck?" She flexed one mega bicep for me. "I'm the police."

"Mike says that even the mayor gets ticketed in L.A."

"Sure," she snickered. "The mayor gets ticketed all the time. He left his limo unattended at the airport—in front of the Tom Bradley Terminal, no less—and it got towed. But that's the mayor. I said, I'm the police."

She locked her truck and met me on the sidewalk. "So, where's your squint?"

"Mike isn't a squint," I said. "He spent about fifteen years patrolling the streets. He's that dear old thing in the gray suit, the one accosting housewives."

"Gray suit?" she sneered. "Not only a squint, but a pogue."

I laughed. "Come and meet him."

When Mike saw me, he started running for me. It was too TV. All we needed was a field of flowers and a slo-mo camera. His first words, however, weren't greatly romantic.

"Shit, Maggie, where the hell have you been? I've had the coroner up my ass all afternoon."

"Hi, Mike," I said, grabbing him under the chin and kissing his face. "I want you to meet Officer Paula Ericksen."

"Yeah," he said with a curt nod in her direction. "What the hell happened at the academy?"

"Paula, here, bench-pressed one-eighty," I said. "Some guy took a shot at me and somehow got himself blown up."

He let out a lot of saved-up air and folded me into his arms. It felt awfully good. I let my head fall against his hard shoulder, made the back of my neck available for kissing, if he felt so moved. Fortunately, he did.

"Flint?" Paula said, narrowing her eyes to look Mike over. "You ever work canines?"

"No," Mike said, coming up for new air. "My old partner does."

"Doug?" she squealed. Truly. She even blushed a little.

"Yes," Mike said, relaxing his hold on me. "You know Doug?"

"We were partners for a while, in Southeast. He ever tell you about busting an old hooker named Queen Esther?"

"That was my bust," Mike said, blushing himself.

"Ohhh." She waggled a finger at him. "You're *that* Flint?"

"Everything he told you about me is a lie," Mike said.

"Oh yeah?" Paula nudged me. "Ask him to tell you about Queen Esther. I'll see you guys around."

I caught her hand. "Aren't you eating with us? I told you, Mrs. Lim is a great cook."

Paula looked at Mike and winked. "Maybe another time."

"What division you working out of?" Mike asked her.

"Best duty in town," she answered, thrusting up her chin. "Rootin' shootin' Newton. Never a dull watch."

"I'll call you," Mike told her. "There's a decent taco place on Tenth."

"Lechuga's?" she asked.

"Right."

"Sure. I'll meet you there. We'll swap some lies." She made a gun with her thumb and forefinger and aimed it at his chest. "See ya', then."

"Thanks for everything, Paula," I said.

"Been an education." She glanced at Mike, then gave me a wicked leer. "Maybe we should have waited around to get some pointers from Celeste Smith."

"Honey," I said, "I don't think you and I need any pointers."

"Got that right," she laughed and jogged off to her truck.

I liked Paula. I was sorry to see her go. Dinner at Emily's would have been fun with the three of us. And I knew she would know when to disappear afterward.

As she roared down Broadway in her truck, Paula beat out "Shave and a Haircut" on her horn for us.

"Sweet young thing," I said, watching her exhaust. Mike was quiet, watching me watch her. When I looked up at him, he covered my mouth with his. I lost track of everything else for a moment.

Traditional Chinese are very reticent about public display of affection. The women skittering home to start dinner all seemed moved to giggles as they passed us.

I came up for air. "Hi, Mike."

"When the report came in about what went down at the academy, I was scared to death," he said. "I tried to find you. Where did you go?"

"Paula took good care of me. First, I got my head sewn up. Then she drove me out to Celeste's house."

"What happened to your head?" he snapped.

"No big deal. The important thing is what I learned at Celeste's."

"What?"

"The Smiths are a lovely family. The two younger children have red hair and freckles, just like their mother."

"Funny how that works out," he said.

"But that's not the good part."

"Go ahead."

"The elder boy, Paix, is the spitting image of Ho Chi Minh."

Chapter 20

"What?" Mike asked. "The kid has a long white beard?"

"No. Paix is a very nice-looking young man." I took Mike's arm. "He is also very Asian."

"So? This tells you something?"

"Yes. It means Marc was not Paix's father."

Mike drew away to give me a narrow-eyed glare. "I'm lost. Could you back it up a little?"

"Celeste inferred that Marc fathered her son."

"And you believed her?"

"Never. I remember what Marc used to say about Celeste. He had no interest in her. Marc could be a wild man, but he was cast in a Beau Geste mold. He believed in true love."

"But you believed her enough to worry about it."

"To think about the implications, anyway." I sat on the base of Sun Yat-sen's statue. "What Garth said about Celeste was true: she's full of shit."

"The things that come out of your mouth," he tsk'ed. He quickly grew serious again. "Just watch your backside. She's a powerful woman in this town, and she has a bad reputation for the means she uses to get her own way."

I looked up at him. "For example?"

"I've heard stories." He shrugged. "Why do you say she's full of it?"

"She told me this sad tale about how she enrolled Paix in an exclusive preschool, but when he showed up, the place was suddenly full. The little guy, she said, had been a victim of conspiracy—someone had gotten to the school."

"You don't buy it?"

I started to shake my head, but it was throbbing, so I thought better of it. "Maybe Paix didn't get into the school. I can think of more ordinary reasons why that might have happened. We're talking twenty years ago. Here's the equation: single mother with a bad rep, fatherless Asian child, high-dollar baby school. Can you make succotash out of that?"

"Maybe not."

I looked up at Mike. "Where was Celeste when Emily was shot?"

"All over town, getting ready for her party. We can't pin her down very well. No one close to her will give us a goddamn thing."

"Makes you wonder, doesn't it?"

"A lot of things make me wonder." He stood up and offered his hand. "Let's go get you an ice pack."

"I thought we were going to skulk around the wishing well and Hop Louie's for a while."

He shrugged. "No need. The area has been staked out since the shooting."

"Then why did you say you would meet me here?"

He grinned. "Because it's where you said you would be."

I stood up too fast and made myself woozy.

"You okay?" Mike asked.

"Yes." I took a deep breath and walked beside him, trying not to jar my head. "I like your new tie. The hula dancer is just true art."

"Thanks. I like it, too. Made me think all day about where my other tie was."

We were just passing Hop Louie's on our way over to Hill Street. I turned to look over my shoulder toward the mouth of the alley where Emily had been shot. I had walked past the same spot maybe half a dozen times in the last couple of days. Though I had given it considerable thought, I hadn't been able to bring myself to go into the alley and see for myself where it had happened. In my mind's eye, I saw Emily lying there among the crates of trash, alone, in the rain. It may sound spooky and superstitious, but I believe I felt she was still in there.

Mike had my hand. He, also, was looking down the alley. "I'll show you, if you want."

"Not yet," I said. "It's pretty dark in there."

"No it isn't." He tugged a little. "You'll feel better if you look, Maggie. Let's get it over with."

He was already walking. I could have kept going right on toward Hill Street, but I followed him as far as the mouth of the alley. I stopped to tuck in my shirt. I looked up at the sky to make sure it wasn't going to start raining anytime soon. I remembered three or four phone calls I had to make that really could not wait a few more minutes.

Mike stopped opposite Hop Louie's back door and waited. "Don't be afraid. There's really nothing to see."

"For crying out loud," I said. "I am not afraid."

"Then get to steppin'."

I ventured in. The alley was just like any alley behind a restaurant. There wasn't room for a dumpster. Instead, there were lots of full trash cans, a stack of wood-slat lettuce crates, a couple of up-ended milk crates surrounded by cigarette butts, some broken Naugahyde chairs. Pots clattering inside the kitchen covered most of the street noise.

"Where did it happen?" I asked.

"Down here." Mike walked on past the door to a small nook where the alley made a dogleg. He moved a couple of boxes and stood in the angle. "This is where she was found. A couple of busboys came out for a smoke and found her in a heap. The boss tells them all the time to keep bums from sleeping back here because they make a mess that gets him in trouble with the health department. So they came over to get her to move along."

"Did they know her?" I asked.

"She was the doc," he said matter of factly. "They

took good care of her until the paramedics came, put a cover over her to keep the rain off."

He crossed the narrow alley and ran his hand along the back wall of the opposite building, a china shop. He laid his finger next to a spot where a chip had been gouged out of the stucco.

"See this?" he asked. "It looks like a bullet impact. Emily was shot at fairly close range; we saw significant gunpowder tattooing on the skin, scorching of the hair around the wound. The bullet made a through and through wound to the head, and still had enough juice left to ding the wall here. A slug, looked like a .38, was recovered from the pavement. There was very little bleeding, virtually no other physical evidence."

I went back and sat down on one of the up-ended milk crates. I did some more deep breathing, but I was okay. It was just another alley after all, and I felt terribly let down. There was no stain on the pavement where Emily had been found. The bullet impact on the wall was nothing. For all the damage that had been done, all the pain, there wasn't enough to show for it. I thought there should be a wreath, at least.

"Thanks, Mike," I said.

"Anything else I can do?" he asked.

"Tell me what you see here with your trained eye."

"It's what I can't see. Come here." He gestured me over to the angle in the wall. "Take a look. From here, you can't see either end of the alley, right? And unless someone comes out the kitchen door, no one can see you, either. The shooter did his homework, picked a good spot."

"You think it was a local?"

He shrugged. "It's easy homework. The trick is getting Emily in here."

"Not much of a trick for a friend to pull off, is it?"

"You're right." He took my hand again. "Seen enough? Or would you like to sit here for a while longer?"

I took a last careful look around. Mike had been right

to get me into the alley. Emily was not there. A kitchen worker came out and dumped a pot of cabbage ends into a can. He glanced up at us as he tried to force the lid back down.

"Think he speaks English?" I asked Mike. "Maybe he saw something."

"Maggie, he's been questioned. Everyone has been questioned."

"May I see their statements?"

"No need." He put an arm around my shoulders and impelled me back out toward Gin Ling Way. "Maggie, the answer will not be found in fingerprints, or eyewitnesses, or sock fibers left at the scene. We won't need any of that until we get to court. If we get this to court."

"What are you saying? You aren't investigating?"

"Of course we are," he said, with some heat. "I've been doing this work for a lot of years. I've learned a thing or two. I know that the vast, vast majority of murder victims know their killers. Emily knew her killer. Right now, in the county morgue, a forensic pathologist is trying to identify the burned corpse of the person who took a shot at you this afternoon. When he makes that ID, it will be someone you know. And when we figure out who, why will follow right along."

"You're saying all we can do is wait for the pathologist."

"We have to wait." He smiled slyly as he ran his hand down my back. "But that's not all we can do."

"You're a pushy guy, Flint."

"Trust me," he said. "Go home. Close your eyes and think about what you know, and you'll get a whole lot closer to the truth than you ever would reading police reports."

"If I close my eyes, I'll go to sleep."

Caesar, with his dog dragging behind, accosted us when we were about halfway across Hill Street.

"Evenin' pretty lady. How's it hangin', officer?"

Mike started for his pocket, but I stayed his hand.

"So, Casesar," I said. "Have you had dinner yet?"

"I was just about thinkin' about it."

"Why don't you join us?" I said. If looks could kill, Mike . . .

Caesar seemed incredibly suspicious. He looked askance at both of us. "What is it you have in mind?"

"Dinner," I said. "Chinese noodles of some kind. Please, be our guest."

"You're not thinkin' nothin', you know, about after dinner, the whole three of us?"

"Just dinner," I said, smiling like Emily Post. "We've come to be such good friends, I'd like to show you some family photos. That's all."

Caesar still seemed suspicious, but he capitulated. Mike was still looking daggers.

"What are you up to?" Mike rasped in my ear.

"Maybe you wouldn't mind picking up a nice bottle of wine," I said. "What goes with noodles?"

Caesar was finally smiling again. "I like a little wine with dinner. Up at the Center, they don't serve nothin'."

"We'll see," Mike said, sticking close to me.

The vile graffiti on Mrs. Lim's front wall had been painted out. The heavy-cover paint wasn't exactly the same color as the original, but it was a definite improvement. Caesar looped the dog's clothesline leash over the rail along the front steps and ordered it to stay. The dog lay down and closed its eyes.

Once again, Mrs. Lim must have been lying in wait. As soon as I bolted the front door, she was out of her apartment. She didn't seem very happy to see Caesar, but she said nothing about him. I knew that Emily brought people home all the time.

"New door," she said, handing me a small brown envelope. "New key."

"Thank you," I said. "Send the repair bill to me."

She waved me off, went back into her apartment and locked her own door.

The new key fit the new door smoothly.

"Caesar, Mike, make yourselves comfortable," I said

as we went inside. Everything was as it should be. And spotlessly clean.

Caesar took off his hat and looked around. "Nice place you have, pretty lady."

"This is Emily's apartment."

"The doc?"

"Yes."

"Nice-lookin' shower in there."

"Caesar," I said, "would you like to take a shower while I get dinner ready?"

"There a lock on the door?"

"Yes, there is."

"Don't mind if I do."

"Wait just one second," I said. I ducked into the closet and found Em's navy sweats. They would fit Caesar better than they had fit me. I handed them to him. "There are clean towels on the rack. We'll be in the next room when you've finished."

As Caesar locked himself in the bathroom, I took Mike by the hand and led him into the sitting room. I sat him on the sofa, straddled his lap, and kissed him. I met no resistance.

"Nice," he said. "But what are you up to?"

"Just what I said. I'd like to show Caesar the family album. You going to get us a bottle of wine?"

"I don't think it's a good idea. You shouldn't have anything if you're on painkillers. And he shouldn't have anything, period."

"Whatever you say." I kissed his cheek and got up to go heat the noodles.

There was rather more than noodles. Mrs. Lim had made a beautiful chicken chow mein, with a green salad, fried wontons and sweet rice balls. It was more than enough for three. I heated what needed heating, tossed the salad, and found three plates in the cupboard over the sink.

Emily had no kitchen table. I imagined her eating in the living room, as we had been. I set the plates, forks, paper napkins and a pitcher of water on the coffee table.

"Can I help?" Mike asked.

"Yes." I handed him the photograph of the Honolulu airport meeting that Jaime had given me and an album I had found in the bookcase of Emily's study. "You know the A list of suspects. See if you can find a picture of each one."

"Maggie, what were we just talking about down there?"

"What can it hurt?"

When Caesar came out of the shower, I hardly recognized him. He was redolent of Yardley complexion bar, peach-stone shampoo, Colgate toothpaste. I don't know what he used for a toothbrush—I had been using Emily's—but I planned to burn whatever was in the rack. With his hair slicked back and his beard groomed, he was a fairly nice-looking man. He padded in on cleanish white socks, preening a bit.

"Caesar," I said, "why don't you sit on the sofa beside Mike. Mike wants to show you some pictures."

I made three trips, bringing in food and water glasses. While I fussed, Caesar went through the photographs like polite company stuck with vacation snaps. I knelt on the floor across the table from them and began to serve the food.

"See anyone you know?" I asked.

"No'm. 'Cept for the doc." Caesar took a gulp of his water and shivered all over.

"Sorry," I said. "We're all out of wine."

He was being the considerate guest. He smiled, but I saw that it cost him.

"You don't recognize anyone else?" Mike asked.

"No," Caesar said, nudging a picture of Rod Peebles with the end of his fork. " 'Cept maybe him. Take off his hair, an' he look like this dude keep runnin' for boss aroun' here. Keep his picture up all over town."

"That's how you know him?" I asked. "From his political billboards?"

Caesar nodded as he stuffed his mouth with chow mein. "Like you say. From his signs."

"Maggie." Mike grinned. "Like I say, just close your eyes and think."

"Caesar, have some more rice," I said. I pushed a nice full-face shot of Celeste closer to his plate. He looked at her, smiled, and popped a whole rice ball into his mouth.

Mike was looking very smug. He finished his chow mein; then he leaned back on the sofa and grinned at me. "You're quite a cook."

I glared at him. "I think I'm getting a headache."

"Chinese food sometime' give me a headache, too," Caesar said. "Pretty lady, think there might be some extra I could take down to my dog?"

"Yes." I got up. "I'll wrap some for you."

"Excuse me, pal," Mike said. He picked up his plate and followed me into the kitchen. While I picked chicken bits out of the chow mein for the dog, he leaned against the sink beside me.

"Who did you think he'd recognize?" Mike asked.

"The man with the skinny nose. The woman who walked the walk."

"They're old pictures. I'm surprised he knew Rod."

"Rod cheats," I said. "I saw one of his billboards today. He uses old pictures and has them airbrushed. As Caesar said, take off the hair and they look the same."

A buzzer went off somewhere close by, and I jumped. First I checked the oven timer; then I looked around for an alarm clock.

"It's me," Mike said. He pulled off his pager and checked the readout. "Borrow the phone?"

"Try the study." I wrapped the chicken and carried it in to Caesar.

"How was your dinner?" I asked.

"An elegant sufficiency," he said, grinning.

"I hope your dog likes this."

"Thank you," he said, rising to take the bowl from me. "You were real nice to ask me in."

"My pleasure. I hope we didn't bore you with the pictures."

"Just one thing," he said. He set down the bowl and

began rummaging through the pictures scattered among the dishes.

Mike came in from the study with a deep, serious expression on his face.

"That was Bronkowski," he said. "The coroner called in. They're still working on the ID, but they found something tangled with the body that was interesting."

"What?" I said.

"It was really charred and they had some trouble cleaning it up enough to read, had to use the infrared in the end."

"Mike." I was out of patience. "What was it?"

"Dogtags."

Caesar tapped my arm, and when I turned, he handed me a snapshot. I took it without looking at it.

"Mike," I said, with some heat. "Whose?"

"Marc Duchamps, USMC."

"Say that again?" I said.

Caesar was pulling on my sleeve. "See him?"

"Who?" I snapped.

"That's him who I saw at the wishin' well that time. I told you, he was lookin' for the doc."

I held up the picture. Caesar had handed me a snapshot Marc had sent from Vietnam. He was snapped standing in the jungle, in the rain, with his face grinning out of an olive drab poncho. I had never noticed before how thin his nose was.

Chapter 21

A giant plastic wreath hanging on the Boyle Heights Holiday Inn was the only color showing against the night sky as we drove along the wrecking yards on Mission Road. It was a bleak landscape, leftover land among the railway tracks at the edge of the city.

"The best thing to do when you first go inside is to take a deep breath," Mike said. "Get used to the smell in a hurry."

"Is it bad?" I asked. I was past having second thoughts and was well into the acceptance of the idiocy of bravado.

"It's not so much bad. I mean, things in your refrigerator can smell worse if you leave them too long. This is just different, and you won't ever forget it."

"Good to know." I rolled down my window a few inches to let in some air.

"And don't expect things tidy like *Quincy*. Not sheet-covered bodies with toe tags sticking out."

"No toe tags?" I asked.

"Toe tags, yes. No sheets."

"Gross."

"I told you it wouldn't be nice," he said gruffly. "But you're so damn determined to see for yourself. So you have to walk down highway one between the deep freeze and the autopsy rooms. There's no way to detour around the cadavers waiting to be processed."

"Listen, Mike," I said, turning in the seat to face him. "If the body taken from the wreckage is my brother, Marc, then this time I'm going to have a good look at him before he's sealed up in his box. So stop trying to scare me."

"I am not trying to scare you," he snapped. "But you have to be prepared for what you're going to see in the morgue. Forewarned is forearmed, right?"

"I'm a big girl. Remember me, the correspondent from the front lines in El Salvador?"

His laugh was smug. "How many bodies did you see?"

"Plenty." Two, actually, not counting livestock. I was not about to tell him that.

Mike had slid into his tough-cop shtick during the short drive from downtown. "There are more bodies picked up every weekend on the streets of Los Angeles than most G.I.'s saw during their entire tours in Vietnam."

"And you personally pick up every body, right?"

"Damn right." He reached across the seat and took my hand. "Why are you mad at me?"

"No one else is available."

"I can live with that."

He pulled into the parking lot beyond the delivery entrance of the county morgue. "Last chance. I can back right out of here and take you home."

"Let's just get on with this."

The morgue sits on a downslope corner of the vast campus of the L.A. County–USC Medical Center Hospital, tucked among the oldest, occasionally condemned, buildings of the facility. All around the morgue corner, it was very dark, except for the green-tinged lights of the loading bay. We got out of the car and walked past technicians garbed in rubber aprons, boots, and gloves who were hosing down battered fiberglass gurneys and washing the residue into a sump hole. A coroner's van with its doors open was parked in the cargo bay. In sum, it was a proper entrance for a charnel house.

"Maggie, there's a little office up front here. The pathologist can bring you pictures and talk to you there."

"Mike, pictures aren't good enough."

"It's not a pretty cadaver."

"I know that," I said. "I was there, remember? I saw the fire. Quit fussing."

"Any time you want to change your mind . . ."

"I'll let you know." If he had shut up, I probably would have backed out. He had to make an issue, so I had to prove something. Now I was fated to take a look at a corpse that had been both exploded and charred. The closer I got, the worse I knew it would be. Some things have to be done.

The box that came home from Vietnam with Marc's name on it had been put into the ground without anyone looking inside to make damn sure Marc was in there. There were health and esthetic reasons why we were not to break the seals. It was a mistake I still had difficulty living with.

I never knew exactly how Marc had died. No one would talk to me about it. Not knowing fed many fantasies. Now and then, Marc still comes into my dreams. At first, I'm always glad to see him. Many nights I drift away from my dream reassured, happy to have spoken to him again, simply to have seen him. But there are other, darker nights when Marc comes to me in his sealed coffin. He begs me to open the box and let him out. I wake up in a hot sweat, afraid to sleep again for days.

I have always known that unless I found some way to see inside the box, I would dream about Marc for the rest of my life. It was a long shot, but as I walked into the morgue, I felt this might be my only chance to put him, finally, to rest.

Mike opened a side door and we went into a small, unadorned lobby. He clipped his photo ID to his lapel and signed us in.

"Ready?" he asked.

"Yes."

When he opened the inner door, I took a handful of his elbow and filled my lungs. The air was cold and heavy with an odor that was at the same time sweet and repulsive. It seemed to lodge at the back of my throat so I smelled it even when I breathed through my mouth.

Naked dead on gurneys lined the hallway on both sides. Their skin was often paler than the beige-painted walls, so anything with color, pubic mound, the red-staining of morbid lividity, bruises, vivid holes, stood out. I found it difficult to look at their faces and quit looking altogether when I saw that the gurney closest to the first autopsy room held a body with no face at all.

The first autopsy room was a hive of green-gowned workers. Mike had been right—it wasn't *Quincy*. There was no clinical gleam. The tools were pruning shears and soup ladles, electric saws and meat scales. Debris of towels and tools and pans littered the floor. There were four cadavers in various stages of processing: tops of skulls removed and the brains gone, the torsos sliced in long and wide cruciforms and laid open from pubis to throat, until they look like anatomical kits disassembled. When I thought about what was happening in there, I felt something rise in my throat. There wasn't much left at that point that seemed obviously human.

The hall angled right and there was a second autopsy room. Here the bodies were waiting three deep, heaped like discarded rag dolls rather than laid out on their gurneys. There were so many, we had to walk single-file past them. I was worried that the people walking ahead of us might come back and try to squeeze past us. There wouldn't be room for them to go by me without forcing me against a gurney. I was afraid to touch anything.

The man lying on my right was young, uncircumcised, well-muscled. He had a good haircut, and a bullet hole in the middle of his forehead. I couldn't look anymore. I scooted closer to Mike's shoulder and studied the weave of his tweed jacket until we came to the room at the end of the hall.

"Is there a short-cut out?" I asked.

"No, sorry. Seems to be a full house tonight. Everyone's working overtime."

"Where are we going?"

"Right here." Mike led me into a small side room. Everything I had seen to this point looked like a public health clinic whose massive client load had been left waiting too long. But upon entering this room we seemed to have moved into something more exclusive, more private. There was one cadaver: a blackened, grotesquely contorted figure.

Mike leaned his face close to mine. "Okay?"

"I'm all right." I lied.

A woman in green surgical drapes shuffled over to us in her paper booties. She was beyond middle-age, somewhere approaching Hallmark's version of grandmotherly. It bothered me that I couldn't see her eyes behind the protective goggles. She held an X-ray film in her left hand.

"Are you Miss MacGowen?" she asked.

"Yes." I didn't offer my hand because hers were encased in soiled rubber gloves. "This is Detective Flint."

"I know." She nodded. "Hi, Mike. Glad you made it."

"I could have passed on this one, Winnie," he said. "What do you know?"

Winnie, whoever she was, chucked the X ray into a light frame. I could see the crushed bones in the pelvis, a grossly fractured femur.

Winnie looked from the X ray to the subject on the table.

"Male," she said, beginning with the obvious. "Between mid-thirties and late-forties, five-ten to maybe six-one, Caucasian, fair complexion, well-nourished, upper income brackets but nouveau riche, complete asshole."

"Wait a minute," I said. "You lost me on the last two."

"They were the easiest characteristics to determine," she said, gesturing me closer to the corpse. With a stainless probe she retracted what was left of the top lip and tapped the front teeth.

"Fused by the fire," she said, "Good quality enamel caps. He had thousands of dollars of dental work in his mouth to correct problems that should have been taken care of when he was a kid."

Then she lifted his pinkie finger. It had somehow escaped massive damage. She looked at me and smiled expectantly, but I didn't see what seemed obvious to her. I shrugged.

"He had a manicure," she grinned. "Did you ever know a man with capped teeth and a manicure who wasn't a complete asshole?"

"Never," I said. "Winnie, I didn't get the rest of your name."

"Kasababian," she said. "Senior pathologist. I was told you might give us some help identifying our friend here."

The corpse was an abomination. It was a feat of some sort for me to even be in the same room with him. The face looked something like King Tut's mummy, with its seared skin stretched tight across the skull bones, little tufts of frizzled hair over the ear holes.

Marc and Emily had always been very thin. Their skin seemed tailored to their bones with great precision, nothing loose, nothing left over. I had thought I would be able to recognize their naked skeletons. I could not see anything familiar in one single feature of this dead man.

"How tall did you say?" I asked Winnie.

"The forensic anthropologist will come closer, but my best estimate is five-ten to six-one."

"My brother was at least six-four," I said. "Could you stretch your estimate that far?"

"That would be a stretch," she said. "Wait and see what the anthropologist says."

She had gone back over to the X ray. Her goggles hung around her neck as she peered closely at it. "We're considering the possibility this is your brother?"

"Yes," I said.

"We'll ask you for the names of the family physician and dentist, but in the meantime, do you remember your brother having any broken bones?"

I thought for a minute. We all take lumps as kids because of the stupid things we do. Marc had been a daredevil par excellence. He had also been a superb athlete, graceful and agile like a cat. And with the same inner gyroscope.

I shook my head. "Sorry. I can't remember Marc breaking anything."

"No legs? No elbows?"

"Sorry," I said. "Nothing."

"Don't be sorry." Winnie smiled. She touched her probe to the right shin of the X-ray subject. "Youthful fracture of the tibia. Well-healed. Heavy calcification. Ditto the elbow. Probably was beginning to cause some pain."

Em, Marc and I all went to different summer camps, and now and then away by ourselves to friends and relatives for a few weeks, maybe a month or two at a time. One break might have gotten by me. But not two.

"Where were the dogtags found?" I asked.

"In the pelvis," she said, "mixed with some melted coins and the remains of a seatbelt buckle. I'm not an explosives expert. I don't know much about debris patterns, and so on. But if you asked my opinion, I would say the dogtags were in the victim's right front trouser pocket."

"Not around his neck?" I asked.

She shook her head. "Not at the time of the explosion."

I went over to Mike and put my hand on his shoulder. "He isn't Marc."

"What about the dogtags?" he asked.

"I think I remember that they were sent home from Vietnam with some of Marc's personal effects. They used to hang on a statue of the Virgin in my mother's bedroom. But I haven't seen them for years."

"Remember what I told you this afternoon?" Mike asked. "This character we pulled out of the Volvo is someone you knew. Any ideas?"

I went through Winnie Kasababian's descriptive parameters again. Sort of tall, but not very, not very old, not exactly young. Could fit a lot of candidates.

"I have some ideas," I said. "I need more information to make them fit."

Chapter 22

It was late and the Cha Cha Topless Bar on Pico was nearly deserted. A few dedicated drinkers were hanging in, watching without passion as a slender young woman bumped and ground on the small stage behind the bar. The dancer outclassed the clientele by a wide margin— she looked like a graduate student with a night job.

I found Lester Rowland sitting alone at a corner table with his back to the room. He had his hand wrapped around a tall drink—the ice was melted, and the glass was full.

I never liked the man, so I wouldn't volunteer, but he looked as if he desperately needed a good friend. I was here only because he had called all over town with the message that he wanted to talk to me. As it was, I was willing to talk to just about anyone. I only wished he hadn't picked such a dive.

The smoky air helped cover the stench of the morgue that still lodged at the back of my throat. I pulled out a chair and sat opposite him. "Hello, Lester."

He glanced up with vacant, watery eyes. "Maggie."

"You heard about what happened up at the academy this afternoon?"

"I heard." Everything about him seemed heavy, his shoulders, his voice, even the stagnant smoke-filled air around him. "You okay?"

I touched the patch job on my head. I was okay, but having been given a little time for the adrenaline to pass off, some space to think about what had happened, and what could have happened, I had a bad case of the shakes.

Lester lit a cigarette from the glowing butt in the ashtray and took a long drag. Angrily, he tamped the ash. "I haven't had a smoke for ten years," he said.

"You invited me here to talk," I said. "So talk."

"I'm sorry," he said, gruff but earnest. "That's all I wanted to say. I'm just so damn sorry. If I'd thought for one second that anyone would get hurt, we would have gone about bringing Aleda in a whole lot differently."

"Why go through the bother of bringing her in at all?" I asked. "What difference did it make? She came in, the judge let her right back out."

"I wanted a little justice to be done." His face was very close to mine. "Has everyone forgotten what really happened back then? An innocent kid was killed. And for what? Peace and freedom? No. For nothing."

"It was a long time ago," I said. "Let it go."

"Tell that to the Potts family. You have any idea how they must feel when Aleda shows up out of nowhere and becomes a fucking media hero? Everyone gets all misty-eyed for the good old days—remember when Abbie Hoffman showed up? There's big bucks potential in book and movie deals, 'My Life on the Lam'? People have short memories. Aleda Weston wasn't a fucking hero. Any more than your sister Emily was."

"Take it easy," I said.

"Fucking instant media heroes." He had worked himself into a red-faced sweat, and he wasn't ready to quit. "For twenty-two years, Aleda evaded a fugitive warrant for conspiracy to murder. She could have come in anytime and faced the charges like Emily and the others. You ever wonder why she didn't?"

"Shit happens," I said.

A waitress hovered nearby until Lester came up for air. She was topless, with little fried-egg breasts. She emptied the ashtray and wiped the table. Though the woman was wearing nothing except a G-string and an appendectomy scar, she got no notice from Lester.

"Need anything here?" she asked.

"Two scotch and sodas," I said. "Easy ice."

"Easy ice I can do." She made a dip, wiped the table again around Lester's untouched drink, then jiggled away.

He seemed chagrined after his outburst. I gave him a moment to collect himself. He sank back in his chair and blew out a long breath.

"Everything turns to shit, doesn't it?" he sighed.

"For instance?"

"Everything. The way Aleda set up her surrender, we thought it would go down so smooth. I'm sorry. I'll say it again. I'm sorry."

"No one blames you," I said.

"I should have known better." He shrugged; then he tapped the table beside my hand, shying away from actually touching me. "I'm glad you're okay."

"That's two of us." I smiled at him, feeling sorry for him for some reason.

"Are we clear now?" he asked. "You know, I'm not such a bad guy. And it's not that I don't have a lot of respect for what Emily has been doing. She came a long way from the days of 'burn, baby, burn.' A whole lot further than some of the others. It breaks my heart to know what happened to her. And you."

I smiled. "You have a heart?"

"Don't let it get around, will you?"

The waitress came back with drinks and a cash register tab. I put a twenty on the tab and she went away. I didn't want a drink, but ordering was like paying rent for our seats.

Lester ran his damp hand over the stubble on his cheeks. When he looked at me finally, his eyes were rimmed in red—fatigue, the smoke, guilt, tears, could have been any of them.

I pushed my drink aside. "Detective Flint and I just spent the most interesting hour at the county crime lab, talking to an explosives man," I said. "You know something about homemade bombs, don't you?"

He shook his head, but I knew better.

"Emily's car was nearly vaporized by the blast up at the academy," I said. "It's amazing what the technicians were able to reconstruct with the tiny bits they had to work with. The device was a masterwork. Beautifully simple. Four sticks of dynamite taped to the gas tank, with a sound-activated detonator. It would have taken a big sound, like the firing of a gun at close range, to set off the explosion.

"Elegant, don't you think? The driver fires a shot and *kaboom*—double play, if he hits his target. The flaw was, he only got one shot. If he'd been a decent marksman, I wouldn't be here."

Lester managed a wry smile. "Can't get good help these days."

I smiled, glad he was in a better frame of mind. I had something more to talk about. I pushed my chair out a little so I could stretch my legs. I needed a long soak in a hot tub. Emily didn't have a tub. I wondered whether Mike did. Business first, I thought, and looked up at Lester.

"Remember Jaime Orozco?" I asked.

"Sure." He furrowed his brow, seemed suspicious.

"He told me someone in their group of activists was on the FBI payroll."

"So?" He shrugged. "That's the way the game is played."

"Was Rod Peebles on your payroll?"

He chuckled. "Funny, isn't it? Question like that starts going around about a politician, he's in trouble. If I say yes, the liberals will kill him; say no and any good conservative will do the job."

"Either way, then, he's doomed. So why don't you just tell me the truth."

"Truth is relative," he said.

"Fuck that," I said.

He laughed, loud enough for the stripper to look our way. "Okay. So maybe we gave young Peebles a little federal scholarship. A little work-study."

"You show him how to build a bomb?"

"No bombs. He gave us information, and that's all."

"That's a lot," I said. "He was a traitor to the Movement. He betrayed his friends. For what? Only money?"

"Rod was a true patriot, unlike the rest of them."

"So was Benedict Arnold, if you were British."

"Then call me a Brit," he said. "Look, Maggie, it was no big thing. Rod didn't have a fat-cat daddy to make things easy for him like the rest of them did. He didn't have strong political convictions one way or the other. He just wanted to get through school the best way he could. So we helped each other. That's the way the game is played."

"He must have had some political attitude," I said. "He's a career politician."

"He has a good face and he reads his lines well."

"Is Rod still on your payroll?"

He shook his head slowly. "Doesn't mean he isn't on someone else's."

"Any ideas?"

"Lots of them. And none of them worth a damn." He rose from his seat. "I have a plane to catch, Maggie. I'm glad we had this little talk."

"It's been an education," I said.

He smiled again. "See you around, kid. Maybe out at the pool sometime, huh?"

He touched my shoulder, his hand lingering just long enough to be noticed as lingering. Then he turned away and headed for the exit.

"Did he talk to you?" Mike asked. He had been waiting outside, as Lester had instructed.

"He talked. I'll tell you on the way home. Lester picked a great place to meet. Did you peek inside there?"

"Not me," Mike said innocently. "But why didn't he get you a waitress with better tits?"

I laughed. "Take me home or lose me forever."

In the car, I pulled off my boots. "Any word on Rod Peebles?"

"Can't find him. You think he was the driver, don't you?"

I nodded. "Rod Peebles, the man who wasn't there."

"What does that mean?"

"Something Lester said. Rod was never anything but a front man. I think he still is. Just a billboard-pretty face. If he tried to shoot me, my guess is it wasn't his own idea."

"Who then?"

"You're the detective. You tell me."

By the time we arrived back at Emily's apartment, it was much too late to call Denver. But I hadn't had a chance to talk to Casey all day. So I dialed anyway.

"Hello," Linda answered, breathless as if she had run.

"It's Maggie. Sorry about the hour. May I speak with Casey?"

There was a pause. She hadn't said a thing after hello. I began to think she had simply walked away to find someone else to deal with me. Then I heard her breathe.

"Linda?"

"Casey isn't here," she said.

"Oh? Where is she?"

"Skiing."

"At this hour?"

"No." Another long pause. That's when I began to panic. "Scotty went to pick her up. They probably stopped for something to eat. Maybe they went to a movie."

"Is Casey all right?" I demanded.

"Well of course," she snapped back. "She's with her father. You think we aren't capable of caring for her?"

"No matter how late it is, would you please have her call me the minute she gets in? I'm still at Emily's."

"Certainly. Merry Christmas." And she hung up.

Mike was coming in from the kitchen with a beer. "Everything okay?"

I nodded, but I had a horrible feeling. The morgue

had been bad. Nearly getting shot down had been terrifying. This was worse. Borderline hysteria. I tried to shake the feeling off as maternal paranoia tempered by shock hangover. While my day had been a nightmare, Casey was a long way away from everything that had happened. Safe with her father. At the same time, too far away from me.

I looked at the clock. I would give her until midnight L.A. time; then I would call her back.

I looked up at Mike. "So?"

"So you should go to bed. I'd like to stay to tuck you in, but I have some ends to tie up. Mrs. Lim is on patrol. There are two new locks on the door. Think you'll be okay?"

"I'm fine. Call me."

As nice as Mike was to have around, I was glad to have a little time alone. To take a really long shower. To think. To wait for Casey's call.

We embraced at the door. It was more familial than anything. I was too distracted to give much thought to passion. He lingered over the kiss on my cheek.

"Call me," I said again.

"Lock up and stay inside," he said. I closed the door after him and didn't hear his footsteps down the hall until I had turned the second bolt.

I was exhausted. I showered, skipped the painkiller, and slid into bed with Em's extension phone half an arm's reach away. I closed my eyes knowing I wouldn't sleep until I had spoken to Casey.

In my mind, the blur of events began to clear, like the Sambo story in reverse, individual tigers taking form out of the yellow mass of butter. A lot of butter, and a lot of tigers.

I had been thinking all along that the catalyst was Lester Rowland, because he would not let events from the past silently slide into oblivion. He had wanted a show trial. That's why he helped Aleda come in out of hiding on her own terms. But I was wrong. From the beginning, the party belonged to Aleda and Emily. He was left out like the fat kid at the park who gets the merry-go-round spinning, but no one will give him a hand up.

It should have been a good party. Emily had gathered in Max, Lucas, me, and Rod, and warned my parents. There were three no-shows: Jaime, Celeste, and the four o'clock appointment at the wishing well by Hop Louie's. Still, it would have been interesting.

I may have drifted off. When the telephone rang I jolted upright and knocked the instrument to the floor. I managed to find it in the dark.

"Casey?" I said.

"This is the GTE operator. I have a collect call for Mom from Casey. Will you accept the charges?"

"Yes."

"Go ahead please," I heard the operator say. There was a lot of background noise.

"Casey? Where are you?"

"Mom, promise you won't be mad."

"Just tell me."

"I heard Linda yelling at Daddy this morning about how I was messing up their first Christmas together."

"I'm sorry you heard. She was probably just blowing off steam."

"Mom, I'm at the airport."

"Is Dad there?"

"He doesn't know."

"Jesus, Casey, he must be worried sick. Tell me where you are and I'll call Dad and have him pick you up right now."

"I'm outside the Delta terminal. But Mom?"

"What?"

"I'm in Los Angeles."

I was awake then. "Listen to me. You go inside and wait for me by Delta check-in. You talk to no one, and you don't move. I'll be there in twenty minutes."

"You're really mad, aren't you?"

"Yes, baby, but not at you. I'll be right there."

I hung up, found my clothes, and put them on while I dialed Denver.

"Linda," I said, "Casey flew herself to L.A. I'm going to pick her up at the airport right now."

"The little brat."

"You just better hope that Scotty's next wife is more generous to your little bambino when she goes to visit Dad for the holidays."

I didn't wait for a response. I went out on the street and managed to flag down a cab outside one of the big Chinese restaurants.

"LAX, please," I said. "Delta terminal. I'm in a hurry."

"Everyone's always in a hurry," he said, but he stepped on it.

As we sped toward the freeway, I pulled out what was left of my cash. I had just about thirty-five dollars. I leaned forward in the seat.

"What's the fare?" I asked.

The cabbie half-turned to talk. "Airport's a flat rate, run you twenty-four dollars."

I could get there okay, even manage a tip. Coming back was beginning to look like a problem. There were people I could call, but it would be a whole lot easier on everyone if I could make a quick turnaround. The driver seemed like a nice enough sort, a family man. I hoped we could work something out. I got his name off his permit.

"So, Kareem," I said, "are you licensed to pick up fares at the airport?"

"Yes, ma'am, but I don't like to do it. Too many taxis means I have to wait in line twenty, sometimes thirty minutes before they give me my fare. Most the time, I just come straight back downtown. Time is money in this business."

"Then maybe we can help each other here. I'll offer you thirty-five dollars for a round trip."

"I'm not supposed to do that. It's a flat rate, twenty-four dollars each way."

"My daughter just called from the airport. She's only twelve. I didn't know she was coming in, so I'm caught a bit short of cash. Anyway, if you don't wait to pick up a fare at the airport, you just deadhead all the way home, right? I'm asking you, who's to know my daughter and I are with you? And you go in tonight with an extra eleven dollars for Christmas."

He turned and grinned at me. "You sure are a hard talker, lady. You got yourself a deal."

"You're a prince."

"I'm a daddy. You could have quit your speech as soon as you said it was your little girl."

He talked almost nonstop all the way to the airport, most of it about kids and the dumb stuff they do. He was a hard talker himself. And he knew how to drive. We were in front of Delta in just under twenty minutes.

"There she is." I pointed out Casey's worried little face pressed against the glass inside the terminal, by the check-in stations just as I had instructed her. She was still wearing ski clothes. Kareem pulled to the white curb and I made a dash for the door.

Casey started crying as soon as she saw me. Sobbing, she gathered together her things, jet-packed skis and boots and a backpack, and ran out to meet me.

"Oh, Mom." She had to stoop a little to wail against my shoulder because she is already taller than I am. I hugged her, skis and all, and tried to move her into the cab before a taxi dispatcher came along and busted Kareem. He got the skis wedged in catty-corner from front window to back, and Casey and I slid in next to them.

"All set?" he asked.

"Let's go."

I pushed Casey's face up and wiped it with one of the leather mittens still attached to her jacket.

"How did you pull this off, Case?" I asked.

"Dad dropped me off at the slopes this morning." She looked into my face and started to cry again. "I'm so sick of skiing. I hate it. But there was nothing else to do when Dad went to work. Linda didn't want me hanging around the house all day."

"And . . ."

"So, I went into this little village up there to get some things for Christmas. And I was paying for some stuff and I saw my airplane ticket in my wallet. I just started thinking. I saw the Denver bus, and went to the airport."

"Your ticket is for San Francisco. They let a kid change a ticket?"

She winced. "I bought a new one."

"With what money?"

"Dad gives me money." She opened the front of her backpack and started pulling out wads of bills. "Everytime we do something, he gives me money. I said I wanted to take something home to you, so he asked me to pick out something from him, too.. He gave me this." She handed me a roll the diameter of a Havana cigar. I started counting fifties, quit when I realized I had more than five hundred dollars in my hand.

"Merry Christmas, from Dad," she said.

"This is insane."

"Dad's having a tough time."

"Aren't we all?"

"How's Aunt Emily?"

"She's the same, Casey." I kept out a fifty for Kareem and jammed the rest of the money back into her pack. I pulled her against me. "I want to hold you for a minute before we talk about what a stupid stunt this trip was."

"Could I just say I know it was dumb, and skip the lecture?"

I laughed, so did Kareem.

"Kids," he said, shaking his head. "Wouldn't live without 'em. But they sure do keep you hoppin'."

Chapter 23

I woke up first. Casey was sprawled over more than her share of the bed, sound asleep, with a little drool drying at the side of her mouth. She's too old and teenagery to cuddle in bed anymore. Risking her wrath, I brushed her long hair from her face and kissed her forehead. Then I dragged myself up.

My first coherent thought was that there were only two more days until Christmas. I had promised my mother I would be home in time. Now, with Casey here, I couldn't think of many reasons to stay in L.A. any longer.

I wasn't doing the investigation much good, but I still had some business to take care of. Emily's apartment needed to be closed up. Whatever had begun between Mike Flint and me needed some resolution. Both of those, I decided, might best be dealt with after the holidays. My film crew wasn't leaving for Ireland until the middle of January. If I was very organized about preparations for the trip, I could maybe squeeze off a few days after the First and come back to L.A.

I went into the bathroom and pulled the tape off the gauze covering my stitches, losing a few hairs in the process. The stitches didn't look too bad, but they were still stitches, so, after I combed my hair, I cut a new piece of gauze to cover them up again. I was taping the gauze down when Casey, yawning and stretching, came in and leaned against the sink beside me.

"What did you do to your head?" she asked, squinting without her glasses.

"I bumped it."

"How?"

I looked at her sleepy face in the mirror. "The usual way. I was running from a man who was trying to shoot at me from Aunt Emily's Volvo. When he fired the first shot, it set off a bomb in the car that had so much force that it set afire six cars, including Uncle Max's BMW, threw me into the air and then dumped me on my head. That's how."

"Uh huh," she yawned. "You always tell the stupidest stories, Mom."

"I try my best to entertain you," I said. "Feel like breakfast?"

"I'm starved."

"Do you have anything to wear besides ski pants?"

"I have some jeans in my backpack."

"Go call Daddy, then get dressed. We'll use some of his money and eat out, anywhere you like."

"What am I going to say to him?"

"Try the truth."

"What if he gets mad?"

"Start crying and hang up. Always works for me."

"You are so weird, Mom." She went into Emily's study and shut the door. I was sorely tempted to pick up the extension and eavesdrop. As I made up the sofa bed, I actually touched the receiver two or three times. It's a good thing the conversation didn't last very long, or I would have lost all self-respect.

Casey came out dressed in jeans and a blue sweater just the color of her eyes.

"How'd it go?" I asked.

She shrugged. "He apologized for Linda. He's sending me a check."

"A check for what?"

She raised her hands, perplexed. "You know the man better than I do."

At least she was smiling again. She's a resilient kid, but she's taken a number of good bounces during the course of the last couple of years. I always worry that the next trauma will be one too many.

"Where do you want to eat?" she asked.

"How about, we call Uncle Max at the Bonaventure and have him join us," I said. "He knows about his car, but I haven't faced him yet. If you're there, he won't get as mad at me."

"What happened to his car?"

"I told you. It burst into flames when the man driving Aunt Emily's Volvo took a shot at me and set off a bomb."

"Right," she said, but the sarcasm held just a tinge of doubt.

"Moms don't tell lies," I said. I put my arm around her and led her out the door.

I called Max to meet us. Then Casey and I caught the Dash bus up to the Bonaventure on Figueroa. By the time we got there, Max had a table in the hotel coffee shop and had already ordered juice and coffee for us. When he spotted Casey behind me, he jumped up and wrapped her in a bear hug, swung her around a couple of times, imperiling a goodly number of water glasses and coffee cups with her long legs.

"You're one hell of a good-looking kid, kid," he said. "You look like a stretch model of your mother when she was your age. I think you're going to be as tall as your Aunt Emily."

Casey lifted a corner of her lip with dismay and looked at me. "How tall is Aunt Emily?"

"Six feet."

"Gross." She broke free of Max and slumped into a cushy chair. "I don't like being taller than everybody."

"You will," Max said. He sat down and took one of her hands. "How was skiing?"

She rolled her eyes. "Don't say snow to me, and don't mention skiing."

He turned to me and laughed. "Déjà vu. That's you exactly at twelve. Chip off the old block, Maggie."

I poured myself a cup of coffee. "Glad to see you in such good humor, Max. After what happened to your car, I was afraid you would come gunning for me, too."

Very swiftly, he became deadly serious. "My God, Maggot. Are you okay?"

"Do I look okay?"

He leaned back and gave me a good going over. Then he smiled again. "You look a hell of a lot better than my car."

"I'm sorry, Max," I said.

"Forget it."

Casey had been listening to this exchange while she drank her juice and then chased it with mine. "What *did* happen to your car, Uncle Max?"

"I told you," I said.

"Let's eat," Max said. I saw a deep furrow appear between his heavy brows before he hid behind his menu. I touched his arm.

"You okay?"

"I think you should take Casey and go home, Maggie," he said with a husky voice. "Every time I even think about what happened to you yesterday, or what might have happened . . ."

"If we can get a flight, we'll leave L.A. this afternoon. Okay with you, Casey?"

"Sure." She was looking between Max and me, borrowing Max's serious mood.

"Let's eat," I said.

Casey ate eggs Benedict, a short stack of pancakes, a side of bacon, and finished my bran muffin. Max, lingering over half a grapefruit and dry whole-wheat toast, watched her with amusement.

"Want some dessert, Casey?" he asked when she folded her napkin beside her plate.

"Dessert for breakfast?" she asked brightly.

"He's teasing," I said. "Are you ready?"

"Yes. I saw this shop in the lobby. Can I go look?"

"Go ahead. I'll meet you in the lobby."

We watched her dash out. Casey has never walked. Except once, when she was maid of honor at her father's wedding to Linda. She went down the aisle so slowly that the minister had to go out and fetch her. Or so I hear. I wasn't invited.

"She's going to be a beauty," Max said. "I'm surprised you had her come, Maggie, with all this shit going on."

"She came all by herself. Had some problems with Linda, it seems, so she put herself on a plane last night. And here she is."

He was smiling wickedly. "How sweet it is. Finally, you will learn what I went through when you were her age."

Because of his wicked smile, I let him sign for breakfast without putting up even a token argument.

"How long are you staying in town?" I asked as we walked out to find Casey.

"I had planned to fly up to the Bay Area today, but I need to deal with the insurance company. I'll be home for Christmas."

I took his arm and leaned against him as we walked into the lobby. "Max, I am so sorry about your car. I shouldn't have left it at the academy overnight."

"None of it was your fault, Maggot. Don't give it another thought. Anyway, it was better the bomb went off at the academy than in the middle of town. Have you seen the crater it made?"

We met Casey coming out of a gift shop carrying a paper bag. She was finally smiling again.

"All set?" I asked her.

"In a minute." She walked up to Max, grinning, and handed him the bag. "I know how much you liked your car, Uncle Max. So I want to replace it."

It was a very small bag. Max hesitated, a bit nonplussed, but very flattered by this attention, whatever its payoff. Slowly, he opened the bag. Then he erupted in laughter and hugged Casey again.

"Thanks, you little creep," he said. He pulled out a two-inch-long cast metal replica of a black BMW, just like his late car.

"Low maintenance," I said. "Quite an improvement."

"Quite." He held Casey close to him as he walked us

out. "To hell with the insurance people. If it's okay with you two, maybe I can get all of us on a flight together tonight. What do you think?"

"I think it's a great idea. We'll be at Emily's. Call us."

We said our good-byes on the sidewalk and he waited for us to catch the Dash. He waved to us as the bus pulled into traffic.

"Giving him that little car was a sweet thing to do, Casey."

"I saw it when we were walking in," she said. "Poor Uncle Max. Things always happen to him."

"Poor Max," I chuckled. I should have his problems. "So, we have a whole day in L.A. What do you want to do?"

"Nothing."

"Good idea."

I had seen a large stationer at the bottom of Broadway. We got off near there and bought a dozen large, collapsed cartons with lids. As long as we were doing nothing, I thought, we might as well begin packing Emily's personal things. After the break-in, I was nervous about leaving her apartment unattended over the holidays.

The cartons were awkward to carry. Between us, we were managing all right until Caesar came up behind me and startled me. I spilled the lids.

"Hey, pretty lady," he said. The sweats I had given him last night were caked with filth and torn on one knee. He reeked of wine and alley hovel. "You got you a pretty young friend."

"Caesar, this is my daughter, Casey."

"How you doin' little lady?" He tipped his grubby cap.

"I'm okay," she said, moving closer to me.

"I seen the man with the skinny nose," he told her, his step faltering. "Skinny as your own nose."

Casey seemed nervous about Caesar. I would have put my arm around her, but my hands were full. I just smiled and said, "He also saw the woman who walked the walk."

"Yes ma'am I did. I ain't got me no watch, but I say it wasn' so long ago."

"Mom," Casey breathed. "You know him?"

"Friend of Aunt Emily's"

"Oh," she said flatly, understanding all too well.

I set down the rest of the cartons and fished a five out of my pocket. "Merry Christmas, Caesar."

The bill disappeared into the folds of his coat. "Merry Christmas to you, pretty ladies." He quick-stepped down the block.

"What was he talking about?"

"It's a long story. I'll tell you later."

We re-balanced the boxes and made it back to Emily's without further adventure. I stopped at Mrs. Lim's apartment and knocked on the door. I could hear her talking to us in rapid Chinese as she hustled to answer. A few days earlier, I would have thought she was scolding and been put off. But she wasn't, so I wasn't. She had grown on me.

Mrs. Lim opened her eyes wide when she saw Casey.

"Mrs. Lim, my daughter, Casey."

There was a lot of bowing. Casey bowed back and laughed a little, shyly.

"We're going to start packing Emily's things. I may go home tonight. In January, I'll come back and finish. You should start looking for a new tenant."

She shook her head and waved her arms, giving a strong negative to the suggestion. "No rent," she said. "No rent."

"Mrs. Lim, Emily won't be coming back here to live. She's up north with our parents. So you might as well find someone else to live there. It's a nice apartment."

"No rent," she said again, and tears ran down her lined face. "Emily has long lease. All paid."

"Suit yourself, then," I said. Casey and I picked up the boxes again. "It's your building. But you know what Emily would say about leaving the apartment vacant when someone might need it. Even if the rent is paid, I think it would be all right to find a new tenant."

She seemed to cave in upon herself. "Not now," she said firmly, and shut the door on us.

Casey and I walked upstairs, hassling the boxes and the slippery lids. Everything seemed normal and quiet around Emily's door. I unlocked both bolts and we went in.

"Let's put the boxes in the study," I said. "Anything of importance is there. There are a few things in the closet that we should pack for Grandma. Later, I think I'll call one of Aunt Emily's friends, Sister Agnes Peter, to come for the clothes. She'll know what to do with them."

Casey chose to work in the study because she could move in the TV to watch. She was busily sorting through Emily's books when I went into the closet.

It was difficult for me to handle Emily's material remains because of the finality of it. It was acknowledgment that Emily no longer needed anything, was not coming back, ever.

As I went through the drawers, I tried to think as she would, trying to be more practical than sentimental. Emily would not approve of storing away good, warm clothes that could be used. She would not mind if they became soiled and torn like Caesar's new sweats. A few really nice things gave me pause, but I let Em persuade me to leave them for Agnes Peter's multitude.

Emily had a box with some nice jewelry, some of it gifts from our parents, perhaps some of it gifts from Jaime or lovers who followed him. Mother would have to decide what should be done with it. My job was simply to pack it.

The closet was quick work. Emily was not a saver. I had less than a boxful of things to carry home when I finished. I put the box in the hall, intending to take it into the study after I washed off some shoe polish I had gotten into.

As I passed the front door, I heard what sounded like metal scraping against metal outside. Old buildings make all sorts of noises all the time. I didn't pay it any attention. Until I heard it a second time.

Casey was still in the study. She slammed a drawer shut and opened another.

I listened at the door for a moment; then, very quietly, I slipped the bolts.

At first, I saw nothing. Then I spotted a small figure huddled in the little alcove at the very end of the hall.

"Mrs. Lim?" I said, thinking maybe she was scrubbing the corners of the alcove floor.

The person there froze, and I knew it wasn't Mrs. Lim. Slowly, back toward me, the figure began to rise.

"Celeste?" I said, puzzled. "What are you doing out here?"

She had a small screwdriver in her hand. On the floor beside her I saw a coffee can, a small length of copper wire, electrical tape, crimpers, a wind-up alarm clock, and a big Gucci handbag.

"Casey," I called. "Come here please."

"I'm busy."

"Come here now."

Casey must have heard something in my voice. She was out in a hurry. she looked at celeste and put on her I'm-going-to-meet-another-one-of-Mother's-strange-friends face.

"How long do we have, Celeste?" I asked.

"I don't know. I think I've messed up the mechanism."

I took Casey's arm. "Go down and get Mrs. Lim and take her out of the building. There's a phone across the street. Call nine-one-one and tell them there's a bomb. They won't believe you, so you argue with them until they decide to come. Got it?"

"A bomb?" Casey said, sarcastic.

"A bomb," I said. "From across the street, have Mrs. Lim call anyone who might still be in the building and tell them to get out. Now."

"This is a weird joke, right?"

"No joke."

Casey looked at Celeste and decided to believe me. "Aren't you coming?"

"I'll be down," I said, giving her a little push. "Now hurry."

As I said before, Casey never walks. And when she runs, she runs hard.

I squared off with Celeste. "Drop your tools and come down with me," I said.

"It's too late, Maggie."

People facing death often say a lovely calm settles over them at the last moment. I hoped that impending death was not the reason I wasn't incoherent with panic. More likely it was because Celeste was the most unlikely looking bomber imaginable. How many bombers wear silk and pearls to do their work?

"What were you planning to do," I asked, "blow up the whole building?"

"No. Just you." She held the screwdriver in her perfectly manicured hands. "And it wasn't me. I mean, I didn't make this thing. I saw you come in with your daughter. I didn't want her to get hurt. I'm trying to disarm the damn thing, but I don't know how."

She was so mellow, so emotionally flat, that I knew she had to have taken something pretty heavy before she got here.

"If you didn't make the bomb, who did?"

"The resident pro. Made the one that got Rod, too." She touched the coffee can with her shiny pump, made me real nervous. "I have the old book they used to use," she said. "But all the research was done in the Cal library, and it's a good thing no one was graded on it, because they made some terrible mistakes."

"Mistakes?" My stomach made another somersault. I was remembering the *whummp* that kicked me after Rod fired his gun.

Celeste frowned, disapproving. "They got the explosives charts all wrong. Political types are not usually very good in physics, you know. You saw what happened in Berkeley."

"How do you know the same thing won't happen right here?"

"I don't. According to the book, it's only supposed to make a smallish fire." She smiled at me coyly and shrugged, a matron puzzled by a new recipe. "Of course, this is the same device Arty Dodds was putting together when he was atomized."

"Using the same directions?"

"Fragments of the book were found in the rubble. We all laughed about it, remember?"

"Let's go down," I said, moving toward the stairs.

She picked up the big Gucci bag, opened it, and dropped in her screwdriver. I expected her to follow me. I was no more than eight feet from the top of the stairs.

"Maggie," she said in her sweet, cultured voice.

I turned and saw the automatic in her hand, and the little red dot on its side that warned that the safety was off.

I tried to sound calm. "You don't want to make my daughter motherless, do you? Let's go."

"Oh, Maggot, I'm so tired." She was stoned. I don't know whether the drugs she had taken were kicking in or were wearing off, but I thought she wouldn't be upright much longer. The disconcerting thing was that the hand that held the gun was steady, and she was intact enough to keep the sight aimed at my sternum.

I moved slowly toward her. Her pupils were soulless holes that held a beam on my face with the same black stare the gun held at my chest.

"Let's go outside, Celeste."

"What's the point?" she sighed. "We can die here, or we can die out there. She'll never leave us alone."

"Who?"

"Who do you think? Aleda."

This was a bomb of another sort. "You lie," I said.

Celeste nodded. "I have to. Rod, too. My life may rest on a tissue of lies. But it's my life. Emily had no right to decide for all of us that it was time to stop telling lies."

"What lies?"

"About everything," she snapped. "We all knew a firebomb had been set in the Berkeley labs. We all knew there were people working inside the lab. Aleda said it would be just a lot of smoke. We all knew she was lying. For twenty-two years, a whole generation, we covered for each other, we covered for her. One lie, and another, and another. A tower of lies. And I can't climb down." She rolled her eyes and seemed to lose her balance a little.

I had my eye on the gun barrel. "We'll talk about it outside."

She shook her head. "She'll hear. She always knows things. All that time, she blackmailed us. And you know what we all did?"

"Tell me," I said.

"Nothing. We did nothing."

I shook my head. "Emily would never go along."

"She did. Aleda had Em by the balls, too." She thought about that a moment and waved it off. "You know what I mean."

"No, I don't."

"Marc!"

"Marc was dead," I said. I was edging backward toward the stairs.

"Baby Marc. Aleda had Marc's baby. She was preggers when she took off. Or so she said. All those years, Emily had investigators looking for him. Couldn't find him anywhere. You want to hear the weird part? Last week, someone claiming to be Marc found Emily."

Something in the coffee can went click. I lunged, caught Celeste's gun hand and forced it up and back until her grip released. She wasn't very strong. The automatic fell to the floor and I kicked it away.

Like tugging a big rag doll, I pulled her down the stairs and out the front door.

"How'd you know what to do?" Mike asked as the fire trucks drove away.

"I watch TV," I said. I was crushed against his chest and enjoying it very much.

Celeste sat quietly in a black-and-white police unit parked ten feet away at the curb, her hands cuffed and resting in her lap, her trim legs properly crossed at the ankles. After the bomb squad had gone, Celeste was the only curiosity left for the assembled crowd to gawk at. As they grew bored—she hardly blinked for them—they drifted off.

Casey, who had been answering questions posed by a handsome young sprig of the law, walked over and shook my arm.

"Were you scared, Mom?" Casey asked.

"I was a little nervous about what Celeste had in that can, but she just didn't seem to have enough wits about her to be dangerous. Besides, I'm bigger than she is."

Mike laughed. He was hanging on very tightly.

Caesar came stumbling along with two pals, passing a bottle in a brown bag among them. When he saw me, he took a long pull from the bottle and ambled over sociably.

"Hey, pretty lady," he said.

"Hey, yourself," I said.

He aimed the neck of the bottle toward Celeste. "See you found your friend you was lookin' for. Fine lookin' lady, ain't she?"

I looked at Celeste's trim legs again. "The lady who walks the walk? That's her?"

"Like I say," he nodded and passed his bottle on to a thirsty friend.

I looked up at Mike. "If Caesar's right, Celeste was at the wishing well by Hop Louie's just about the time he last saw Emily."

I could see his mind was already clicking.

"I'm going in with Celeste," he said. "Just to make sure everything's done right. I'll call you when I'm finished with reports and we'll argue some more about whether you should leave tonight or not."

Even with Casey standing on the sidewalk behind me, making faces, I kissed Mike. "Write fast," I said.

Grinning, he walked over to the black-and-white car, gave some instructions to the uniformed officers there, then climbed into the back seat beside Celeste. The car immediately pulled away and sped down Hill Street.

"Jeez, Mom," Casey said, watching after the car. "First Dad, now you."

"I'm not getting married."

"Well, you're kissing him aren't you? And probably other things, too."

"How'd you get so wise? Or is that wiseass?"

I put my arm around her and we crossed the street back to Emily's building. I don't know whether Celeste had managed to somehow defuse the incendiary device that had been built into the coffee can, or whether it had been a dud to begin with. When it did its thing, there was a pop and a fizz and a spark big enough to char a hole through the old wool carpet runner under it. The bomb squad had come, caught up on gossip with the detachments of both police and firemen, and, eventually, carried away the remains of the can in a big lead box. For the kids waiting on the sidewalk, they had used lights and sirens when they drove away. As a source of pre-holiday excitement, the event had been as big a dud as the bomb.

Firemen had dragged the smoldering carpet out to the sidewalk and left it there for the trash haulers. A few lower floor tenants had snuck in behind the firemen to save a few precious pieces of furniture. The furniture now blocked the front steps and cluttered the hall inside. With the front door hanging open, an assortment of nosy neighborhood people had come inside for a better look at the burn mark on the floor upstairs. They still lingered about, finding the furniture more interesting than the damage.

"Think Ireland can be any more fun than this?" I asked Casey as we pushed aside a hand-carved, inlaid chest that stuck out into the landing.

"I hope so," she said. "Poor Mrs. Lim."

"I think she enjoyed the fuss." We had left the door of Emily's apartment standing open. "Shall we finish packing?" I said.

"I'm hungry, Mom. There's nothing in the refrigerator to eat."

"Let's lock up and go out for a while. We'll get something to eat, maybe see a movie. Something with more kissing than shooting, okay?"

"Gross," she said. "I want my jacket. It's cold."

While Casey went to get her jacket from the chair in the sitting room where she had left it after breakfast, I waited in the little entry, trying to figure out how many boxes, and which ones, we would carry home on the plane.

"What do you want to eat?" I called. "Chinese, Mexican, burgers?"

Casey, white-faced, backed out of the sitting room and grabbed for me. "Mom."

"What?" I went in to see what she had seen.

There was a man sitting on the sofa. He rose. At first, he was in front of the window, backlit by the glare so I couldn't see his face. He wore jeans and loafers and a long windbreaker. He was tall and straight. I knew I hadn't seen him around the neighborhood.

"How did you get in?" I asked.

He shrugged. "The door was open. I hope it's okay."

He moved slowly toward me, away from the window. "I'm glad you're okay," he said. "I got real worried when all the police came. Until you came out, I didn't know what to do. I've been waiting for the right time to talk to you. I was thinking I might be too late. Again."

"Again?" I asked.

"Like Emily," he said.

He seemed nervous, but more expectant than worried. He had a nice, deep voice that sounded so familiar I didn't want him to stop talking. I had listened to his voice on Emily's answering machine tape for hours a few nights earlier. Even without the tape, I would have heard a familiar quality in his voice.

I could not ever have passed him on the street without recognizing that I had known him all my life, though he was no more than twenty-two years old. My father had passed to my sister and brother and I a distinctive long, narrow nose with a hump at the bridge. Casey had my father's skinny nose, too. Caesar had recognized it when he saw Casey. And when he saw this young man.

I reached out for the young man with the skinny nose.

He took a deep breath and touched my outstretched hand. "Maggot?"

"Hello, Marc. This is Casey."

Chapter 24

When I looked up, we were somewhere past Riverside, just at the cusp between new tract house development and open desert. Mike drove, with Casey napping in the front seat beside him. I was in back with Marc, hearing the story of his life. You can learn a lot about a person in an hour. Marc seemed to have a very solid core.

Mike turned to me. "Want to find a telephone?"

"No," I said. "Stopping would just take time. I know Jaime is fine."

"You're sure? We could call the sheriff."

"No. I'm sure," I said, touching Marc's shoulder. "He's with Aleda."

Marc had been telling me the story of his life with his mother. I had filled in for him details about my family—his family—that his mother either didn't know or had misremembered. It was spooky how much he knew about us. He had followed my career from the beginning. He had collected articles Emily had published in medical journals, and the occasional pieces about her and her adventures that showed up in the press. He played the flute, like my father.

Marc's shadow life with his mother, moving frequently, changing his name between schools, leaving friends behind, had been populated by mythic characters—largely, my family. He was incredibly like his father, my brother, his namesake. I felt I had always known him.

"Why did you keep running?" I asked him. "The government wasn't very interested in your mother after a while."

He shook his head. This part of his story wasn't clear to him. "At first, I think, Mom was afraid the Feds would take me from her, put her in prison. Then, when she sent out feelers to see whether it was safe to come in, someone threatened us and started looking for her. We hid. After a while, it was habit. I can't explain it. It was just the way we lived."

"Didn't your mother know we would have helped her?"

"She was afraid you would be hurt. It was like you were all held hostage." He pulled nervously at his ear. "It was true, too, wasn't it? As soon as Mom and Aunt Emily made arrangements for Mom to surrender, look what happened."

I did look. Emily shot, Rod immolated. To protect whom? From what?

When we drove into Jaime's gravel driveway, Lupe was on the porch, sweeping. She went to the screen and yelled something. Tires on the gravel made too much noise for us to hear what she said. The collie nosed open the screen and ambled down the steps, with Jaime and Aleda slowly following him. Two uniformed Riverside County sheriff deputies came outside behind them and waited on the porch with Lupe.

Aleda Weston had once been very beautiful, not so much because of her features, which were regular and refined, but because of the grace and confidence of her carriage. People would stop to watch her go by, or listen to what she had to say.

As she came down the steps, there was still something left of the old confidence, just a shadow you had to know to look for. I was looking for it very hard, the way I had looked for a spark of life in Emily's eyes a few days before.

Aleda was painfully thin. Her thinness added emphasis to the beginnings of a dowager's hump forming between her shoulder blades. The hump gave her posture a stoop, made her seem burdened. I suspect that anyone seeing her for the first time would see only a rather plain, middle-aged woman.

What had Max said? Everyone had been in love with Aleda. I know I still was. Celeste, no matter how wild her stories were, couldn't change that. In my heart, Aleda was an echo of my sister, Emily.

I had heard all of Celeste's invective, her accusations against Aleda. While I had suffered some lingering doubts, as soon as I saw Aleda again, I knew the truth. Mike had said I would. Celeste had created a tower of lies in which to dwell. Now that it had come crashing down around her, I wondered whether she could sort out any truth for herself. Not that I cared in the least.

Aleda picked up her pace when I got out of the car, though her gait seemed pained. She smiled at Marc, but reached for me. I carried a wrapped package under my arm and nearly dropped it to embrace her.

"Oh, Maggot," she said, tears welling in her pale eyes. The skin of her hand felt dry and thin, like old silk. Like my grandmother's hand. "Look at you. All grown up."

I glanced at Casey in time to see her roll her eyes at this comment.

"Aleda," I said, "this is my daughter, Casey."

Aleda reached toward Casey. "You look so much like your Aunt Emily."

Casey didn't know whether this was a compliment, but she managed a polite smile.

Jaime grabbed Casey around the middle, like the old days, and gave her a spin, albeit a tamer one than when she was smaller. "What happened to my little girl? She's just a big hunk of junk now."

Casey giggled.

Aleda pointed at Mike. "I know you. You were with Maggot at the jail when I was brought in."

"Mike," he said, offering no official title. "I've heard a lot about you."

Aleda laughed. "No doubt."

The air was clear and crisp. The sky a dusky blue. We all sat on the porch steps to watch the color show of the desert sunset. The package I had brought was wedged between Mike and me.

"I miss Lucas," Aleda said. "Shouldn't we have one of his awful hymns about now?"

Jaime smiled. "Where is Lucas?"

"He's Santa Claus tonight at the shelter Christmas party," I said. "He'll be in Berkeley by dinnertime on Christmas day. He promised."

"I have a Lucas hymn," Jaime said. "One of his favorites. He taught us when we were in the Alameda County Jail for unlawful assembly."

Jaime began to sing a morbid dirge, and Aleda, laughing, joined in:

> *Plunged in a gulf of dark despair,*
> *We wretched sinners lay,*
> *Without one cheering beam of hope,*
> *Or spark of glimmering day. A-Men.*

Before the last phrase, Aleda began to weep softly. Jaime and I held her between us.

"I feel so bad about Emily," she sobbed into my neck. "It's all my fault."

"How is it your fault?" Mike asked. "Celeste shot Emily. Celeste hired a pro to rig a bomb to do in Rod Peebles. What does it have to do with you?"

"Marc and I were okay where we were. If we had just left things alone, we would still be okay."

"Okay how?" I said. "You would stay in hiding forever? Marc told me he graduates from college in June. I think its high time you both moved out into the world."

She didn't seem convinced. "I knew what Celeste was capable of. Don't underestimate her power and influence. Or her perversity. She killed Tom Potts because she wanted to. And he wasn't the only one."

"Emily knew the risks," I said. "She must have felt they were worth taking."

I handed the package I had brought to Marc. "Emily

had this made for you. I don't think you need to wait until Christmas morning."

Mike was beaming. It was through his efforts that this item had been released—liberated—from the collection of Emily's possessions the police had found in the trunk of Celeste's car. Mike speculated that when Celeste broke into Emily's apartment, among other things, she had taken Marc's dogtags and had given them, or planted them, on Rod before she sent him to his explosive end. A little detail to add drama to her scene.

Marc hesitated before he began to slowly remove the brown paper wrapping. He refolded the paper deliberately before he picked up the framed photograph inside. He glanced at his mother, confused it seemed, before he held it up for the rest of us. I had given him the enlargement Emily had made of Marc's snapshot, the one she had airbrushed.

"Where's Dad's joint?" Marc asked.

"Purged," I said.

Aleda was smiling again. "Poor Marc. Right to the end, Emily got the last word."

"One thing still bothers me," I said. "Why did Emily get her boobs done?"

Mike laughed and pulled me against him. "Because she wanted to."

Chapter 25

Mother sat at the table in her big kitchen, in a stream of bright morning sunlight, folding red linen napkins fresh from the laundry. It was a beautiful picture, the contrasts of the red napkins, her shiny silver hair, the pale, well-scrubbed pine table. She is a tall slender woman who holds herself very straight. But her hair was soft wisps, the collar of her cotton shirt was open at the throat, and there was a hole in the toe of her right sneaker.

She was facing the big bay windows, and now and then she looked out through the redwood trees in the backyard, gazing off toward Grizzly Peak. Through the window, I could see my father in a far corner of the yard, kneeling with a trowel in his hand at the edge of the small herb garden that was planted in the patch of yard that catches only the morning sun.

It was a beautiful morning. More like spring than Christmas Eve.

"Grandma," Casey said softly. When Mother turned, Casey took Marc by the hand and led him over to the table. Max, Jaime, Aleda, Mike and I stayed back, voyeurs.

"Grandma, this is Marc."

"Of course it is." Mother stood up and pulled out a chair for him. Her eyes were very moist, but she remained composed as she looked at him. She put her slender hand on his shoulder. "You are very like your father. Anyone can see that. But I can see your mother in you, too. She has always been my favorite."

266

He smiled. "You're just the way my mother described you."

"Well," she laughed. "We'll have to hear about that! Everyone come and sit. I have Bloody Marys ready. Casey, honey, please go tell Grandpa that his grandson has come home."

Don't miss Wendy Hornsby's next
Maggie MacGowen mystery,
Midnight Baby, coming soon in a
Dutton hardcover edition.

Under a full moon and sodium-vapor streetlights, the girl
was all silver: her pale cropped hair, her face with its
heavy matte makeup. The parts below her face, small,
pushed-up bosom, narrow hips, muscled, serviceable
legs, were banded in stretch jersey and black mesh and
could have belonged to any undernourished, overused
hooker between puberty and menopause.

At first, I had no attitude about her. Through the
viewfinder of my videocamera, she was no more than a
photogenic image, good filmic contrast to the fat toddlers
I had spent the day recording in Encino.

Guilt, or maybe the impulse of universal motherhood,
I don't know what, took over when I learned the girl was
only six months older than my own daughter, Casey.
That made her fourteen and a half.

My documentary project was nearly in the can, until I
met her. Over-budget and overdue as always, but under
control. Until I met her.

"I'll do women," she said, trying to keep her face away
from my camera. "There's no extra charge."

"What's your name?" I asked.

"You can call me Pisces."

"Where do you live, Pisces?"

"Here," she said, vaguely indicating MacArthur Park
with her cigarette as a pointer. "I don't like having my
picture taken. Not for free."

"How long have you been on the streets?"

She shrugged, glanced back at the red Corvette that
had been following us along the curb as we walked. I
couldn't see the driver; he could have been a potential

date, her pimp, or her dealer. Or an undercover cop doing his job. Whatever he was, when I turned the camera on him, he sped off.

I knew better than to get involved with the girl, just as I had known better than to finish off the bottle of wine the previous night before driving home, or to put myself into debt well into the next millennium to buy a house directly atop the San Andreas fault. Wisdom and action don't necessarily intersect on the same plane.

The street around us was a midnight carnival. Derelicts, hypes, a broad assortment of the ambulatory insane, spilled out of MacArthur Park like leakage from Pandora's box, to panhandle or rage against internal demons, to look for another fix. Among them, skittery but tolerant, were little family groups of refugees to El Norte, whose lighted food wagons sold the same spicy meat pies I had bought once in San Salvador, Coca-Cola bottled in Mexico, and dysentery on a stick—crushed fresh fruit frozen in someone's home kitchen.

It was April in L.A. The day had been warm, the usual monotonous seventy-six degrees, but the night had turned cold. My partner, Guido Patrini, had walked down to the corner to buy hot coffee from a torta vendor. I could see him leaning against the cart, practicing his Spanish while the coffee cooled. I felt impatient, not because I wanted the coffee, but because the neighborhood scared me shitless.

The girl, Pisces, wanted my attention again. Dramatically, she pulled out a dark lipstick and redid her full lips. "We can go in an alley, or there's a motel on the corner if you want to get a room."

"All I want is your face in my film," I said, dropping the camera from my shoulder. "Pisces, are you okay out here?"

"You mean, do I have a man?"

"I mean, are you okay? Does your family know where you are?"

The way she shrugged reminded me of my daughter, Casey, who, if things were going according to plan, was at home tucked in her bed under the watchful care of our housemate, Lyle. In our house that lies over the San Andreas Fault.

The same red Corvette passed us again, tight by the curb and moving slowly. Pisces moved to put me between her and the street.

"I know a shelter just off Hollywood Boulevard," I said to her. "It doesn't cost anything to stay there and they won't ask questions. If you want to get off the street tonight, I'll drive you over."

"And what do you get?" she smirked. "A free piece on the way?"

"All I get is peace of mind. I have a daughter your age. I wouldn't want her to be out here unprotected, either."

"Oh, a mother," she taunted, but she didn't walk away. "I remember mothers. They want you to wash behind your ears and eat your peas and carrots before they fuck you over."

I hefted the camera back to my shoulder. "Tell me about home, Pisces."

"I get paid by the half hour," she said. "Even if all you want is talk."

Four gunshots exploded into the night nearby—bam-bam, bam-bam, two pairs. I ducked. Every one on the street ducked. And Pisces slipped into my arms.

Three punks in gang-banger uniform—black jeans and Raiders T-shirts—crashed through the shrubs around the park and scattered out toward the street, two of them dodging cars while the third lagged to fumble with something caught in his jacket. The police were right behind them, two sleek officers in pressed uniforms. They caught the laggard with a flying tackle and slammed his face to the sidewalk at the feet of a drunk, who didn't even notice when the batons came out to beat the kid to quiescence.

The entire show took less than two minutes. When it was over, the police raised their handcuffed quarry by the elbows and quickstepped him down the block to the police substation in the park. One of the officers held a semiautomatic pistol he hadn't had when he breached the shrubbery.

I have seen, through the lens of my camera, the conditions at home the Salvadorans fled from: chaos, hunger, war. As I looked around this carnival, I couldn't see the improvement.

Guido walked up just then with two plastic cups of coffee. I traded him the camera for one of the cups.

"Took you long enough," I said sharply, relieved to see him intact. "Did you have to harvest the coffee beans on the way?"

"I was trying to explain to this guy why he should start using paper cups." He didn't mention the shooting. "Shit, Maggie, don't they know that plastic is killing us?"

"Maybe you should start bringing your own cup, Guido," I said, blowing on my coffee, blowing off steam. "I'll get you one you can hook to your belt loops. Better yet, I'll get you a little solar-powered coffee maker you can carry around with you. You know, make your own, drink it right out of the pot. No, forget that. Just carry a bottle of water with you and some No Doz. Your body won't know the difference. I read in *Geographic* how they're burning the rain forests to plant coffee."

"Always the smart-ass, Maggie," Guido said.

"And you love it."

He raised his cup to cover his grin.

Guido isn't a very big man, about my height, five-seven or five-eight. He weighs maybe 130 pounds after a big lunch. He has that tight-wired intensity that little men often have; borderline hyper. I love having him work on film projects with me because of the energy he injects. Guido's biggest professional problem is that while he's a gifted filmmaker, he isn't much of a salesman. You have to be both if you want to get funding to do independent investigative film projects. And that is my livelihood.

So Guido found himself a decent alternative: he teaches at the UCLA film school. It's a good job, and he has made a name for himself. But he misses being out in the trenches so much that I have found him to be a bit of a slut—he never turns down my invitations to work.

I tasted the coffee, strong and bitter, and took back the camera from him. Pisces was still standing close beside me. The fireworks across the street were over. It should have been apparent I wasn't going to hire her services. So I had expected her to walk away. It surprised me when she didn't. She just stood there, eavesdropping, watching me fuss one-handed with the camera's battery pack, spilling some coffee as I fussed.

"Guido," I said, glancing up, "meet Pisces."

He nodded to her. "How's it going?"

"Well enough," she said. She had her eyes on my coffee cup, or the steam rising from it. I was cold in jeans and a wool jacket. Her exposed arms were all goose bumps. I held out my cup to her.

"Would you like some?" I asked.

"Cream and sugar?" she asked.

"Cream, no sugar."

She shrugged, condescending, but she took the offered cup. Sugar wouldn't have hurt her figure. She was skinny, but very muscular. When she moved her body had the assertive thrust of an athlete.

"So, Pisces," I said. "It's late and there doesn't seem to be much business out here. Can I give you a lift to that shelter I mentioned?"

"I don't know. It is pretty cold tonight, but I hate going to those places. Do you live around here?"

"No. I live in San Francisco. I'm only in L.A. working for a few days."

"You have a hotel?"

"I'm staying at Guido's."

She looked at Guido and waited for him to say something. He turned to me.

"Why do you always do this to me, Maggie?"

"Do what?" I asked with *faux* innocence.

"We were going to Langer's to get some pastrami," he groused. "We saw *her* on the way, so we detoured to get her on film. That's great. But do we have to do a Mother Theresa shtick, too?"

"I love it when you're forceful," I said, patting his cheek. "Pisces, you want to get something to eat with us?"

"That would be fine," she said, and smiled wryly at Guido. "Nice of you to ask."

We walked the half block to Langer's Deli like a little family group out for the evening: Mom, Dad, and baby hooker.

The restaurant is a New York–style neighborhood eatery, 1950s linoleum and glass meat cases, an institution left behind when the old neighbors moved out of MacArthur Park and El Salvador moved in. Guido claims it has the best pastrami in the world.

As soon as we got inside, Pisces excused herself to go to the rest room. Guido and I found a booth in the middle where she could find us when she was finished.

Guido pried a half-sour pickle out of the pot on the table, and took a bite. He smiled at me while he chewed.

"What?" I said.

"I was just thinking," he said. "There any kids hooking on the street in San Francisco?"

"Of course."

"And chubby little bambinos up there in model daycare palaces?"

"What's your question?"

"Just curious why you had to come to L.A. to film."

"The child psychologist who is consulting on the script agrees with me that it would be best—we want to depict a broad range of child-raising experiences. You're always so cautious, Guido. I want to take the lid off on this one. I want to include some kids most people never see."

"So go to Natchitoches, Louisiana, or Bismarck, North Dakota," he said. "You didn't have to come to L.A. to film a face in the dark, or kids on a slide. You could have taken care of that shit in your own neighborhood."

"You sound like the grant coordinator. Are you asking me to defend the project?"

"Nope." He leaned forward and used the pickle as a pointer aimed at my nose. "Have you called Mike Flint?"

"Hadn't occurred to me to do so," I said, defensive. Another thing that makes Guido such a good filmmaker is his unerring insight. Sometimes I just hate him.

Guido reached into his pocket, fiddled through some change, and slid two dimes across the table toward me.

"Should I know what the dimes are for?" I asked, knowing full well.

"Make the call."

I thought about it. I had been thinking about it for six months. Mike Flint and I had started something about a year earlier that had never been resolved. As hard as I had fallen for Flint, from the beginning I knew that anything beyond *carpe diem* was hopeless. He was a detective with twenty-two years on the LAPD. A big-city dick, with a full share of the reactionary attitudes that implies. Beyond that, he was a true and loyal friend, a man with deep compassion, great thighs. He made me laugh.

I could live with his opinions—I love a good argument and he always offered plenty to argue about. The sticking point was that until he had put in his twenty-five years on the force he was stuck in L.A. And after that, he envisioned himself retiring to a cabin so deep in the woods that the sound of drive-by gunfire could only be heard on the six-o'clock news. He longed for quietude.

Simply put, Mike and I had incompatible geography. I hate L.A., but I'm not big on flannel shirts and bear meat. As I said, it was hopeless. I had had six months to get used to that reality. What I could not understand was why I kept having this running conversation with Mike Flint in my head. Why my eyes began to roll back every time I thought about the texture of the soft hair at the back of his neck.

Pisces came back from the rest room. I slid deeper into the booth to make room for her beside me. Once she sat down, I couldn't get out to use the telephone. I pushed the dimes back to Guido.

"Guido says the pastrami here is worth risking your life for," I said to Pisces. "How do you feel about pastrami?"

"It's all right," she said. "May I have some salad with it?"

"Anything you want," I said, glaring at the tooth-sucking expression on Guido's chiseled face.

"Thank you," Pisces said. "I'm really hungry now that I smell food."

Guido turned his attention to the girl, studied her with his quick intensity. In the rest room she had brushed her hair back from her face, wiped off most of the makeup, and pulled up the top of her skimpy dress to cover her shoulders. Without all the goo she was a pretty little girl with wide, dark brown eyes and good skin. She seemed to have transformed her streetwise attitude as well as her appearance.

"You have nice manners for a lady of the evening," Guido said as she spread a paper napkin on her lap. "Where you from, kid?"

"Here," she said, shrugging.

"Here, like L.A.?"

"Sort of."

"Southern California, anyway, right? You sound like a local."

She giggled a little. "You can't tell that. Everyone knows there is no California accent."

"Wrong," he corrected. "It's Brooklyn that has no accent. Unless you're from Chicago."

She laughed politely. She picked up a pickle, bit off the end of it, and screwed up her face at the sourness.

If I had felt at all protective of her before, I felt doubly so as I watched her. This was not a child raised in the streets. Guido had been correct about her manners. There was a sophistication about her, a social easiness, that comes with a certain careful upbringing. She did not appear to be on drugs. This kid was somebody's baby girl. The question that began to eat away at me was: Who had lost her?

A senior-citizen waitress came and rested her soft hip against the end of the table. She gave us a long, nosy inspection. "Have you decided?"

Guido looked at Pisces and me. "Can I order for everyone? There's an art to eating pastrami. It has to be done just right to get the full effect."

"We're in your hands," I said, and Pisces giggled again.

Guido faced the waitress. "We'll have three pastramis on rye, with yellow mustard—none of that gray poop. Three cream sodas, and one dinner salad, not slaw, on the side. And that's all."

"A man who knows his mind," the waitress said. "Be right back with the salad."

She was true to her word; the salad came immediately. While Pisces ate, Guido and I talked about the footage we had shot in Encino at a model day-care center. I